The Folded Leaf

The Folded Leaf

WILLIAM MAXWELL

NONPAREIL BOOKS
David R. Godine · Publisher · Boston

This is a NONPAREIL BOOK published in 1981

David R. Godine, Publisher, Inc.
Horticultural Hall, 300 Massachusetts Avenue
Boston, Massachusetts 02115

Library of Congress Cataloging in Publication Data
Maxwell, William, 1908–
    The folded leaf.
    (Nonpareil books ; 20)
    "Slight revisions have been made by the author."
    Reprint of the ed. published by Vintage Books, New York.
    I. Title.   II. Series.
PS3525.A9464F6 1981   813'.54   80–67031
ISBN 0-87923-351-6

For this edition certain slight revisions have been made by the author.

Manufactured in the United States of America

Fifth printing, January 1991

For Louise Bogan

Lo! in the middle of the wood,
The folded leaf is woo'd from out the bud
With winds upon the branch, and there
Grows green and broad, and takes no care,
Sun-steep'd at noon, and in the moon
Nightly dew-fed; and turning yellow
Falls, and floats adown the air.
Lo! sweeten'd with the summer light,
The full-juiced apple, waxing over-mellow,
Drops in a silent autumn night.

ALFRED TENNYSON
1833 (aet. 24)

Contents

The Folded Leaf

BOOK ONE

The Swimming Pool

I

The blue lines down the floor of the swimming pool wavered and shivered incessantly, and something about the shape of the place—the fact that it was long and narrow, perhaps, and lined with tile to the ceiling—made their voices ring. The same voices that sounded sad in the open air, on the high school playground. "Lights! Lights!" it seemed as if they were shouting at each other across the water and from the balcony stairs.

All of them were naked, and until Mr. Pritzker appeared they could only look at the water; they couldn't go in. They collected on the diving board, pushed and tripped each other, and wrestled halfheartedly. Those along the edge of the pool took short harmless jabs and made threats which they had no intention ever of carrying out but which helped pass the time.

The swimming class was nearly always the same. First the roll call, then a fifteen-minute period of instruction in the backstroke or the flutter kick or breathing, and finally a relay race. Mr. Pritzker picked out two boys and let them choose their own teams. They did it seriously, going down through the class and pointing to the best swimmers, to the next best, and in diminishing order after that. But actually it was the last one chosen that mattered. Whichever side had to take Lymie Peters lost. Lymie couldn't swim the Australian crawl. Week after week the relay began in the greatest excitement and continued back and forth from one end of the pool to the other until it was Lymie's turn. When he dived in and started his slow frantic side stroke, the race died, the place grew still.

Since he was not any good at sports, the best Lymie could do was to efface himself. In gym class, on the days when they played outdoor baseball, he legged it out to right field and from that comparatively safe place watched the game. Few balls ever went out there and the center fielder knew that Lymie couldn't catch them if they did. But in swimming class there was no place to retire to. He stood apart from the others, a thin, flat-chested boy with dark hair that grew down in a widow's peak on his forehead, and large hesitant brown eyes. He was determined when the time came to do his best, and no one held it against him that he always decided the race. On the other hand, they never bothered to cover up that fact.

This day two things happened which were out of the ordinary. Mr. Pritzker brought something with him which looked like a basketball only larger, and there was a new boy in the class. The new boy had light hair and gray eyes set a trifle too close together. He was not quite handsome but his body, for a boy's body, was very well made, with a natural masculine grace. Occasionally people turn up—like the new boy—who serve as a kind of reminder of those ideal, almost abstract rules of proportion from which the human being, however faulty, is copied. There were boys in the class who were larger and more muscular, but when the new boy stepped into the line which formed at the edge of the pool, the others seemed clumsy, their arms and legs too long or their knees too large. They glanced at him furtively, appraising him. He looked down at the tile floor or past them all into space.

Mr. Pritzker opened his little book. "Adams," he began. "Anderson . . . Borgstedt . . . Catanzano . . . de Fresne . . ."

The new boy's name was Latham.

Mr. Pritzker, separated from the rest by his size and by his age, by the fact that he alone wore a swimming suit and carried a whistle on a string around his neck, outlined the rules of water polo. Lymie Peters was bright enough when it came to his studies but in games he was overanxious. The fear that he might find himself suddenly in the center of things, the game depending on his action, numbed his mind. He saw the words *five men on a side;* saw them open out like the blue lines along the floor of the swimming pool and come together again.

Eventually it was his turn to slip into the water, but instead of taking part in the shouting and splashing, instead of fighting over the ball with the others, he stayed close to the side of the pool. He went through intense but meaningless motions as the struggle drew near and relaxed only slightly when it withdrew (the water flying outward in spray and the whistle interrupting continually) to the far end of the pool. Once every sixty seconds the minute hand on the wall clock moved forward with a perceptible jerk, which was registered on Lymie's brain. Time, the slow passage of time, was all that he understood, his only hope until that moment when, without warning, the ball came straight toward him. He looked around wildly but there was no one in his end of the pool. From the far end a voice yelled, "Catch it, Lymie!" and he caught it.

What happened after that was entirely out of his control. The splashing surrounded him and sucked him down. With arms grabbing at him, with thighs around his waist, he went down, down where there was no air. His lungs expanding filled his chest and he clung in blind panic to the ball. After the longest time the arms let go, for no reason. The thighs released him and he found himself on the surface again, where there was light and life. The ball was flipped out of his hands.

"What'd you hang onto it for?" a boy named Carson asked. "Why didn't you let go?"

Lymie saw Carson's face, enormous in the water in front of him.

"If that new guy hadn't pulled them off of you, you'd of drowned," Carson said.

In sudden overwhelming gratitude, Lymie looked around for his deliverer, but the new boy was gone. He was somewhere in that fighting and splashing at the far end of the pool.

2

Miss Frank, pacing the outside aisle between the last row of seats and the windows, could, by turning her eyes, see the schoolyard and the wall of three-story apartment houses that surrounded it. The rest of them, denied her freedom of movement, fidgeted. Without realizing it they slid farther and farther down in their seats. Their heads grew heavy. They wound their legs around the metal column that supported the seat in front of them. This satisfied their restlessness but only for a minute or two; then they had to find some new position. In the margins of their textbooks, property of the Chicago Public School System, they drew impossible faces or played ticktacktoe. And all the while Miss Frank was making clear the distinction between participles and gerunds, their eyes went round and round the room, like sheep in a worn-out pasture.

The door was on the right, opposite the windows. In front on a raised platform was Miss Frank's desk, which was so much larger than theirs and also movable. If she stepped out of the room, the desk alone restrained them, held them in their seats, and kept their shrill voices down to a whisper. Behind the desk and covering a part of the blackboard was a calendar for the month of October, 1923, with the four Sundays in red. Above the calendar was a large framed picture. It had been presented to the school by one of the graduating classes and there was a small metal disc on the frame to record this fact; also the subject and the artist, but the metal had tarnished; you could no longer tell what class it served as a memorial to. At certain times of the day, in the afternoon especially, the picture ("Andromache in Exile," by Sir Edward Leighton) was partly obscured by the glass in front of it, which reflected squares of light and the shapes of clouds and buildings.

Miss Frank abandoned her pacing and stepped up to the blackboard in the front of the room. A sentence appeared, one word at a time, like a string of colored scarves being drawn from a silk hat. It was beautiful and exciting but they hardly altered the expression on their faces. They had seen the trick too often to be surprised by it, or care how it was done. Miss Frank turned and faced the class.

"Mr. Ford, you may begin."

"*At* is a preposition."

"That's right."

"*First* is an adjective."

"Adjective, Mr. Ford?"

"Adverb. *First* is an adverb, object of *at*."

Ford had remembered to take his book home after football practice but he had studied the wrong lesson. He had done the last four pages of the chapter on relative pronouns.

"Prepositions do not take adverbs as their object, Mr. Ford . . . Miss Elsa Martin?"

"*First* is a noun, object of *at*. *Men* is a noun, subject of the verb *were*—"

"Of what else?"

"Subject of the sentence. *Were* is a verb, intransitive. *Delighted* is an adjective modifying *men*. *When* is a conjunction—"

"What kind?"

By reversing each number and reading from right to left, the *203* on the glass of the classroom door, which was meant to be read in the corridor, could be deciphered from the inside. Carson—third row, second seat—did this over and over without being able to stop.

"Not you, Miss Martin. I can see you've prepared your lesson. . . . Mr. Wilkinson, what kind of a conjunction is *when*?"

"*When* is . . ."

Janet Martin, Elsa's twin sister, but different, everyone said, as two sisters could possibly be, opened her blue enameled compact slyly and peered into it.

"Mr. Harris?"

"*When* is . . ."

"Mr. Carson?"

"I know but I can't say it."

Miss Frank made a mark in her grade book abstract-edly, with an indelible pencil.

"Very well, Mr. Carson, I'll say it for you. But of course that means I get an 'S' for today's recitation and you get an 'F'. . . . *When* is a conjunction introducing the subordinate clause: *when they heard what brave Oliver had done* . . . Miss Kromalny, suppose you tell us as simply and briefly as possible what *they* is."

In spite of every precaution the compact closed with a snap. All over the room, heads were raised. Wide-eyed and startled, Janet Martin raised her head at exactly the same moment as the rest. She made no effort to hide the compact. There it was, in plain sight on top of her desk. But so were a dozen like it, on a dozen other desks. Miss Frank glanced from one girl to another and her frown, finding no place to alight, was dissipated among the class generally. She walked around to the front of her desk.

"That's right, Miss Kromalny. *What* is a relative pronoun used as object of the verb *had done. Brave Oliver had done what.* Go on, please."

"*Brave* is . . ."

But who knows what *brave* is? Not Miss Frank. Her voice and her piercing colorless eye, her sharp knuckles all indicate fear, nothing but fear. As for the others, and especially the boys—Ford, Wilkinson, Carson, Lynch, Parkhurst, and the rest of them—it would appear that bravery is something totally outside their knowledge or experience. They look to Miss Kromalny for enlightenment.

"*Brave* is an adjective modifying the proper noun *Oliver. Had* is . . ."

In the second row on the aisle there is a boy who could tell the class what none of them, not even Miss Kromalny, knows. But it is not his turn to be called on, and besides, he isn't listening. His face is turned to the windows and his jaw is set. Two hunkies from the West Side are waiting for him where Foster Avenue runs under the elevated. At three o'clock he will go to his locker and get the books he needs for his homework—a Latin reader, a textbook on plane geometry—and find his way out into the open air. There will be time as he stands on the school steps, dwarfed by the huge doors and the columns that are massive and stone, to change his mind. Wilson Avenue is broad and has traffic policemen at several of the intersections. It is perfectly safe. Nothing will happen to him if he goes that way. But instead he turns up the collar of his corduroy coat and starts walking toward the elevated. . . .

"What is *done*, Mr.—ah—Mr. Charles Latham?"

Caught between two dangers, the one he had walked into deliberately and this new, this unexpected peril, Spud clenched and unclenched his hands. He had all of a sudden too many enemies. If he turned his attention to one, another would get him from behind. His mouth opened but no sound came out of it.

"I could have sworn that Mr. Latham was with us at the beginning of the hour. Excuse me while I mark him absent."

The class was given time to titter.

"Miss Janet Martin, what is *done?*"

The blood drained slowly from Spud's face. His sight and then his hearing returned. With an effort he pulled himself up into his seat. Now that he was sitting straight, no one bothered to look at him. He had had his moment and was free until the end of the hour. He could think about anything he pleased. He couldn't go back and attend to the hunkies under the elevated because they weren't there now. They never had been, actually. He had invented them, because he was homesick and bored and there was no one to take it out on. But it was all right for him to think about Wisconsin—about the tall, roomy, old-fashioned, white frame house the Lathams had lived in, with thirteen-foot ceilings and unreliable plumbing and a smell that was different from the smell of other houses and an attic and swallows' nests under the eaves and a porch, a wide open porch looking out over the lake. Or he could think about the other lake, on the other side of town. Or about the sailboats, in summer, passing the church point. Or about the railway station, with the morning train coming in from Milwaukee and the evening train from Watertown. Or about the post office and the movie theater and the jail. Or—it was all the same, really —he could think about Pete Draper and Spike Wilson and Walter Putnam; about old Miss Blair and the Rimmerman girls; about Arline Mayer and Miss Nell E. Perth, who taught him in first grade, and Abie Ordway, who was colored; about Mr. Dietz in the freight office, whose wife ran off with a traveling man, and his son Harold; about the Presbyterian minister and Father Muldoon and Fred Jarvis, the town cop, and Monkey Friedenberg and the Drapers' old white bulldog that rolled in dead fish whenever he found some and had rheumatism and was crazy. . . .

After a minute or two Spud's eyes came to rest on the mournful figure of Andromache. The class went on without him. When they had finished the sentence about brave Oliver, they opened their books to page 32 and the paragraph dealing with the subjunctive.

3

The ringing, brief but terrible, reverberated throughout all the corridors at five minutes before the hour. After the first bell no one, not even Miss Frank, could prevent them from talking out loud or from yawning openly.

They were permitted to stand in the aisles and stretch. The girls could pry open their compacts and, without fear of being reprimanded, apply spit to their bangs and rouge to their thin young cheeks. The boys could poke each other. Hurrying from the school library—second floor at the front of the building—to an algebra class or a civics class or gymnasium or hygiene or Spanish 2B or commercial geography, Adams could step on Catanzano's heels, and if deFresne saw a friend climbing the stairs ahead of him, he could quietly insert a ruler between the familiar legs and so make them trip and sprawl. The relief this afforded was only partial and temporary. By the ringing of the second bell, they were once more in their seats. The door was again on the right, the windows on the left —unless, as occasionally happened, they were reversed— and the calendar hanging behind the teacher's desk at the front of the room. The picture, of course, had been changed. It was sometimes King Lear's daughter Cordelia, in white, taking leave of her two evil sisters; sometimes the chariot race from *Ben-Hur*. Or it might be some old monotonous ruin like the Parthenon, the temple at Paestum, the Roman Forum—they hardly noticed which, once they had settled down and become resigned to another hour of inactivity.

The ringing at five minutes to three in the afternoon was different. Although it was no louder than the others, it produced a nervous explosion, a discharge of every ounce of boredom, restlessness, and fidgeting stored up during the long school day. Classrooms were emptied and this time they did not fill up again. The doors of lockers were opened, revealing pictures of movie stars, football players, cartoons, and covers of *College Humor*. Books were tossed in blindly. Caps, plaid woolen scarves, and autographed yellow slickers were taken out.

They all had something to do, some place to go.

The Martin twins met at their lockers—second floor

near the head of the center stairs—and parted again almost immediately. Elsa and her friend Hope Davison put on smocks and went down to the assembly hall where, with large brushes and buckets of paint, the stagecraft class was creating the seacoast of Illyria. Janet Martin went down the corridor to another stairway and out a side door of the building. When she appeared, Harry Hall left the cement pillar he was leaning against and came to meet her.

Carson and Lynch went to a movie on Western Avenue. It was called "The Downward Path" and a large sign outside the movie theater said no one under eighteen would be admitted. Carson and Lynch were only sixteen but they were large for their age. They stood and looked at the stills outside. Necking parties and girls half dressed, confronting their parents or the police. The blonde woman in the ticket booth accepted their two dimes without interest.

Rose Kromalny, whose family did not understand about art and music, waited for Miss Frank, to walk home with her.

The three boys who were trying out for assistant football manager met in Mr. Pritzker's office at one end of the gymnasium and tried not to look at one another.

The crack R.O.T.C. squad, consisting of Cadet Corporal Cline and Cadets Helman, Pierce, Krasner, Beckert, Millard, Richardson, and Levy, appeared in the schoolyard, in uniform, and commenced drilling. As always, there were those who stayed to watch.

There was a Junior Council meeting in Room 302 and a meeting of the business staff of *The Quorum* in 109. The Senior Sponsors held a brief meeting in the back of the assembly hall. The orchestra, as usual, practiced in 211. They had two new pieces: Mozart's "Minuet in E Flat" and the "Norwegian Rustic March" by Grieg.

Spud Latham, who had nothing to do and was in no hurry to go home since it wasn't home that he'd find when he got there, stood in front of his wooden locker and twiddled the dial. He was in the throes of another daydream. The school principal, on looking back over Spud's grades, had discovered that there had been some mistake; that they should all have been S's, not C's and D's. So he had the pleasure of coming home and announcing to his incredulous family that he was valedictorian of his class and the brightest student in the history of the school.

The pointer slipped by the last number of the combination and he had to work it over again. The second time he was successful. The locker flew open. His English grammar landed on the floor beside his gym shoes. He reached for his corduroy coat and, forgetting both the Latin reader and the textbook on plane geometry, closed the door of the locker. While he was moving the dial he glanced over his shoulder and saw a boy in a leather jerkin. The boy was waiting for him, apparently. For a moment Spud thought it was somebody he'd never seen before, but then he remembered. In the swimming pool when they were playing water polo. The kid who didn't have sense enough to let go of the ball. . . .

Spud turned quickly and walked away.

4

The way home from school led Lymie Peters past Le-Clerc's pastry shop. Without turning his head he looked in and saw Mark Wheeler in a coonskin coat, although the weather was mild, and Bea Crowley and Sylvia Farrell, who were trying to make a brown-and-white fox terrier sit up and beg for peanut brittle. And Bob Edwards, and Peggy Johnston, standing next to him in a dark red dress with a wide black patent leather belt.

And Janet Martin and Harry Hall, sitting side by side, their hands almost touching, on a dead radiator.

There were a lot of others at LeClerc's that afternoon. Lester Adams, Barbara Blaisdell or a girl who looked like Barbara Blaisdell, Bud Griesenauer, and Elwyn Glazer were standing in one little group. Beyond their group was another one. A third group was over by the counter. In the eleven or twelve steps that it took Lymie to pass the shop window, he saw them all, including Mrs. LeClerc with her dark skin and her polished black hair. Other parts of his long walk home were accomplished miraculously, without his hearing or perceiving a single detail of all that was going on around him. He made his way blindly across busy intersections. Streetcars, taxicabs, and double-decker busses passed unseen before his eyes. Signboards, filling stations, real estate offices he ignored. He went under the elevated and came out again without knowing it. But LeClerc's was something else again. The girls in LeClerc's were like wonderful tropical birds, like parrots and flamingos, like the green jungle fowl of Java, the ibis, the cockatoo, and the crested crane. They may possibly have realized this themselves. At all events, their voices were harsh and their laughter unkind. They parted their hair in the middle sometimes, sometimes on the side, and encouraged it to fall in a single point on their cheeks. Their dresses were simple and right for school, but came nevertheless from Marshall Field's or Mandel Brothers, never the Boston Store or The Fair. And their eyes, framed in mascara, knew everything.

The boys who hung out at LeClerc's had broad shoulders, or if they didn't, the padding in their coats took care of it. They wore plus fours as a rule, but some of them wore plus eights. Their legs were well shaped. Their bow ties were real and not attached to a piece of black elastic, like Lymie's. The little caps that clung to the backs of their heads matched the herringbone or the basket weave of their very light, their almost white suits. They had at their disposal a set of remarks which they could use over and over again, and the fact that there were a great many things in the world about which they had no knowledge and no experience did not trouble them.

The year before, they went to a Greek confectionery half a block up the street. Although the food in the school lunchroom was cheaper and more nourishing, so many of them insisted on eating at Nick's at noon that getting in and out of the door could only be achieved through force of character. You had to brace yourself and then shove and squirm and have friends make a place for you so that, together, you could elbow your way up to the counter. Once there, if you were lucky or if you had the kind of voice that outshouts other voices, you might come away with a bottle of milk and a ham sandwich or a cinnamon bun. But in the spring something (the same instinct, could it have been, that governs the migrations of starlings?) caused them to abandon the Greek confectionery and settle in LeClerc's, which was even smaller. Here every afternoon were to be found all the girls who never made the honor society or served as Senior Sponsors or took part in dramatics or played the viola; and yet who were, Lymie couldn't help noticing, so much better looking than the ones who did.

In the late afternoon LeClerc's was seldom over-crowded. If Lymie had pushed the door open and walked in, nobody would have indicated any surprise at seeing him. Mark Wheeler would have said "Hi there," over the heads of several people, and Peggy Johnston, who was in his division room, would probably have smiled at him. Her smile seemed to mean more than it did actually, but there were others. There were undoubtedly three or four groups he could have stood on the outside of, without anybody's minding it. After all, that was how it was done.

Ray Snyder and Irma Hartnell and Lester Adams had all had to stand around on the outside before they were taken in. But Lymie didn't try.

He was too proud perhaps and at the same time too uncertain of himself. The fact that his legs were too thin for him to wear knickers may have had something to do with it; or that he had no set of remarks. Also, the one time that he had screwed up his courage to ask a girl for a date, she had refused him. Considering how popular Peggy Johnston was, he should have asked her at least two days before he did. She said she was awfully sorry but she was going to the Edgewater Beach Hotel that night with Bob Edwards, and Lymie believed her. It wasn't that he doubted her word. But deep down inside of him he knew as he hung up the phone what would have happened if he'd called earlier. And because he still carried that heavy knowledge around with him, when he got abreast of LeClerc's big plate glass window he looked in and saw everything there was to see but kept right on walking.

Perhaps it was just as well; Lymie was only fifteen.

But why, since he was so proud and in many ways older than his years, did he let himself be drawn into the Venetian Candy Shop farther up the street and come out half a minute later with a large red taffy apple and proceed to smear his whole face up with it, in public, walking along the street?

5

Mrs. Latham reached up and turned on the bridge lamp at her elbow, though it was still daylight outside, and the lamplight fell upon her lap, which was overflowing with curtain material. There were piles of it on the sofa and on the floor around her, and it was hard to be-

lieve all this white net could hang from the four living
room windows that now were bare and looked out on
a park.

She sat with her back not quite touching the back of
the big upholstered chair and her head bent over her sewing. In shadow her face was expressive and full of character but when the light shone directly on it, although the
features remained the same, it seemed wan. It was the face
of a woman who might be unwell. Her soft brown hair
had very little gray in it and was done on top of her
head in a way that had been fashionable when she was a
girl. Anyone coming into the room and seeing her there
in the pale yellow light would have found her very
sympathetic, very appealing. Without having the least
idea what was in her mind as she raised the spool to her
lips and bit through the white cotton thread, he would
have felt sure that she had been through a great deal; that
she had given herself heart and soul to undertakings
which ought to have turned out well but hadn't always;
and that she was still, in all probability, an innocent person.

Near the center of the park—it was no more than an
open field with young elm trees set at regular intervals
around the edge—boys were playing touchball. Their
voices penetrated to the living room, through the closed
windows. Mrs. Latham may or may not have heard them;
she did not commit herself. A bakery truck passed in the
street, and several cars, one of them choking and sputter-
ing. The sound of footsteps on the cement walk caused
Mrs. Latham to raise her head and listen. Whoever it was
that she was expecting, this couldn't have been the one,
for she went back to her sewing immediately and did not
even bother to look out.

In spite of the solid row of front windows, the living
room was dark. It was the fault of the wallpaper and of
the furniture, which had obviously been acquired over

many years, at no great expense, and perhaps even accidentally. There was barely enough of it here and there in the room to make it livable. A plain grayish-blue rug covered most of the floor. The sofa and the chair Mrs. Latham sat in were upholstered in a subdued green. There was a phonograph and three wooden chairs, none of them wholly comfortable. The table was mission, with a piece of Chinese embroidery for a runner, and a pottery lamp with a brown shade. Also a round ashtray with cigar bands glued in a garish wheel to the underside of the glass, and a small brass bowl. The bowl was for calling cards. It had nothing in it now but a key (to a trunk possibly, or to the storeroom in the basement) and thumbtacks. On the shelf under the table were two books, an album partly filled with snapshots and a somewhat larger one containing views in color of the Wisconsin Dells.

The opposite wall of the living room was broken by a fireplace of smooth green tile made to look like bricks. The gas log had at one time or other been used. It was not lit now. At either end of the mantelpiece were two thin brass candlesticks, each holding a battered blue candle. Between them hung a framed sepia engraving of an English cottage at twilight. The cottage had a high thatched roof and was surrounded by ancient willow trees. The only other picture in the room hung at eye level above the sofa. It was a color print of a young girl, her head wound round with a turban, a sweet simpering expression on her face, and (surprisingly) one breast exposed.

Beyond the living room was the hall, with the front door bolted and chained, and then a rickety telephone stand. On the right was a door with a full-length mirror set into it, and another door that opened into Mr. and Mrs. Latham's bedroom. The hall opened into the dining room, which had two large windows looking out on a blank wall (this was not the apartment Mrs. Latham would have

chosen if they'd had all the money in the world) and was
a trifle too narrow for anyone to pass easily between the
table and the sideboard at mealtime. In the center of the
dining room table, on a crocheted doily, was a small house
plant, a Brazilian violet which showed no sign of blooming.

After the dining room came the kitchen, and right
beside it a bedroom—a girl's room by the look of the
dressing table and the white painted bed. On the dressing
table there was a letter. The room had a single window
and French doors at the far end. The curtains must have
been intended originally for some other room than this,
since they did not quite reach the window sill. They were
organdy and had ruffles. The glass in the French doors
was covered with white net.

It was easy to guess that the door in the hall, the one
with the mirror set into it, would, if opened, have
revealed a closet. But these two French doors were
tightly shut and without the help of Mrs. Latham there
would have been no telling what lay beyond them. When
the street lamps were turned on outside, something
prompted her to stand up, brush the threads from her lap,
and walk back here. She put her hand on a glass knob
and turned it slowly. The door opened, revealing a boy's
body lying fully clothed except for shoes, on a cot that
was too small for it. The position—knees bent awkwardly,
right arm dangling in space—seemed too inert for sleep.
It looked rather as if he had a short time before been
blindfolded and led out here to meet a firing squad. But
such things seldom happen on a sleeping porch, which
this clearly was, and besides, there was no wound.

6

When Mrs. Latham spread a blanket over Spud he turned and lay on his back. His face, freed for the time being of both suspicion and misery, was turned toward the ceiling.

It was too bad, Mrs. Latham thought as she bent over him, it was a great pity that they had to leave Wisconsin where they knew everybody and the children had so many friends. But at least Evans had been able to find another job. That wasn't always easy for a man his age. And in time he'd probably get a raise, like they promised him, and be making the same salary he had been making before. The children were still young. They'd have to learn to make new friends, and be adaptable.

She raised one of the windows a few inches and then closed the door behind her softly.

It was nearly six when Spud awoke. He drew the blanket around his shoulders without wondering where it had come from. For a moment he was quite happy. Then the room identified itself by its shape in the dark, and with a heavy sigh he turned on his side and lay with his hands pressed palm to palm, between his knees.

The light went on in the next room and he saw his sister Helen through the curtained doors. She seemed to be at a great distance. Remote and dreamlike, she was reading a letter.

The letter was probably from Pete Draper's brother Andy, Spud thought. "Gump" they called him. For three years now he had had a case on Helen, but his family didn't want him to marry her because she wasn't a Catholic. Every Friday night along about seven-thirty Andy used to appear at the front door with his dark blue suit on, and his hair slicked down with water. Sometimes he'd take Helen to a movie and sometimes they went to a basketball game. Once when Spud was coming home from a Boy Scout meeting on his bicycle, he saw them walking along the edge of the lake, and Andy had his arm around Helen. He was an awfully serious guy. Not like Pete. The night before they left Wisconsin, Helen sat out on the front porch talking to Andy for a long time. Spud was in bed but he wasn't asleep yet. Nobody was asleep in the whole house. His father and mother were in their room, and his mother was packing. He could hear her taking things out of the closet and opening and closing dresser drawers, and he kept tossing and turning in bed, and wondering what it was going to be like when they got to Chicago. His window was right over the porch and he could hear Andy and Helen talking. Several minutes would pass with no sound except the creak of the porch swing. Then they'd begin again, their voices low and serious. Spud thought once that Andy was crying but he couldn't be sure. And at a quarter to twelve his father came down, in his bathrobe, and sent Andy home.

By the way Helen tossed the letter on the bed, without bothering to fold it and put it back in the envelope, Spud could tell that his sister was not satisfied. Something she wanted to be in the letter wasn't in it, probably, but whatever it was, he'd never find out. She didn't trust him any more than he trusted her.

There was six years' difference between Spud's age and his sister's, and in order to feel even kindness toward her, he had to remember what she had been like when he was very small—how she looked after him all day long, defending him from ants and spiders and from strange dogs, how she stood between him and all noises in the night. Now, without either kindness or concern, he watched her dispose of her hat and coat in the closet, and brush her hair back from her forehead. His mother would have brushed her hair in the dark, so as not to waken him. Or if she needed a light to see by, she would have turned on the little lamp beside the bed, not the harsh overhead light. Helen never spared him. She didn't believe in sparing people.

The glare of the light raised Spud to a sitting position. He threw the blanket to one side, put his stockinged feet over the edge of the bed, and stretched until both shoulder blades cracked. The air that came in through the open window was damp and heavy and smelled of rain. He rubbed his eyes with the heel of his hand, yawned once or twice, and bending down, found his shoes. Having got that far he hesitated. All remembrance of what he was about to do with them seemed to desert him. He picked one of them up and stared at it as if by some peculiar mischance his life (and death) were inseparably bound up with this right shoe. When the light went off in the next room, the shoe dropped through his fingers. He yawned, shook his head feebly, and fell back on the bed. There he lay with his eyes open, unmoving, until Mrs. Latham came to the door and called him.

After she was gone he managed to sit up all over again, to put both shoes on, and to stand. Like a sailor wakened at midnight and obliged to make his way in a sleepy stupor up lurching ladders to the deck of the ship (or like the ship itself, pursuing blindly its charted course) Spud passed from room to room of the apartment until he found himself in the bathroom in front of the washstand. He splashed cold water on his face and reached out with his eyes shut until his hand came in contact with a towel. It was hanging on the rack marked SISTER but before he discovered that fact the damage had been done. He folded the towel, now damp and streaked with dirt, and put it back in what he imagined was the same way it had been before. Then he combed his hair earnestly, made a wild tormented face at himself in the bathroom mirror, and said, "Oh fuss!" so loudly that his mother and Helen heard him in the kitchen and stopped talking.

Their astonishment did not last. When he appeared in the doorway they hardly noticed him. He drew the kitchen stool out from under the enamel table and sat down and began to tie his shoes. When he finished, he straightened up suddenly. There was something that bothered him—something that he had done, or not done. Before he could remember what it was, Helen made him move so that she could get the bread knife out of the table drawer, and the whole thing passed out of his mind.

The kitchen smells, the way his mother took a long fork and tested the green beans that were cooking in a kettle on the top of the stove, the happy familiarity of all her movements, reassured him. It seemed almost like the kitchen of the house in Wisconsin. But then there was the rattle of a key in the front door, and Mr. Latham came in, looking tired and discouraged. Before Mr. Latham had even hung up his coat in the hall closet, the atmosphere of security and habit had vanished. Nothing was left but a bare uncomfortable apartment that would never be like the house they were used to. And when they sat down, the food seemed hardly worth coming to the table for.

7

Evans Latham was an honest and capable man. He had worked hard all his life, and with no other thought than to provide for his family, but somehow things never turned out for him the way they should have. There was always some accident, some freak of circumstance that couldn't possibly have been anticipated or avoided. Bad luck dogged his heels wherever he went. It was not the work of his enemies (he had none) and must therefore have been caused by a disembodied malignancy.

If bright and early some morning the Lathams had left their apartment, which was not what Mrs. Latham would have chosen anyway, and had set up some kind of temporary quarters in the park across the street, among the nursemaids and the babies in their carriages; if Mr. Latham, with advice and assistance from the old men and the boys who gathered in the late afternoon to play touchball, had offered sacrifices—the phonograph, perhaps, or the garish ashtray; if he had then called upon all their friends, or since they had no friends, their neighbors, to join them by moonlight with faces blackened or with masks, and wearing swords or armed with shotguns and revolvers or shinny sticks or golf clubs or canes; and if, at a signal from Reverend Henry Roth of St. Mary's Evangelical Lutheran Church, they had rushed into the deserted apartment firing guns, overturning everything under which a malignant spirit might lurk, tossing the furniture out of doors, beating against walls and windows; and if the old men and the young boys had marched nine times around the outside of the apartment building throwing torches about, shouting, screaming, beating sticks together, rattling old pans, while the nursemaids ran up and down, up and down the cellar stairs; if all this had been done properly, by people with believing hearts, it is possible that the spirit would have been driven off and that, for a time anyway, prosperity would have attended the efforts of Mr. Latham. Unfortunately this remedy, tried for centuries on one continent or another and always found helpful, never occurred to him. He went on day after day, doing the best he knew how. And it wasn't seeing other men get rich off his ideas (oil had been found on the ranch in Montana two years after he had sold it) or any single stroke of bad luck, but the terrible succession of them, large and small, which had changed him finally, so that now he was seldom hopeful or confident the way he used to be.

When, like tonight, he was not inclined to be talkative, the others felt it and did not attempt to be cheerful in spite of him. Helen addressed an occasional remark to her mother but Mrs. Latham's replies were not encouraging and led nowhere.

Except when he was obliged to ask for the butter or the bread or the jelly, Spud ate in silence. Much of the time he was not even there. Mr. Latham had to ask him twice if he wanted a second helping. Spud managed to pass his plate without meeting his father's eyes and said, "What are we going to have for dessert?"

"Baked apple," Mrs. Latham said.

"I wish you'd make a chocolate cake sometime. You know the kind—with white icing?"

Mrs. Latham felt the earth around the Brazilian violet and then poured the water that was in her glass over it.

"When we get straightened around," she said.

"I don't think I want any baked apple," Spud said. "I don't feel hungry."

"First time I ever knew you to make a remark like that," Mr. Latham said. "Are your bowels clogged up?"

"No," Spud said, "they're not. I just don't seem to be hungry any more. Not like I used to. I haven't felt really hungry since we moved to Chicago."

Mrs. Latham signaled to him to be quiet but he paid no attention to her. "It's the atmosphere," he said. "All this smoke and dirt."

Mr. Latham stabbed at a couple of string beans with his fork. "Perhaps you'd better move back to Wisconsin," he said sharply. "I seem to remember that you ate well enough when we lived there."

"I would if I could," Spud said.

"There's nobody stopping you," Mr. Latham said.

Mrs. Latham frowned. "Please, Evans," she said. "Eat your supper."

"Well," he said, turning to her, "it's very annoying to come home at the end of a hard day and find all of you glum and dissatisfied."

"If you call this home," Spud said.

"It's the best I can provide for you," Mr. Latham said to him. "And until you learn to accept it gracefully, maybe you better not come to the table."

Spud put his napkin beside his plate, kicked his chair back, and left the room. A moment later they heard the front door slam. Helen and her mother looked at each other. Mr. Latham, carefully avoiding their glances, picked up the carving knife and fork and cut himself a small slice of lamb, near the bone.

8

Two pictures stood side by side on Lymie Peters' dresser. The slightly faded one was of a handsome young man with a derby hat on the back of his head and a large chrysanthemum in his buttonhole. The other was of a woman with dark hair and large expressive dark eyes. The picture of the young man was taken in 1897, shortly after Mr. Peters' nineteenth birthday. The high stiff collar and the peculiarly tied, very full four-in-hand were bound to have their humorous aspect twenty-six years later. The photograph of Mrs. Peters was not a good likeness. It had been made from another picture, an old one. She had a black velvet ribbon around her throat, and her dress, of some heavy material that could have been either satin or velvet, was cut low on the shoulders. The photographer had retouched the face, which was too slender in any case, and too young. Instead of helping Lymie to remember what his mother had looked like, the picture only confused him.

He had come into the bedroom not to look at these pictures but to see what time it was by the alarm clock on the table beside his bed. The room was small, dark, and in considerable disorder. The bed was unmade. A pair of long trousers hung upside down by the cuffs from the top drawer of the dresser, and the one chair in the room was buried under layers of soiled clothes. On the floor beside the window was a fleece-lined bedroom slipper. There was fluff under the bed and a fine gritty dust on everything. The framed reproduction of Watts' "Hope" which hung over the dresser was not of Lymie's choosing. During the last five years Mr. Peters and Lymie had lived first in cheap hotels and then in a series of furnished kitchenette apartments, all of them gloomy like this one.

The grandfather's clock in the hall and the oriental rug on the floor in Lymie's room had survived from an earlier period. The rug was worn thin and curled at the corners, but when Lymie turned the light on, the childlike design of dancing animals—dogs, possibly, or deer, worked in with alternating abstract patterns—was immediately apparent, and the colors shone. The grandfather's clock remained at twenty-five minutes past five no matter what time it was, but the alarm clock was running and it was seven-twenty.

Lymie went into the bathroom and moved the pieces of his father's safety razor, the rusted blade, the shaving brush, and the tube of shaving soap, from the washstand to the window sill. He let the hot water run a moment, full force, to clean out the bowl, and then he washed his face and hands and ran a wet comb through his unruly hair. The arrangement was that if his father didn't come home by seven-thirty, Lymie was to go to the Alcazar Restaurant on Sheridan Road and eat by himself.

At exactly seven-thirty-one he let himself out of the front door of the apartment building. The other boys in the block had had their dinner and were outside. Milton Kirshman was bouncing a rubber ball against the side wall of the building. The others were in a cluster about Gene Halloway's new bicycle. They nodded at Lymie, as he went by. The bicycle was painted red and silver and had an electric headlight on it which wouldn't light. A slight wind blew the leaves westward along the sidewalk, and there were clouds coming up over the lake.

The Alcazar Restaurant was on Sheridan Road near Devon Avenue. It was long and narrow, with tables for two along the walls and tables for four down the middle. The decoration was *art moderne*, except for the series of murals depicting the four seasons, and the sick ferns in the front window. Lymie sat down at the second table from the cash register, and ordered his dinner. The history book, which he propped against the catsup and the glass sugar bowl, had been used by others before him. Blank pages front and back were filled in with maps, drawings, dates, comic cartoons, and organs of the body; also with names and messages no longer clear and never absolutely legible. On nearly every page there was some marginal notation, either in ink or in very hard pencil. And unless someone had upset a glass of water, the marks on page 177 were from tears.

While Lymie read about the Peace of Paris, signed on the thirtieth of May, 1814, between France and the Allied powers, his right hand managed again and again to bring food up to his mouth. Sometimes he chewed, sometimes he swallowed whole the food that he had no idea he was eating. The Congress of Vienna met, with some allowance for delays, early in November of the same year, and all the powers engaged in the war on either side sent plenipotentiaries. It was by far the most splendid and important assembly ever convoked to discuss and determine the affairs of Europe. The Emperor of Russia, the King of Prussia, the kings of Bavaria, Denmark, and Württemberg, all were present in person at the court of the Emperor Francis I in the Austrian capital. When Lymie put down his fork and began to count them off, one by one, on the fingers of his left hand, the waitress, whose name was Irma, thought he was through eating and tried to take his plate away. He stopped her. Prince Metternich (his right thumb) presided over the Congress, and Prince Talleyrand (the index finger) represented France.

A party of four, two men and two women, came into the restaurant, all talking at once, and took possession of the center table nearest Lymie. The women had shingled hair and short tight skirts which exposed the underside of their knees when they sat down. One of the women was fat. The other had the face of a young boy but disguised by one trick or another (rouge, lipstick, powder, wet bangs plastered against the high forehead, and a pair of long pendent earrings) to look like a woman of thirty-five, which as a matter of fact she was. The men were older. They laughed more than there seemed any occasion for, while they were deciding between soup and shrimp cocktail, and their laughter was too loud. But it was the women's voices, the terrible not quite sober pitch of the women's voices which caused Lymie to skim over two whole pages without knowing what was on them. Fortunately he realized this and went back. Otherwise he might never have known about the secret treaty concluded between England, France, and Austria, when the pretensions of Prussia and Russia, acting in concert, seemed to threaten a renewal of the attack. The results of the Congress were stated clearly at the bottom of page 67 and at the top of page 68, but before Lymie got halfway through them, a coat that he recognized as his father's was hung on the hook next to his chair. Lymie closed the book and said, "I didn't think you were coming."

"I got held up," Mr. Peters said. He put his leather brief case on a chair and then sat down across the table from Lymie. The odor on his breath indicated that he had just left a prospective client somewhere (on North Dearborn Street, perhaps, in the back room of what appeared to be an Italian *pizzeria* but was actually a speakeasy); his bloodshot eyes and the slight trembling of his hands were evidence that Mr. Peters drank more than was good for him.

Time is probably no more unkind to sporting characters than it is to other people, but physical decay unsustained by respectability is somehow more noticeable. Mr. Peters' hair was turning gray and his scalp showed through on top. He had lost weight also; he no longer filled out his clothes the way he used to. His color was poor, and the flower had disappeared from his buttonhole. In its place was an American Legion button.

Apparently he himself was not aware that there had been any change. He straightened his tie self-consciously and when Irma handed him a menu, he gestured with it so that the two women at the next table would notice the diamond ring on the fourth finger of his right hand. Both of these things, and also the fact that his hands showed signs of the manicurist, one can blame on the young man who had his picture taken with a derby hat on the back of his head, and also sitting with a girl in the curve of the moon. The young man had never for one second deserted Mr. Peters. He was always there, tugging at Mr. Peters' elbow, making him do things that were not becoming in a man of forty-five.

"I won't have any soup, Irma," Mr. Peters said. "I'm not very hungry. Just bring me some liver and onions." He turned to Lymie. "Mrs. Botsford come?"

Lymie shook his head. "Maybe she's sick."

"She always calls the office when she's sick," Mr. Peters said. "More than likely she's quit. It's a long way to come and she may have found somebody on the South Side to work for. If she *has* quit, she'll get in touch with me. She's got four weeks' wages coming to her."

"But I thought you paid her last week," Lymie said.

"I was going to," Mr. Peters said, "but I didn't get around to it." He glanced at the next table. "What kind of a day did you have at school?"

"All right," Lymie said.

"Anything happen, specially?"

A whistle blew faintly, Mr. Pritzker's whistle, and for a moment the splashing surrounded Lymie and sucked him down. He decided that it wasn't anything that would interest his father. School was one world, home was another. Lymie could and did pass back and forth between them nearly every day of his life, but it was beyond his power to bring the two together. If he tried now, his father would make an attempt at listening but his eyes would grow vague, or he would glance away for a second and hardly notice when Lymie stopped talking.

"No," Lymie said, "nothing happened."

Mr. Peters frowned. He would have liked the people at the next table to know how smart Lymie was and what good grades he got on his monthly report card.

There was a long silence during which Lymie might as well have been studying, but he didn't feel that he should when his father was sitting across from him, with nothing to read and nobody to talk to. When Irma reappeared with the liver and onions, it was a great relief to both of them. Mr. Peters cut a small piece of meat, stuck his fork into it, and raised it to his mouth. Just as he was about to take the meat from the fork, Irma leaned across the table and set a glass of ice water at his place. He put the fork down, broke off a piece of bread, buttered the bread carefully, and then put it on the tablecloth beside his plate. After that he raised the piece of liver to his mouth again, but instead of taking it he said thoughtfully,

"Irma is a very fine girl. Too capable to be doing this kind of work. She ought to be in an office somewhere making twenty-five dollars a week."

Lymie, who had observed his father bending forward slightly so that he could see inside the neckline of Irma's uniform, said nothing. The fork remained poised. After a moment Mr. Peters lowered it with the piece of liver still on it, took a drink of water, and then after a moment picked the fork up as if this time he had every intention of eating. The front door opened and a man and woman came in. Mr. Peters turned to look at the woman's legs as she walked back through the restaurant. The liver fell off the fork, so he took a piece of fried onion and raised that halfway to his mouth.

This comedy went on for nearly twenty minutes and then Mr. Peters signaled to Irma to take his plate away.

"You haven't eaten anything," Lymie said.

"I wasn't hungry," Mr. Peters said. "All I want is some coffee," and once more there was a long silence, during which each of them searched vainly through his whole mind for something to say to the other.

9

Continuing the argument at the supper table, finding answers that made a monkey out of his father, Spud left the park, where he had been sitting all alone on a bench for the last hour and a half, and came to a neighborhood where the apartment houses no longer presented a continuous brick front to the street. Instead there were open spaces where the light from the street lamp shone on a cluster of shabby For Sale signs and signs beginning This Choice Building Site, with the rest of the lettering submerged in weeds. Sometimes there was only one three-

story building to a square block, and no trees, no bar-
berry bushes or bridal wreath to soften the hard outlines
of the masonry. Here the air, although tainted with coal
smoke, was freer, more like the air of open country.

Occasionally a car drove past, changing the aspect of
the street by its headlights, making everything look thin
and theatrical. The people Spud overtook on foot might
have been young and beautiful and willing to hand over
their lives to him, or they might have been older than
death. So far as he was concerned they were shadows. He
walked past them without even a sidelong glance. When
he came to an iron bridge he loitered for several minutes,
watching the water flow underneath, and no one caught
up with him, which was odd. Possibly the others—the girl
with the cloth rose on her hat, the Christian Science prac-
titioner, the young boy with a canvas bag stuffed full of
handbills, the piano tuner, and the woman whose blood
pressure was higher than it should have been at her age—
perhaps all these people had some destination or were
expected somewhere. Spud was sailing before his own
anger.

He walked on past a paint and varnish factory where,
at the gate, an electric bulb shone down on the night
watchman's empty chair. Across the street stood a row of
ramshackle two-story frame houses, each with the same
peaked roof, the same high sagging front porch. The
houses extended for two blocks. Then the future asserted
itself over the past and there were more apartment buildings with vacant lots between them, more signs, more
weeds growing up through unfinished foundations.

A big Irishwoman in a black coat came toward Spud
on the wrong side of the walk. She was feeling the effects
of liquor and self-pity, and the least people could do, it
seemed to her, was to get out of her way. Spud came
straight on. At the very last moment her truculence
turned to panic and she stepped off the sidewalk. But he

was not, as she had thought, a blind man, so she shouted after him: "Damn kids! Think they own the earth . . ."

Spud turned and looked back, seeing the drunken woman for the first time. He shook his head and walked on. The members of his own family—his father, his mother, and his sister—all were against him; it was not surprising that, without knowing how or why, he should bring on himself the ill will of strangers.

At Christiana Avenue the sidewalk gave out abruptly and rather than continue through mud and have to clean his shoes when he got home, Spud turned south. After one long block, Christiana Avenue also gave out, and he turned back east again, zigzagging until he found another bridge and a street that brought him to the western edge of the park. In the park at the drinking fountain Spud found what all day long he had been searching for.

The other boy was astride a bicycle and apparently deep in conversation with two girls. He looked up as Spud walked past. Neither gave any sign of recognition. The other boy balanced himself on his bicycle with the front wheel turning this way and that, and his right foot resting against the cement base of the drinking fountain. His straight blond hair was parted in the middle and trained back like an Arrow collar ad, but it kept falling forward, and he had a nervous habit of tossing his head back.

Spud sat down on a bench near a young maple tree and crossed his legs so that his right ankle rested on his left knee. The girls giggled, which was to be expected, and when they bent over the drinking fountain, the blond boy made the water spurt up in their faces. After having this ancient trick played on them, they decided to turn the water on for each other, but the blond boy promised, and crossed his heart to die, and said honestly, until at last they gave him one more chance. Spud could have told them what would happen. He knew also that the argument by the drinking fountain was for his benefit. If the blond boy had been sure of himself, he wouldn't have wasted valuable time spurting water on girls and pretending to run over their feet with the front wheel of his bicycle.

Tilting his head back until he could look up at a street lamp that was directly behind him, Spud ignored the whole performance. His throat was dry and he could feel his heart pounding inside his shirt. He watched the moth millers beating against the glass globe, which was large and round and made the yellow leaves of the maple glow with light.

After a while the two girls (whether in real or mock anger there was no telling) walked away. Left to himself, the blond boy circled once around the drinking fountain and then rode past Spud so slowly that the bicycle wavered and nearly fell. Spud waited until he tossed his hair back, and then said quietly, "Why don't you get a violin?"

The blond boy didn't answer. He rode on about fifteen feet, made a sudden swift turn, came back, and stopped directly in front of Spud. One foot was on a pedal, the other resting on the sidewalk. "I don't like your attitude," he said.

Spud cleared his throat and spat carefully, so that it just missed the front wheel of the blond boy's bicycle. The wheel was withdrawn a few inches.

"You looking for trouble?"

"If I saw some," Spud said, "I don't know as I'd get up and walk away from it."

They were in position now, their moves as fixed and formal as the sexual dancing of savages.

"Because if you're really looking for trouble," the blond boy said, "I'd be only too happy to beat the shit out of you."

"You and how many other Swedes?"

That did it apparently, for the blond boy let go of

his bicycle, which fell with a clatter, and Spud rose from the bench to meet him. They stood sizing each other up. The blond boy was taller than Spud, thicker through the waist, and larger boned. They each waited for the sudden twitch, the false movement which would release their arms and set them slugging at one another. They could not fight until the willingness to fight, rising inside them like mercury in a glass, reached a certain point; and that, rather than what they said or did or any ability to discriminate between a disparaging remark which could with dignity be allowed to pass and an insult which must be challenged if one is to maintain honor, cast the decision.

"There's a better place over there," the blond boy said, pointing to a dark clump of shrubbery.

"Okay," Spud said.

They walked into an open space among the bushes, took off their coats, their ties, unbuttoned their shirt collars, and rolled up their sleeves as if they were about to inspect each other's vaccination marks. There was a moment when they stood helplessly. Then the mercury began to rise again. The blond boy tossed the hair out of his eyes and shifted his balance, and Spud knew as definitely as if it had been announced over the radio what was coming. He ducked just in time.

No longer was it necessary to imagine two bohunks waiting under the elevated. He had an enemy now, a flesh and blood Swede with a cruel mouth and murder in his pale blue eyes. The Swede got through Spud's guard and landed one on the end of his chin. It only made Spud feel stronger, more sure of himself. All the rancor against his father for uprooting him, all his homesickness, his fear of Miss Frank's sarcasm, his contempt for the dressy boys who sat around him in the classrooms at school, his dislike for girls who painted their faces and for the other kind who knew their lessons and were superior, his resentment at being almost but not quite poor, at having to

go through his sister's bedroom to get to his own—
everything flowed out through his fists. At each impact
he was delivered of some part of his accumulated misery
and he began to feel larger than life size.

10

Janet Martin with her hair in curlers and her face
scrubbed clean of rouge and powder and lipstick was not
so different from her sister Elsa, after all. In the dark they
talked across the narrow space that separated their two
beds, and yawned, and broke the sudden silences with
more talk. Their voices grew drowsy and the things they
had to say to each other more intimate.

Carson and Lynch, in spite of what they had seen in
the movie house on Western Avenue, fell into a dreamless
sleep the moment their heads touched the pillow.

At quarter after eleven Lymie Peters was still awake.

On the way home from the Alcazar Restaurant Mr.
Peters had stopped in at a cigar store and made a telephone
call, the results of which were obviously satisfactory. As
soon as they got back to the apartment he went out to the
tiny kitchen and from one of the cupboards he produced
two green demijohns, one containing alcohol, the other
a little less than half full of distilled water. Then he made
a trip to the linen closet, where he kept the glycerin and
also a very small bottle containing oil of juniper. When
alcohol, juniper drops, and glycerin had been added to
the distilled water, in proper proportion, Mr. Peters took
the bottle in his hands and shook it vigorously up and
down, from side to side in wide sweeping arcs. After a
time his arms grew tired and he called Lymie, who came
and took turns swinging the demijohn.

To Lymie the word *party* had once meant birthday presents wrapped in white tissue paper, ice cream in the shape of a dove or an Easter lily, and games like London Bridge and pin-the-tail-on-the-donkey. Now it meant a telephone call from the corner cigar store and the shades drawn to the window sills. The women who came to see his father had bobbed hair that more often than not was hennaed, they smoked cigarettes, their voices were raucous and hard, and their dresses kept coming up over their knees.

If he walked into the living room they usually made a fuss over him, and asked him to come and sit beside them on the sofa. Sometimes they straightened his necktie and slicked his hair down and asked him how many girls he had and if he knew why the chicken crossed the road. He did, actually, but he pretended that he didn't. No matter what he said, they always burst out laughing, and apparently it was about something which wasn't exactly the thing they were talking about, some joke that Lymie wasn't old enough to understand. He didn't stay long. He didn't want to, particularly, and he waited for his father to give him that look which meant it would be a good idea if Lymie said good night and went back to his own room.

Tonight, when the doorbell rang, Lymie raised his head and listened. He was prepared for what was coming. It had happened many times before. But nevertheless the expression on his thin pointed face was of anxiety. He heard his father's footsteps in the front hall. Mr. Peters was pressing the buzzer that released the vestibule door. A moment after he turned the double lock, a voice broke out on the stairs, a woman's voice, and when she reached the landing, Mr. Peters joined in, both of them talking loudly.

"Whee I'm out of breath. Lymon, the next apartment you move into better be on the second floor before I develop heart trouble from climbing the stairs."

"You're getting fat, that's all that's the matter with you."

"I'm not either getting fat . . . Why do you say things like that?"

"What's this right here . . . feel it?"

"Don't be silly, that's just my . . ."

Lymie got up noiselessly and closed the door of his room. It made very little difference. The woman's voice would have penetrated through stone. For a while after he had undressed and got into bed, he lay curled on his right side, listening. Then he began to think about the house where he was born. It was a two-story Victorian house with a mansard roof and trellises with vines growing up them—a wistaria and a trumpet vine. The house was set back from the street and there was an iron fence around the front yard, and in one place a picket was missing. As a child he seldom went through the front gate, unless he was with some grown person. Bending down to go through the hole in the fence gave him a sense of coming to a safe and secret place.

The odd thing was that now, when he went back to the house in his mind, and tried to walk through it, he made mistakes. It was sometimes necessary for him to re-arrange rooms and place furniture exactly before he could remember the house the way it used to be.

The house had a porch running along two sides of it, and the roof sloped down so that it included the second story. The front door opened into a hall, with the stairs going up, and then the door to the library, the door to the living room. Beyond the living room was the dining room, and beyond the dining room was the kitchen. The stairs turned at the landing, and upstairs there was another hall. The door to his room, the door to the guest room, the door to his mother and father's room, and the door to the sewing room all opened off this upstairs hall. And there was a horsehair sofa where he sat sometimes in his nightgown, when there was company and he wanted to listen to what was going on downstairs. The sofa scratched his legs. There was also a bookcase in the upstairs hall, with his books in it, and a desk, and over the desk was a picture of a boy with a bow and arrow and a gas jet that was left burning all night. The bathroom was at the end of a long corridor and up one step. When you got to the end of the corridor you turned right if you wanted to go into the bathroom, and left if you wanted to go into the back hall, where the clothes hamper was, and the door to the maid's room, and the back stairs. The back stairs used to frighten him even in the daytime, and at night he never dared look to the left, as he reached the end of the corridor.

About the bathroom he was confused. Sometimes the washbowl was in one place and sometimes it was in another. The tub was large and had claws for feet, he was sure. But was it at the far end of the room, under the window? Or was that where the toilet was?

He gave up trying to establish the arrangement of the bathroom and thought instead of the butler's pantry, which he had completely forgotten before. It was between the dining room and the kitchen. The butler's pantry was where the door to the cellar stairs was. You opened this door and the stairs went down to the furnace room, which was dark and full of cobwebs. And there was no railing.

There was also a door that opened off the kitchen, and another stairs which led to the cellar where his mother kept all kinds of fruit in jars on open shelves.

The discovery of these two sets of stairs, both of which he had totally forgotten, pleased Lymie. He thought about them for a minute or two and then suddenly the house went out of his mind, leaving no trace. He was back in his own bed, and it was the utter absolute silence that kept him from sleeping.

I I

Mrs. Latham was still awake when Spud came in. She called to him softly from her bedroom. "Is that you, son?" It couldn't have been anyone else and it was really another question altogether that she was asking him. When he answered, the sound of his voice satisfied her apparently. "Turn out the light in the hall," she said. "And sleep well."

"Same to you," Spud said.

With his tongue he touched the cut on the inside of his cheek. There was a slight taste in his mouth which was blood. His shirt was torn all the way down his back. His hair was full of dirt and leaves. He was glad his mother hadn't waited up for him. It would upset her if she knew he had been fighting.

He tried not to make a sound going through Helen's room but he miscalculated the position of a small rocking chair and fell over it. Picking himself up he was as conscious of his sister's irritation as if she had spoken out loud, but there was no sound from the bed, not even the creaking of springs.

When Spud got his clothes off he was too tired to do anything but crawl in between the covers. Too tired and too happy. For the first time the room seemed his. It was a nice room, better than he had thought. It had all these windows. *The blond boy began to give way, to defend himself. Foot by foot they fought their way across the open space in the shrubbery, their breathing and the impact of their fists the only sound, their bodies the whole field of vision. When the blond boy, stepping backward, tripped and lost his balance, Spud fell on top of him.* Carlson, his name was: Verne Carlson. So he must have been a Swede. He was not especially different from a lot of guys in Wisconsin. Guys like Logan Anderson or Bob Trask, who think they are a lot tougher than they really are. But on the other hand (Spud yawned) not bad when you get to know them.

The night sky was split wide open by a flash of lightning and then another paler one. If it rained it would probably get the window sill and the floor wet but it didn't matter. Nothing mattered now. *The blond boy was tired. He got his legs around Spud's waist and then didn't have the strength to cut off Spud's wind. They lay that way, locked and not moving, until a sudden jerk pried the heavy legs apart and Spud rolled free.* He twisted around in the bed until he found the place he was looking for. *The blond boy made a grab for him and missed and grabbed again, but Spud knew what he was doing. He waited and saw his chance and pinned the blond boy's shoulders to the ground. Give up? he asked. Do you give up? The blond boy lay there panting, his eyes closed, his face streaked with sweat and dirt, and didn't answer.* Spud wanted to stay awake until he heard the sound of rain but his eyelids closed of their own accord and it didn't seem worth while opening them. Somewhere down the block a car started up and there were voices, people saying good night. And then his mother's voice saying . . . and the voice of the woman who passed him on the sidewalk. . . . No, that was what his mother said. Sleep well, she said. He flexed his fingers, sighed, and was almost gone when he remembered something. The splashing and the shouting in the pool. But that wasn't it. It wasn't while they were playing water polo, it was afterward. It was that skinny kid who. . . .

was safely past, the shoulder relaxed. With a kind of wonder Spud felt the fragile collarbone moving, and the tendons, and made up his mind to follow trustingly.

The initiation should have been held in a long hut under the darkest trees in a forest, but that couldn't be managed; there are no forests, strictly speaking, anywhere near Chicago. The fraternity had engaged a suite of rooms on the fourth floor of a North Side residential hotel. The committee in charge had come early, bringing with them the paraphernalia for the initiation. They had unfortunately no masks, no slit gongs, no bull roarer. No one had told them about these things. But they had bananas, limburger cheese, a ball of kitchen string, French dressing, soured milk, tartar sauce, oysters, and a quart milk bottle full of stale tea. Because they were obliged to perform in one evening a ritual that, done properly, requires from two to three months, they yanked the shades down and hurriedly pushed the furniture out of the way. It would have saved them embarrassment later and also some expense if they had rolled up the rugs, which were a bloody shade of red, but they didn't think about it. Dede Sandstrom tore an old sheet of his mother's into strips that could be used for blindfolds. The other boys cut several lengths of string and on the end of each one they fastened an oyster.

Shortly after seven o'clock the pledges appeared, one at a time, in the hotel lobby. Their pockets were stuffed with chocolate bars, Life Savers, candy, and chewing gum. Their faces were scrubbed and shining, and they were dressed as for a Friday night date at the Edgewater Beach Hotel. This was a Wednesday—Wednesday, the twenty-fifth of January. The elevator boy delivered them, one at a time, at the fourth floor, where they parted from him reluctantly as though from a friend and made their way along the corridor, reading the room numbers. Lynch's hand sought his striped bow tie, lest it be at an angle, and two minutes later, at almost the same spot, Carson felt his wavy hair, plastered to his skull with water. Catanzano, caught off guard by a Florentine mirror, reassured himself by stretching his bull neck and squaring his heavy shoulders. In spite of the red arrows painted on the wall opposite the elevator shaft, Lymie Peters went the wrong way and had to retrace his steps. His face was flushed and he had a stitch in his side, from running. He had left home in what he thought was plenty of time, but then he had lingered in front of a butcher shop on Sheridan Road between Albion and Northshore Avenues. The shop was closed for the night and the floor was strewn with fresh sawdust, and in a row facing the plate-glass door stood a plaster sow and four little pigs. Caught in a timeless pink light they looked out at Lymie and he looked in at them until the big round clock on the wall of the butcher shop released him from this trap for children and sent him running down the street.

Spud Latham was the last to come, and he was several minutes late. This tardiness was intentional. His clothes had changed since last October. He wore plus eights, like Mark Wheeler and Ray Snyder, whom he counted among his innumerable enemies. He knew that they hated him (or at least that they didn't like his attitude) and he stood and faced the door of Room 418 with his jaw set, waiting for somebody to make a false move. When there was only silence he grew impatient, raised his fist, and rapped on the door with his bare knuckles.

"Who's there?"

The voice that spoke through the closed door was hollow and sinister.

Spud answered according to previous instructions: "Neophyte wishing admission to the Isle of Thura."

"Shut your eyes, neophyte, and face the other way on pain of deadly punishment."

The door was opened behind his back. Hands blindfolded him, and other hands pulled him roughly into the room, where they stripped him and disfigured his body with Carter's drawing ink and tincture of iodine. He submitted to this without protest, but then his coming here at all was an act of submission. Along with Spud's need for enemies was also the need to have friends, to be accepted by the right people.

He was pushed into the straggling line of naked, blindfolded neophytes, between Lymie Peters and Carson. After Carson came Lynch, with his bow tie retied around his bare neck. Then Ford, Catanzano, and deFresne—each with his right hand on the shoulder of the boy ahead of him. They were driven round and round the room, walking, running, hopping on one leg, and squatting duck-fashion until their knees went soft. They were driven over and under chairs, into the next room and out again, to the sound of paddles slapping, feet stomping, voices shouting, the whoosh of a broom descending (on whose buttocks?) and other often inexplicable noises.

The members of the initiation committee were enjoying themselves thoroughly. They had once undergone this same abuse and so it satisfied their sense of justice. But the real reason for their pleasure was probably more obscure. They were re-enacting, without knowing it, a play from the most primitive time of man. In this play the men of the village had a grudge against the nearly grown boys, or were afraid of them perhaps. In retaliation for some crime which the boys had committed or were about to commit (possibly some crime which the men themselves had once committed against men who were older than they) the boys of the village were torn from the arms of their mothers, rounded up, and made to undergo a period of intense torture. This torture may even have been a symbolic substitution for punishment by death. At all events it kept the committee busy from twenty minutes after seven until a quarter of eleven.

The neophytes were only kept in line half an hour. The more refined torment had to be administered singly. Carson wrestled for a long time with temptation. Lynch had to scramble like an egg, and Ford ate a square meal. DeFresne wore the skin off the end of his nose pushing a penny along the red carpet. And Catanzano, who was the biggest of the pledges and played guard on the football team, had to do as many push-ups as he could and then ten more. With the third he felt a hand on the small of his back. The hand pushed down cruelly whenever he pushed up. After a time he collapsed and lay still, not minding the catcalls and the obscene noises. He was a wop. His natural place was with the excluded. He was surprised to be here at all.

The fact that Lymie Peters was no good at games and that he never was seen in LeClerc's should have been enough to keep him from being pledged also, but Mark Wheeler had decided it would be a good thing for the fraternity to have somebody whose grades they could point to, if they ever got called up before the principal, and Mark Wheeler had persuaded the others. Having done that much for Lymie, he now knocked him off his feet with a frying pan. Bob Edwards made Lymie read a section of the classified telephone directory with the hot end of a cigarette directly under his nose. The others were fairly considerate. Lymie without his clothes on looked more delicate than he actually was, and they were afraid of injuring him. Also they were waiting for Frenchie deFresne. They wanted to see if they could make Frenchie cry.

When it was his turn they began by beating him with a broom to teach him that no one was kidding. They made him shadowbox blindfolded, hitting him occasionally and shoving him so that he scraped his knuckles on the rough plaster wall. They rubbed hard on the short hair at the back of his neck and also pounded incessantly on his collarbone (this produced an immediate and subtle pain) and made him do alternate knee-bends while they counted: 1, 3, 4, 7, 8, 2, 10, 6, 14, 19, 9 . . . When he had reached what they hoped was a state of physical exhaustion, Ray Snyder shouted: "Think of a nine-letter word beginning with S and ending with N or you'll be in a hell of a SituatioN. We'll throw you in the SheboygaN River, neophyte. It's damn cold there and no good SamaritaN can save you from pneumonia. The SuspicioN will be thrown elsewhere, neophyte, so don't try for revenge"—all the while pounding Frenchie's biceps and slapping his chest. Frenchie couldn't think of any nine-letter word beginning with S and ending with N, so they slapped him across the face several times. When he flinched, they slapped him harder until he quit flinching. After they had slapped him as hard as they could, fifteen or twenty times on both sides of his face, Frenchie cried and they were free to go on with the next part of the initiation.

The neophytes were lined up once more and subjected to divination to determine whether or not they had been experimenting with sex. All seven of them were found guilty and made to swallow a pill. To test their courage they were pushed one at a time up a tall stepladder from which, at a given signal, they were to throw themselves into space. Their blindfolds were raised for a second only, so that they could look down at the board full of rusty nails that they would land on. Carson's blindfold was not as tight as it should have been. He saw the rubber mat being substituted at the last moment for the board, but Lymie flung himself believing in the rusty nails and trusting that Mark Wheeler would be there to catch him. Nobody caught him. He landed on his hands and feet, unhurt, and the voice that cried out in pain was not his voice.

Spud Latham, who was next in line, jerked his blindfold off and saw that he had been fooled. The committee was astonished by this action, and somewhat at a loss to deal with it. They decided that there was no point in making Spud jump off the ladder after he knew what the trick was, so they tied his blindfold on tighter than before, and shoved him out of the way. Catanzano came next, then Ford, who hesitated when the signal was given and tried to back down the ladder. He had stepped on a rusty nail the summer before, at Lake Geneva, and he kept trying to explain about this; in the end they had to push him off.

The earth is wonderfully large and capable of infinite repetition. At no time is it necessary to restrict the eye in search of truth to one particular scene. Torture is to be found in many places besides the Hotel Balmoral, and if it is the rites of puberty that you are interested in, you can watch the same thing (or better) in New Guinea or New South Wales. All you have to do is locate a large rectangular hut in the forest with two enormous eyes painted over the entrance. You will need a certain amount of foolhardy courage to pass through this doorway and you may never come out again, but in any case once you are inside you will learn what it feels like to be in the belly of Thuremlin (or Daramulun, or Twanyirika, or Katajalina —the name varies in different tribes), that Being who swallows young boys and after the period of digestion is completed restores them to life, sometimes with a tooth missing, and always minus their foreskin.

When you have found your place in the circle on the dirt floor, it will not matter to you that Pokenau, the boy on your right, and Talikai, the boy on your left, are darker skinned than Ford and Lynch, and have black kinky hair. In that continual darkness, the texture of your own hair and the color of your skin and eyes will not be noticeable. The odor that you detect will be that which you were aware of in the Hotel Balmoral. The odor of fear is everywhere the same.

In the belly of Thuremlin a comradeship is established which will last Pokenau and Talikai and Dobo-
mugan, and Mudjulamon and Baimal and Ombomb and
Yabinigi and Wabe and Nyelahai the rest of their lives.
They can never meet one another on any mountain path
or in a flotilla of outriggers and not remember how
month after month they sat in a crouching position, cross-
legged, without moving; how they heard, not with their
ears but through their hands, the strange tones which are
the voices of spirits; how they learned to make the loud
humming noise which so terrifies women; how one by one
the mysteries were revealed to them—the sacred masks,
the slit gongs, the manikin with the huge head and the
gleaming mother-of-pearl eyes.

Along with the singing and eating, the boys are reminded again and again of how, as children, they were
never far from their father's arms, and how their elder
brothers hunted for them. Flutes play in the morning
and evening, and when the boys are led to the bathing
pool, the ghosts of their ancestors bend back the brambles
from the path.

In a primitive society the impulses that run contrary
to the patterns of civilization, the dark impulses of envy,
jealousy, and hate, are tolerated and understood and
eventually released through public ritual, through cutting
with crocodiles' teeth, burning, beating, incisions in the
boy's penis. This primitive ritual of torture is more pain-
ful, perhaps, but no more cruel than the humor of high
school boys. Each stage of the torture is related to a
sacred object, and the novices are convinced that, as a
result of running the gantlet and being switched with
nettles, they will have muscle and bone, they will grow
tall and broad in the shoulders, their spirit will be war-
like, and they will have the strength between their legs to
beget many children.

Occasionally in New Guinea a boy will get into the

wrong stomach of the Being, the stomach that is intended for pigs; and that boy cannot be restored to life with the others. But as a rule when the period of seclusion is over, all of the boys appear once more in the village, splendidly dressed in feathers and shell ornaments. Their eyes are closed. They still have to be led by their guardians and though they feel their mother's arms around them, they cannot respond. Even after they have been commanded to open their eyes, the most ordinary acts of life remain for a time beyond their understanding. If the support of their guardian is withdrawn, they totter. They do not remember how to sit down, or how to talk, or which door you enter a house by. When a plate of food is given them, they hold it upside down. Gradually they learn all over again what to do and how to take care of themselves, and the use of their new freedom. They can carry iron weapons after the initiation, and they are free to marry. And they neither fear death nor long for it, because death is behind them.

All this requires the presence and active participation of grown men. Boys like Mark Wheeler, Ray Snyder, and Dede Sandstrom aren't equal to it. In their hands, the rites of puberty are reduced to a hazing; and what survives afterwards is merely the idea of exclusion, or of revenge. The novices are in no way prepared to pass over into the world of maturity and be a companion to their fathers.

The night that Lynch was born, his father, then a young man of twenty-four, stood and stared at his son through the window in the hospital corridor with the tears streaming down his cheeks. Where was he now? Catanzano's father was dead, but why wasn't Mr. Ford at the Hotel Balmoral that evening? He could have talked to his son quietly and perhaps coaxed him until Ford jumped from the stepladder of his own free will. Where was Carson's father? And Frenchie deFresne's? And what about Mr. Latham? That stupid pursuit of enemies that

forehead against the washbasin, which was cool, though there was no comfort in it. "Oh . . ." he said very quietly, over and over, wanting to die. The minutes passed, and finally there was a sharp rap on the door. This was neither the time nor the place for despair.

He sighed and stood up and took his toothbrush out of the rack. Because there was, after all, nothing else to do, he scrubbed his teeth vigorously, avoiding his reflection in the mirror. Then he untied the strings of his pajama drawers, pulled the coat over his head, and reached for the cold water faucet that was connected with the shower. The cold shock on his face and on his spine kept him from thinking, but afterward, when he stepped out of the tub and began to dry himself, his mind took up exactly where it had left off. The last traces of ink and iodine came off on the towel.

Looking at them, Spud remembered, as though it were something that had happened long ago, how the neophytes, when the initiation was over and the blindfolds were jerked off, looked at one another with surprise and then at their own ink-stained, iodine-smeared, sweating, dirty bodies. Ray Snyder gave them the password (Anubis) and showed them the sacred grip, which turned out to be the same as the Boy Scouts'. After what had happened this morning, none of that mattered in the least.

At breakfast Spud sat with his head bent over his oatmeal and his mind off on a desperate search for some time or circumstance when he could have exposed himself. So far as girls were concerned, there weren't any. In Wisconsin they used to play postoffice at parties, and spin-the-bottle, but he hadn't even kissed a girl since he moved to Chicago. The trouble was, you didn't always need to get it from contact with a girl. The man who lectured in the assembly room of the high school (to the boys only; there was a woman who lectured to the girls) said you could get it in dozens of different ways; from drinking cups even, and from towels. Probably there was no use trying to figure out where he got it, since there were thousands of ways it could have happened. The only odd thing, the part Spud couldn't understand, was how people could wake up happy in the morning and dress and eat breakfast and go about their business all day without ever taking any precautions, without even *realizing* the danger that existed everywhere about them.

When Mrs. Latham said, "Do you feel all right?" he opened his mouth to tell her that his oatmeal dish would have to be washed separately, also the spoon he was eating with, and his eggcup; they'd all have to be sterilized, everything except his glass, which he hadn't touched yet. But he couldn't talk about such things to his mother. It was a part of life she didn't know about, and if he told her now what was the matter with him, it would be just the same as if he had spattered her with filth.

She put her hand on his forehead, and though it felt to him as if it were burning up, she didn't seem alarmed. "I guess you just aren't awake yet," she said, and got up and went out to the kitchen.

The sunlight, shining on the brick wall outside the dining room windows, cast Mr. Latham's face in shadow and also cast a shadow on the *Herald and Examiner*. He complained about this to Mrs. Latham when she returned with the coffee-pot, and Mrs. Latham suggested that he change places with her but he merely frowned and went on reading. Spud watched him, in the hope that his father would look up suddenly and realize that he ought to put the morning paper down and get up and go into some other room, where they could talk in private.

Helen got up from the table first. "What were you doing so long in the bathroom this morning?" she asked Spud, and without waiting for him to answer, went off to finish dressing. After she left, Mrs. Latham sat with a dreamy expression in her eyes as if, during the night, she had gone and done something quite unbeknownst to all of them. She took a sip of coffee occasionally, and the bottom of her cup grated when she returned it to the saucer. That and the rattle of the newspaper were the only sounds at the breakfast table. At last Mr. Latham stood up and, with the paper clutched in his hand, walked past Spud's pleading eyes.

Anyone at all familiar with Mr. Latham's habits could have told, by the sounds which came from the next room, that he had chosen a tie from the rack on the closet door; that he was tying it now, standing in front of the dresser; that now he was using the whisk broom on his coat collar. In a moment he would come out into the hall and open the hall closet and then it would be too late to stop him. With his hat in one hand and in the other his brief case containing samples of insulating material, Mr. Latham would be quite beyond the reach of his family. Spud pushed his chair back and went and stood in the bedroom door.

His father and mother's bedroom was a place that he seldom wandered into, and never at this time in the morning. Mr. Latham was in front of the window with one foot on the low sill, polishing his right shoe with a flannel rag. He switched to the other shoe and Spud went in and sat down on the edge of the unmade bed. It occurred to him, as his father passed between him and the light, that in all probability, since the disease took some time to show itself (ten days or two weeks, the man said) his mother and Helen were already contaminated by him.

Mr. Latham stuffed the flannel rag in a little brown bag which hung on the inside of the closet door. Then he turned to Spud and said, "Do you need some money?"

In a despair so complete that it blurred his vision, Spud shook his head and saw his father go out into the hall. A moment later the front door closed with a click. After a while Spud got up, went back to his own room, and gathered up the books he had brought home the afternoon before. I'll have to get through this day somehow, he decided. I'll have to go to school so they won't suspect anything, and come home, and eat supper the same as usual. When the lights are out and they're in bed and asleep, I can figure out some way to kill myself.

It was ten minutes of eight when Spud reached the schoolyard. The snow had melted in places, leaving patches of gravel exposed. Spud saw Lymie Peters coming up the walk behind him. He walked faster but Lymie hurried too and caught up with him as he started up the wide cement steps. They went into the building together. Neither of them mentioned the initiation but as they passed the door of the boys' lavatory on the first floor, Lymie said, "Did you pee green this morning?" and deprived Spud of the last hope, the one comfort left to him.

The disease showed.

If it had been any of the others, Spud would have swung on him. He couldn't hit Lymie. Lymie wasn't big enough. Besides, he remembered what he saw the night before when he ripped his blindfold off: Lymie, his thin naked body marked with circles and crosses and the letters I EAT SHIT, trying to get to his feet, without help from anyone. The scene had stayed in his mind intact. Also the curious feel of Lymie's shoulder under his hand. Instead of lying, which he would have done if it had been any of the others, he still had enough trust in Lymie to be able to say "Yeah," in a weak voice. "Yeah, I did."

"So did I," Lymie said. "I thought it might be—you know. So I asked my father. He said it must be that pill they gave us."

The sickness receded, leaving Spud without any strength in his knees.

"That was probably it. They figured they'd scare us," he said, with no outward sign that he had, in that instant, gone completely crazy. He wanted to laugh out

loud and prance and dance and kick something (there was
nothing to kick in the corridor) and hit somebody (but
not Lymie) and throw his head back and screech like a
hoot owl. He managed to walk along beside Lymie and to
climb the stairs in the center of the building, one step at a
time.

The door of Room 211 stood open, and high-pitched
voices were swarming out of it. Spud and Lymie walked
in together and down separate aisles. In spite of the babel
and the steady tramping outside in the corridor, each of
them heard the other's footsteps; heard them as distinctly
as if the sound were made by a man walking late at night
in an empty street.

14

The fraternity house which was referred to with such a
carefully casual air in LeClerc's was a one-room basement
apartment that Bud Griesenauer got for five dollars a
month through an uncle in the real estate business.

They took possession on Ground-Hog Day and
spent Saturday and Sunday calcimining the walls a sickly
green. The woodwork, the floor, and the brick fireplace
were scrubbed with soap and water, but there was nothing
much that they could do about the pipes on the ceiling,
and they decided not to bother with curtains even though
small boys peered in the windows occasionally and
had to be chased away.

The apartment was furnished with a worn grass rug,
a couch, a bookcase, and three uncomfortable chairs from
the Edwards' attic. Carson brought an old victrola which
had to be wound before and then again during every
record, and sometimes it made terrible grinding noises.
Mark Wheeler contributed a large framed picture of a

handsome young collegian with his hair parted in the
middle, enjoying his own fireside, his pennants, and the
smoke that curled upward from the bowl of his long-
stemmed clay pipe. The title of the picture was "Pipe-
Dreams" and they gave it the place of honor over the
mantel. The only other picture they were willing to hang
in the apartment was of an ugly English bulldog looking
out through a fence. This had been given to Mr. and Mrs.
Snyder twenty-two years before, as a wedding present.
The glass was underneath the slats in the fence and they
were real wood, varnished and joined at the top and
bottom to the picture frame.

To get to the fraternity from school the boys had to
take a southbound Clark Street car and get off and wait
on a windy street corner, by a cemetery, until a westbound
Montrose Street car came along. It was usually dark
when they reached the apartment and a grown person
would have found the place dreary and uninviting, but
they had a special love for it, from the very beginning.
This was partly because it had to be kept secret. They
could talk about it safely in LeClerc's but not at school,
in their division rooms, where the teacher might overhear
them and report it to the principal. And partly because
they knew instinctively that sooner or later the apartment
would be taken away from them. They were too young
to be allowed to have a place of their own, and so they
lived in it as intensely and with as much pleasure as small
children live in the houses which they make for themselves on rainy days, out of chairs and rugs, a fire screen,
a footstool, a broomstick, and the library table.

Sometimes the boys came in a body, after school;
sometimes by two and threes. Carson and Lynch were almost always there, and when Ray Snyder came it was
usually with Bud Griesenauer or Harry Hall. Catanzano
and deFresne came together, as a rule, and Bob Edwards
and Mark Wheeler. Lymie Peters attached himself to any

group or any pair of friends he could find, and once Spud Latham turned up with a blond boy from Lake View High School, who kept tossing his hair out of his eyes. He didn't think much of the apartment and made Spud go off with him somewhere on his bicycle. Later, without being exactly unpleasant to Spud, they managed to convey to him that he had made a mistake in bringing an outsider to the fraternity house, and after that, when Spud came, which was not very often, he came alone. Ford also came alone. As a result of his refusing to jump off a stepladder blindfolded he was now known as "Steve Brodie" and sometimes "Diver" and he had stopped going to LeClerc's.

The fraternity house was a place to try things. Catanzano and deFresne smoked their first cigars there and were sick afterwards, out in the areaway. Ray Snyder fought his way through "I Dreamt I Dwelt in Marble Halls" on the ukulele, and Harry Hall appeared one day with a copy of Balzac's *Droll Stories* which he had swiped from the bookcase at his grandfather's. It was referred to as the dirty book, and somebody was always off in a corner or stretched out on the couch reading it.

One afternoon when Carson and Lynch walked in they found Dede Sandstrom and a fat-cheeked girl named Edith Netedu side by side on the couch, with an ashtray and a box of Pall Malls between them. The girl sat up and began to fuss with her hair, and Dede said, "Haven't you two guys got any home to go to?"

Carson and Lynch had a feeling that maybe they weren't wanted but they took off their caps and coats and stayed. Dede wound the victrola and put a record on, and after the girl had danced with him a couple of times she asked Carson and then Lynch to dance with her. Both of them were conscious of her perfume and of her arm resting lightly on their shoulders, and they felt that the place was different. Something that had been lacking before (the very thing, could it have been, that made them want the apartment in the first place?) had been found. They went off to the drugstore and came back with four malted milks, in cardboard containers, and it was like a party, like a housewarming.

The other girls who ate lunch at LeClerc's knew about the apartment and were curious about it but they wouldn't go there. Edith Netedu was the only one. She was there quite often. She came with Dede Sandstrom but she belonged to all of them. They dressed up in her hat and coat and teased her about her big hips, and snatched her high-heeled pumps off and hid or played catch with them, and fought among each other for the privilege of dancing with her. She was a very good dancer and the boys liked particularly to waltz with her. She never seemed to get dizzy, no matter how much they whirled. They took turns, trying to make her fall down, and when one of the boys began to stagger, another would step in and take his place. Finally, when they were all sprawling on the couch or the floor, Dede Sandstrom would take over and dance with her quietly, cheek to cheek.

When she was there, the place was at its best. They sang and did card tricks. Ray Snyder's ukulele was passed around, and sometimes they just talked, in a relaxed way, about school and what colleges were the best and how much money they were going to make when they finished studying and got out into the world. Edith Netedu said she was going to marry a millionaire and have three children, all boys; and she was going to name them Tom, Dick, and Harry. When she and Dede Sandstrom put on their coonskin coats and tied their woolen mufflers under their chins and went out, they left sadness behind them.

15

When Spud Latham suggested that Lymie Peters come home with him to supper, Lymie hesitated and then shook his head.

"Why not?" Spud asked.

"Well," Lymie said, "I just don't think I'd better."

They were waiting for a northbound car with the brick wall of the cemetery at their backs, and it was snowing.

"Don't you want to come?" Spud asked.

"Yes, I'd like to very much."

"All right then," Spud said, "that settles it."

Actually it didn't settle anything for Lymie. He liked Spud, or at least he would have liked to be like him, and have broad shoulders and narrow hips and go around with his chin out looking for a fight. But nobody at school had ever asked him to come home like this, especially for a meal, and Lymie had a feeling that it wasn't right. Spud's father and mother would probably be nice to him and all that, but afterwards, when he had gone . . .

A streetcar came along and the two boys got on it, paid their fares, and went inside. The Clark Street car was always slow and this one kept stopping at every block to let people on or off. Lymie had plenty of time to wish that he had said no. He tried to suggest to Spud that maybe he oughtn't to be bringing somebody home like this without asking permission first, but Spud seemed to have no such anxiety. He raised his cap politely to a woman across the aisle who had been staring at them, and this sent Lymie off into a fit of the giggles. The woman was offended.

When the car stopped at Foster Avenue, Spud took Lymie by the arm and, partly dragging, partly tickling him, got him off. They stood and argued then on the corner, while the snow dropping out of the darkness settled in their hair and on the sleeves of their overcoats.

"I'll come some other time," Lymie said. "If I go home with you now, your mother won't be expecting me and she'll—"

"My mother won't mind," Spud said patiently. "Why should she?"

"Well," Lymie said, "it means a lot of extra trouble."

"If you think she's going to send me out for ice cream on your account——"

"That's not what I meant," Lymie said. "She may not be counting on anybody extra and she'll be upset."

"You don't know my mother," Spud said. "Honestly, Lymie, she likes to have me bring kids home. When we lived in Wisconsin I did it all the time. Pete Draper used to eat more meals at our house than he did at his own. When anybody asked his mother how Pete was, she'd say, 'I don't know. You'll have to ask Mrs. Latham.' Jack Wilson and Wally Putnam used to be there too on account of the ring I fixed up in the back yard, to shoot baskets. And Roger Mitchell and a lot of my sister's friends."

Under Spud's persuasion, Lymie gave in once more and then wished he hadn't. A block from the apartment building where the Lathams lived, he and Spud went through the whole argument all over again, stamping their feet and swinging their arms to keep warm. Still certain that it was wrong, that no good would come of it, Lymie watched Spud fit his key into the inside vestibule door and kick it open.

The Lathams lived on the second floor. When they got inside, Spud tossed his coat and muffler in the general direction of the chair in the hall and disappeared. The muffler fell where it was intended to, but the coat landed in a heap on the floor, between the chair and the hall table. Lymie picked it up and put it on the chair, with his own on top of it. When he turned and walked into the living room he knew instantly why it was that he hadn't wanted to come here, and that he ought to get out as soon as he possibly could. There, staring him in the face, was everything he'd been deprived of for the last five years.

He had thought he remembered what it used to be like but he hadn't at all. He didn't even have the house straight in his mind. It had taken on the monotonous qualities, the ugliness of the cheap hotels and furnished apartments he and his father had lived in ever since—all so similar that when he woke in the night he couldn't remember for a second whether he was in the one on Lawrence Avenue or the one on Howard Street or the one on Lakeside Place. He had totally forgotten how different furniture was that people owned themselves from the kind that came with a furnished apartment; and that tables and chairs could tell you, when you walked into a place, what kind of people lived there.

His eyes went on a slow voyage around the room, taking in every detail, fixing it (he hoped) forever in his mind: the curtains, the blue rug, the sofa, the lighted lamps, the phonograph, the Chinese embroidery, the sewing basket with the lid left open, the ashtrays, the brass bowl, the package of pipe cleaners, the fireplace, the brass candlesticks, the English cottage at twilight. This was how people lived, boys his own age, who didn't have to get their own breakfast in the morning, or wash their face in a dirty washbowl, or go to sleep at night in a bed that hadn't been made; boys whose fathers didn't drink too much and talk too loud and like waitresses.

When Spud came back, bringing Mrs. Latham, Lymie turned, ready to apologize and pick up his things and leave. He saw that Mrs. Latham's hair was not bobbed, that she had no makeup on, and that her skirt was well below her knees.

"Mother, this is Lymie Peters," Spud said.

"How do you do, Lymie," Mrs. Latham said, and shook hands with him. Before Lymie could explain that he had changed his mind and wasn't staying for supper after all, she turned to Spud and said, "Show him where the bathroom is, and see that he gets a clean towel. We're all ready to sit down as soon as your father comes." Then she was gone.

"You see?" Spud said, straddling the bowl of the toilet while Lymie washed his hands. "All that fuss for nothing."

16

To know the world's injustice requires only a small amount of experience. To accept it without bitterness or envy you need almost the sum total of human wisdom, which Lymie Peters at fifteen did not have. He couldn't help noticing that the scales of fortune were tipped considerably in Spud's favor, and resenting it. But what gnawed at him most was that Spud should be, besides, a natural athlete, the personification of the daydream which he himself most frequently indulged in.

In this fantasy Lymie was in another place. His father had had to move, for business reasons, and he went along, of course, and they settled down in a nice big house in some place like New York or Philadelphia, where nobody knew them or anything about them. His father stopped drinking and was home every night for dinner, and they had a housekeeper who kept the place spick-and-span and saw to it that they had his favorite dessert (made of pineapple, marshmallows, oranges, maraschino cherries, and whipped cream) at least once a week.

One day, one Saturday morning, he was walking past a vacant lot where some guys were playing baseball, and he stopped to watch. In the last of the ninth inning the pitcher sprained his ankle and had to quit. They asked Lymie if he wanted to play. He didn't want to particularly but he didn't have anything else to do so he said all right and took his coat off and threw it on the ground. Then he tossed his cap beside it, loosened his necktie, and rolled up his shirt sleeves. They asked him if he wanted to pitch and he said "Sure." His side had a slight lead. The score was five to four, but there were three men on bases and no outs. Lymie (who had never pitched before) stepped into the dirt-drawn square which was the pitcher's box and with the heavy end of the batting order coming up, struck out three men, one right after the other, and won the game.

That was the way it was with everything he did in that place he moved to. He didn't care whether people liked him or not, so he didn't try to keep on the good side of everybody, and sometimes he got in a fight because this person or that didn't like his attitude, but he always came out on top, and the other guy apologized afterward and they became good friends.

After the guys found out he was so good at games, they always took him first when they were choosing up sides, and whichever side he was on won. He was never by himself any more because somebody always seemed to be waiting for him by his locker after school, and when the phone rang at night it was invariably for him. The guys were always after him to go to a movie or do something with them but he stayed home night after night with his father, reading or listening to the radio, and went to bed early and got plenty of rest. Because he'd been playing games a lot and exercising, his arm and leg muscles developed. He looked like all the rest of the guys in plus fours, only better. The girls smiled at him when he walked past with his chin in the air but he only nodded; he didn't smile back. He didn't have any time for girls. He hardly had time for his homework but he managed somehow so that he got all S's and was elected president of the senior class and captain of the football, basketball, baseball, and fencing teams, before he grew tired of daydreaming and let himself slip back into the actual world.

With gentle jabbing Spud propelled Lymie through the dining room, and Lymie's head swam for a second with the wonderful conglomeration of long-forgotten cooking smells that met him as soon as he set foot in the kitchen. The predominating one was of roast pork, which he could hear sizzling in the oven. A girl with light hair like Spud's was standing on a stool. In her hands was a large blue platter which she had just taken from the top shelf of the china cupboard.

"Hello, Lymie," she said, when Spud introduced her. "I hope you realize you've come to a bad end." Her voice was cheerful and contradicted her words. Lymie saw that she took his being there as a matter of course. Except for the color of her hair, she had almost no resemblance to Spud. Their dispositions seemed entirely different.

"Don't pay any attention to my sister," Spud said. "I don't listen to her, even. If she bothers you, tell her to go fan herself."

"I'm sure that Lymie doesn't talk to his sister that way," Mrs. Latham said. She had tied a kitchen apron around her waist and was holding a large aluminum basting spoon under the hot water faucet.

"Lymie hasn't got a sister, have you, Lymie?" Spud asked.

Lymie shook his head.

"You don't know how much you have to be thankful for," Spud said. "When do we eat?"

"As soon as your father gets home," Mrs. Latham said. "He may be a little late tonight."

"*O grim-look'd night*," Spud said. "*O night with hue so black! O night which ever art when day is not! O night! O night! alack, alack, alack! I fear my Thisbe's promise is forgot.*"

Helen got down off the stool carefully and pushed it under the kitchen table. "It's bad enough to have you out here in the first place," she said, "without your showing off."

"I wasn't showing off," Spud said. "That's poetry. Shakespeare."

"It's all the Shakespeare you know or ever will know," she said, and then, turning to Lymie: "When he was in seventh grade they did a scene from *A Midsummer Night's Dream*. You should have seen it. Spud was Pyramus and he had to make love to a freckle-faced boy named Bill McCann. They were both done up in old sheets and I've never seen anything so funny in all my life."

Lymie had a feeling that she was trying to use him as a weapon against Spud. He backed against the china closet, where he could hardly be considered more than a spectator.

"They kept forgetting their lines," she continued. "And the teacher had to prompt them."

"Is that so?" Spud exclaimed hotly. "You think you're so smart! What about the time you got up in assembly to make a speech and gulped so loud they heard you clear in the back row?"

"Go in the other room, all of you," Mrs. Latham said, "and stop arguing."

Lymie leaned forward, ready to follow Spud and his sister out of the kitchen; to his surprise neither of them

showed any signs of leaving. There was a look about Mrs.
Latham, a certain firmness in her mouth, which indicated
that she could mean what she said. But apparently this
wasn't one of the times.

Spud pulled the kitchen stool out and began to teeter
on it. "If you won't let us talk about Shakespeare," he said,
"what *do* you want us to talk about?"

"You don't have to talk at all," Mrs. Latham said
severely. "You can get the bread knife and cut the bread
and put it on the table."

This time Spud did as he was told.

Lymie would have liked to take part in the confusion
and bickering but he didn't quite know how. He stayed
close to the china closet until Helen came over and said,
"One side. Have to get in there." Then he moved away
cautiously and stood with his elbows resting on the
kitchen window sill.

A door opened somewhere in the front of the apartment. After a second Lymie heard it close.

"Was that your father?" Mrs. Latham asked, when
Spud came back from the dining room.

"It was," Spud said.

"*Der Papa kommt*," Helen said.

"German," Spud shouted contemptuously at her.
"Who wants to talk German? If I were a Frenchman now,
waiting in a shell hole, and you were a big fat Dutchman
crawling toward me on your hands and knees——"

"Germans and Dutchmen are two different nationali-
ties," Helen said. "Dutchmen are Hollanders. They didn't
take part in the war. They were neutral."

"Yeah, the dirty cowards," Spud said.

Mrs. Latham opened the oven door and took the
roast out. It was a large one, brown and crisp. She made
no effort to prevent Spud from reaching out and snitching
a small piece of fat that was hanging loose at the side.

"Just for that," Helen said, "you don't get any second helping."

"I pity the guy that gets you for a wife," Spud said.

A voice interrupted them, a deep masculine voice saying, "Anybody home?"

"We're all home," Mrs. Latham called out.

Everybody had something to do but Lymie. Helen began to mash the potatoes furiously. Spud let the water run in the sink and filled the cut-glass pitcher. Mrs. Latham transferred the roast to the blue platter and made gravy in the roasting pan on top of the stove. Feeling very much an outsider, Lymie picked up the gravy boat and held it for her, so that all she had to do was tip the pan. She thanked him, and then, as if she knew everything that was going on in his mind, said, "Now you're a member of the family, Lymie. You've been broken in."

She didn't smile, and Lymie realized that he could take what she said quite seriously. With a feeling of sudden and immense happiness he carried the gravy boat into the dining room and set it down in the center of the table.

17

All through dinner Spud addressed his mother formally. "Mrs. Latham," he said, pointing to the roast on the platter, "would you be so kind and condescending as to give me a piece of the outside." "Mrs. Latham, you're losing a very valuable hairpin." "Watch out, Mrs. Latham, you're dipping your elbow in the gravy."

He also announced that somebody was kicking him under the table and kept complaining about it until finally they all leaned over, raised the tablecloth, peered under it, and proved conclusively that nobody's foot was anywhere near him.

Lymie was so amused that his eyes filled with tears. It was the kind of thing that never happened at the Alcazar.

Helen and her mother cleared the table for dessert, and then it was Mr. Latham's turn. He rose and placed the knife blade between the prongs of his fork, transferring the musical sound to Lymie's glass, then to Spud's, and so on around the table. Mr. Latham could also (which was really astonishing) hold the sound back and release it whenever he wanted to. This was something he learned in the Masonic Lodge, he explained solemnly, and Mrs. Latham for the first time burst out laughing. Her face colored and she looked almost as young as Helen.

If Lymie had been told that all meals at the Lathams were not like this one, he would have refused to believe it. The others knew better, of course, but Mrs. Latham attributed the gaiety of the occasion to the roast, which was exceptionally tender and done to a turn. Mr. Latham felt that at last the apartment, which had seemed so dark and unlivable, was beginning to be like home. Spud was not given to analyzing. Helen alone knew the real cause—that Lymie's shyness and his delight at being there had affected all of them, arousing their feeling for one another and drawing them temporarily into the compact family that he thought they were. She felt sorry for him, but she was also suspicious of him. She was suspicious of everybody. The letters from Wisconsin had stopped coming. The last was in December, two days after Christmas. Now, so far as Helen was concerned, there was nothing good or kind anywhere, people lost their youth and grew middle-aged without finding anybody to love them, and happiness was a delusion.

The boys ate two helpings of peach cobbler, pushed their chairs back from the table, and went off to Spud's room. Mr. Latham retired to the living room and the solace of his cigar. Mrs. Latham and Helen cleared the table and got ready to do the dishes.

As Mrs. Latham was stirring the dishwater into a froth she turned and said suddenly, "Where on earth do you suppose Spud found that child?"

"The same place he gets all the others," Helen said. "There's a place he goes to that's like a dog pound and that's where he finds them."

Mrs. Latham shook her head. "I've seen him bring home some mighty strange creatures——"

"Strange!" Helen said.

"—just so he could have somebody to play football with. I suppose that's what he's meaning to do with this one."

"It's the wrong time of the year," Helen said. "You don't play football when there's snow on the ground. Besides, did you notice his hands?"

"No," Mrs. Latham said, "what's the matter with them?"

"Nothing, except that they wouldn't go very far around a football."

"Ummm," Mrs. Latham said, and began to put the glasses one by one into the scalding hot dishwater. "Thinnest youngster I about ever saw. I'd like to keep him here for a month or six weeks."

"Where?" Helen asked, reaching for a dish towel.

"Oh, we could put him somewhere."

"I don't know where. He's too long for the couch in the living room and I won't have him sleeping with me."

"Don't be vulgar."

"I'm not being vulgar," Helen exclaimed. "Just practical. Let him stay at his own house."

"I suppose we'll have to, in any case," Mrs. Latham said. "But he doesn't look to me as if he got the right kind of food. Or maybe he's growing too fast and hasn't any appetite."

"It seemed to me he ate very well," Helen said. "He kept right up with Spud, helping for helping."

Neither of them said anything more for a while. Helen dried the glasses and stood them upside down on an aluminum tray on the kitchen table. Mrs. Latham filled the rack with plates and saucers. While she was pouring hot water over them out of the teakettle she saw a shadow in the doorway and looked up. The shadow was Spud. He had been showing Lymie his favorite neckties and the plaid golf socks with tassels on them that he wore whenever he wanted to pick a fight with somebody. Lymie had admired the Navajo rug on the floor and the picture of a four-masted schooner cutting its way through an indigo ocean. Now, while Lymie sat on the bed looking at the illustrations in *Mr. Midshipman Easy*, Spud was free to come back to the kitchen. He knelt down and began to root around in the bottom shelf of the cupboard. Six bars of Ivory soap came tumbling out on the kitchen floor. The kitchen cleanser, several wire brushes, a Mason jar filled with tacks, a tack hammer, a putty knife, a can of silver polish, and a ball of twine followed.

"What are you after?" Helen asked. "Do you know exactly?"

"Saddle soap," Spud explained.

"Why do you have to have it right now?" Mrs. Latham asked. "Couldn't you wait and use it some other time?"

Spud shook his head. "What have you done with it?" he asked. "It used to be right in here somewhere."

Mrs. Latham opened both doors of the cupboard and took out a cigar box with a heavy rubber band around it. "Did you look in here?" she asked.

The saddle soap was inside the cigar box.

"What about straightening up the cupboard?" Helen

said, as Spud started for the dining room door. He glanced back at the confusion he had made.

"I haven't got time," he said. "We're going to saddle-soap my riding boots now. I'll clean it up later."

"That's a very nice boy you brought home," Mrs. Latham said. "Where does he live?"

"Over by the lake," Spud said.

"He has very nice manners. You can see that his mother has tried to bring him up properly," Mrs. Latham said.

"He hasn't got any mother," Spud said. "His mother is dead."

"What a pity!" Mrs. Latham exclaimed.

"Maybe it's a blessing in disguise," Helen said, but Mrs. Latham was not amused.

"Who looks after him?" she asked.

"I don't know," Spud said. "Nobody, I guess. He and his father eat out."

"No wonder he's so thin. Nothing but restaurant food," Mrs. Latham said.

"I ate at the Palmer House once," Helen said, as she finished the last of the dinner plates. "It was quite good."

"You wouldn't think so if you ate there all the time," Mrs. Latham said. And then to Spud. "You must bring him home with you again, do you hear?"

Spud stopped in the doorway to the dining room. "Who?" he asked.

"This boy," Mrs. Latham said. "Bring him as often as he's willing to come——"

But Spud was already on the way to his own room.

Mrs. Latham poured the dishwater out and it made a loud gurgling noise which prevented conversation for a minute. Then she said thoughtfully, "I'm really very glad. Spud needs somebody. He gets bored when he's alone and doesn't know what to do with himself. Lymie isn't the kind of boy I'd expect him to pick out for a friend, but he's a very well-behaved, nice youngster and maybe he'll be a good influence on Spud." There was a silence, while Helen spread her dish towel on the rack to dry; then Mrs. Latham said, "That explains everything, doesn't it?"

"What explains everything?" Helen asked. She had begun to clean up the mess in front of the cupboard.

"I mean the fact that his mother is dead. I knew there was something wrong the minute I saw him," Mrs. Latham said. She finished rinsing out the dishpan and hung it on a nail under the sink. Then she stood in the center of the floor and listened. The only sounds came from Spud's room, where the two boys were saddle-soaping his boots. Their voices sounded pleased and excited.

18

On the tenth of March, which was the anniversary of Mrs. Peters' death, Mr. Peters and Lymie got up early and went down to the Union Station. From Chicago to the small town they had once lived in was a trip of a little less than two hours, on the Chicago, Burlington, and Quincy Railroad. They made this journey every year. The scenery was not interesting—the cornfields of Illinois in March are dreary and monotonous—and there was no pleasure attached to the trip in the mind of either of them. But to live in the world at all is to be committed to some kind of a journey.

If you are ready to go and cannot, either because you are not free or because you have no one to travel with— or if you have arbitrarily set a date for your departure and dare not go until that day arrives, you still have no cause for concern. Without knowing it, you have actually started. On a turning earth, in a mechanically revolving universe, there is no place to stand still.

Neither the destination nor the point of departure are important. People often find themselves midway on a journey they had no intention of taking and that began they are not exactly sure where. What matters, the only sphere where you have any real choice, is the person who elects to sit in the empty seat beside you from Asheville, North Carolina to Knoxville, Tennessee.

Or from Knoxville to Memphis.

Or from Memphis to Denver, Colorado.

Sometimes it is a woman with a navy-blue turban on her head and pearl earrings, pictures in her purse that you will have to look at, and a wide experience with the contagious diseases of children.

Sometimes it is a man who says *Is this seat taken?* Or he may not say anything at all as he makes room on the rack over your head for his suitcase, his battered gray felt hat, his muffler, and overcoat, and the small square package wrapped in blue paper and tied with red string. Before he gets off the train (at Detroit, perhaps, or at Kansas City) you will know what's in the package. Whether you want him to or not, he will spread his life out before you, on his knees. And afterward, so curiously relaxed is the state of mind engendered by going on a journey, he will ask to see your life and you will show it to him. Occasionally, though not often, the girl or the young man who sits beside you will be someone whose clothes, ankles, hands, gray-blue eyes all are so full of charm and character that, even though they are only there for a short time and never once turn and look at you, never offer a remark, you have no choice but to fall hopelessly in love with them, with everything about them, with their luggage even. And when they get up and leave, it is as if you had lost an arm or a leg.

Accidents, misdirections, overexcitement, heat, crowds,

and heartbreaking delays you must expect when you go on a journey, just as you expect to have dreams at night. Whether or not you enjoy yourself at all depends on your state of mind. The man who travels with everything he owns, books, clothes for every season, shoe trees, a dinner jacket, medicines, binoculars, magazines, and telephone numbers—the unwilling traveler—and the man who leaves each place in turn without reluctance, with no desire ever to come back, obviously cannot be making the same journey, even though their tickets are identical. The same thing holds good for the woman who was once beautiful and who now has to resort to movement, change, continuous packing and unpacking, in order to avoid the reality that awaits her in the smallest mirror. And for the ambitious young man who by a too constant shifting around has lost all of his possessions, including his native accent and the ability to identify himself with a particular kind of sky or the sound, let us say, of windmills creaking; so that in New Mexico his talk reflects Bermuda, and in Bermuda it is again and again of Barbados that he is reminded, but never of Iowa or Wisconsin or Indiana, never of home.

Though people usually have long complicated tickets which they expect the conductor to take from them in due time, the fact is that you don't need to bother with a ticket at all. If you are willing to travel lightly, you can also dispense with the train. Cars and trucks are continually stopping at filling stations and at corners where there is an overhead stop light. By jerking your thumb you will almost certainly get a ride to the next town of more than two thousand inhabitants where (chances are) you will manage to get something to eat and a place to sleep for a night or so, even if it's only the county jail.

The appointment you have made to meet somebody at such and such a day at noon on the steps of the courthouse at Amarillo, Texas, you may have to forget. Especially if you go too long without food or with nothing but stolen ripe tomatoes, so that suddenly you are not sure of what you are saying. Or if the heat gets you, and when you wake up you are in a hospital ward. But after you start to get well again and are able to sit up a short while each day, there will be time to begin thinking about where you will go next. And if you like, you can always make new appointments.

The great, the universal problem is how to be always on a journey and yet see what you would see if it were only possible for you to stay home: a black cat in a garden, moving through iris blades behind a lilac bush. How to keep sufficiently detached and quiet inside so that when the cat in one spring reaches the top of the garden wall, turns down again, and disappears, you will see and remember it, and not be absorbed at that moment in the dryness of your hands.

If you missed that particular cat jumping over one out of so many garden walls, it ought not to matter, but it does apparently. The cat seems to be everything. Seeing clearly is everything. Being certain as to smells, being able to remember sounds and to distinguish by touch one object, one body, from another. And it is not enough to see the fishermen drawing in their wide circular net, the tropical villages lying against a shelf of palm trees, or the double rainbow over Fort-de-France. You must somehow contrive, if only for a week or only overnight, to live in the houses of people, so that at least you know the elementary things—which doors sometimes bang when a sudden wind springs up; where the telephone book is kept; and how their lungs feel when they waken in the night and reach blindly toward the foot of the bed for the extra cover.

You are in duty bound to go through all of their possessions, to feel their curtains and look for the tradename on the bottom of their best dinner plates and stand before

their pictures (especially the one they have been compelled to paint themselves, which is not a good painting
but seems better if you stay long enough to know the
country in more than one kind of light) and lift the lids
off their cigarette boxes and sniff their pipe tobacco and
open, one by one, their closet doors. You should test the
sharpness and shape of their scissors. You may play their
radio and try, with your fingernail, to open the locked
door of the liquor cabinet. You may even read any letters that they have been so careless as to leave around.
Through all of these things, through the attic and the
cellar and the tool shed you must go searching until you
find the people who live here or who used to live here but
now are in London or Acapulco or Galesburg, Illinois.
Or who now are dead.

19

"When you grow up," Mr. Peters said, "there won't be
anybody to make things easier for you."

Lymie, who had brought this lecture on himself by
losing his return ticket, was walking ahead of his father
down the white cemetery path. In his right hand he held
a long narrow cardboard box done up in green florist's
paper. In the other hand he carried a Mason jar filled with
water, which slopped over occasionally. His shoes, which
had been shined in the railway station at the same time
as his father's, were now scuffed and muddy. He had no
hat. The sun was out and it was windy but not cold.

"You'll want to provide yourself with a nice home
and pleasant surroundings and all the comforts and con-
veniences you've been used to," Mr. Peters said. "You'll
want to marry and have a family, which you can't do if

you spend all your time reading and going to art museums."

So far as Mr. Peters was concerned, there was a definite connection between Lymie's absent-mindedness and the fact that he seemed to gravitate toward whatever was artistic and impractical. Mr. Peters wanted to be proud of his son and he was glad that Lymie had a good mind, but he was not a millionaire (how much Mr. Peters made exactly was nobody's business) and he had tried therefore to make Lymie realize that before you have a right to indulge in any kind of activity which is not practical, you must learn the value of money. If earning a living takes all your time and energy, it is something that you must resign yourself to. There is no use pretending that life is one long Sunday school picnic. Nothing is ever gained without hard work and plenty of it. But if a person is ambitious and really wants to make something of himself; if he can keep his chin up no matter what happens to him, and never complains, never offers excuses or alibis; and if, once he has achieved success, he can keep from resting on his laurels (also his equilibrium through it all and his feet on the ground) he will have all the more success to come and he need feel no fear of the future.

This philosophy was too materialistic to be very congenial to Lymie, and as a matter of fact Mr. Peters didn't take much stock in it himself. It was not something that he had learned from experience (his own business methods were quite different) but mostly catch phrases from the lips of businessmen he envied and admired. Where they got it, there is no telling.

Mr. Peters' career in business had never been very successful, never wholly unsuccessful. He was a salesman by accident rather than by disposition. His first job was with a bill-posting concern and had involved free passes to circuses, street carnivals, and moving picture houses.

He still remembered it with pleasure. After that he tried real estate and life insurance, both of which had their drawbacks. When his wife died he decided that he wanted to move, to get away from anything and everything that reminded him of her, so he took a job with a wholesale stationery house, operating in the Chicago area. For the past five years he had remained in that business, though the concerns he worked for changed rather frequently. Each one, for a short while, was a fine company headed by men it was a privilege to work for. This opinion was eventually and inevitably revised, until a point was reached where Mr. Peters, for his own good, could no longer afford to work for such bastards. As a rule he quit before he was fired.

When Mr. Peters stopped on the cemetery path to light a cigarette, Lymie stopped also, his eyes busy with the mounded graves, the faded American flags in their star-shaped holders, and the tombstones, row after row of them, all saying the same thing: *Henry Burdine died . . . Mary his wife died . . . Samuel Potter died . . . Jesse Davis died . . . Temperance his wife died . . .*

"You get out of life," Mr. Peters said as they walked on, "just what you put into it."

Mrs. Peters' grave was at the far end of the cemetery, in a square lot with a plain granite tombstone on it about six feet high. On the stone was the single name *Harris*. Two small headstones marked the graves of Lymie's maternal grandfather and grandmother. A little apart from them were two other graves, one full-sized and one small, as if for a child. The inscription on the headstone of the larger grave said *Alma Harris Peters 1881–1919*.

Lymie set the Mason jar down and tore both string and paper off the box, which contained a dozen short-stemmed red roses. He tried to arrange them nicely in the Mason jar but the wind blew them all the same way and he caught the jar with his hand, just before it toppled. By bracing it against the headstone, in a little hollow, he could keep the jar from falling, but there was nothing he could do about the roses.

"Quit worrying with them," Mr. Peters said. "They look all right."

He stood with his hat in his hand, staring in a troubled way at the grave.

Lymie was embarrassed because he had no particular feeling, and he thought he ought to have. He looked down at the low mound with dead grass on it and tried to visualize his mother beneath it, in a horizontal position; tried to feel toward that spot the emotion he used to have for her. He waited, knowing that in a moment his father would ask the question he always asked when they came here.

Though Lymie could remember his mother's voice easily enough, and how she did her hair, and what it was like to be in the same room with her, he couldn't remember her face. He had tried too many times to remember it and now it was gone. It wouldn't come back any more.

On the other side of the lot the ground dropped away abruptly. The cemetery ran along the end of a high bluff from which you could look off over the tops of trees to the cornfields and the flat prairie beyond. In the whole winter landscape the roses were the only color.

"Your mother has been gone five years," Mr. Peters said, "and I still can't believe it. It just doesn't seem possible."

Lymie remembered how his mother used to say his father's name: *Lymon,* she said, *my Lymon*—proudly, and always with love.

He remembered the excitement of meeting his mother suddenly on the stairs. And the sound of her voice. And the soft side of her neck. And the imprint of her lips on the top of his head after she had kissed him. And being rocked by her sometimes, on her lap, when he had been crying. And being allowed to look at her beautiful long white kid gloves.

He remembered waking at night and realizing that she had been in his room without his knowing it—that room he remembered so clearly and that fitted his heart and mind like a glove. The bed he woke up in, and the dresser with all his clothes in it, and the blue and white wallpaper, and the light switch by the door, and the light, and next to it the framed letter which began *Dear Madam I have been shown in the files of the War Department a statement of* . . . and which ended *Yours very sincerely and respectfully Abraham Lincoln.* And the picture over his head of a fat-faced little boy and a little girl with yellow curls, both of them riding hobbyhorses. And the bear that he slept with . . .

"Before she died," Mr. Peters said, "I was sitting on top of the world. I used to look around sometimes and see somebody I knew who was in a mess or having trouble of one sort or another and I'd think It's his own damn fault."

What became of the bear? Lymie thought. Whatever could have happened to it? Did somebody take it away?

"It didn't occur to me that I had anything especially to be thankful for," Mr. Peters said. "Probably if I had—" And then instead of finishing that sentence he asked the question Lymie had been waiting for: "Do you remember your mother, son?"

"Yes, Dad," Lymie said, nodding.

He remembered the time his mother saw a mouse and screamed and jumped up on one of the dining room chairs and from the chair to the table. She was deathly afraid of mice. And when they went to the circus at night they never could stay for the wild West show because his mother grew nervous as soon as they started loosening the ropes. But she loved lightning and thunder.

He himself used to be afraid of noises in the night,

and of the shadows which the gaslight made in the hall. The gaslight flickered, and that made the shadows move. But it also guided him on that long trip down the hall from the door of his room to the door of the bathroom, which he entered quickly, being careful not to glance to the left, where there was danger, darkness, and the back stairs. He was also afraid, horribly afraid deep down inside of him, when the man leaned over and put his face in the lion's mouth. But these were things that he had never told anybody.

"Your mother was a wonderful woman," Mr. Peters said. "I didn't know what I was getting when I married her. She was just young and pretty and always laughing and tying ribbons in her hair and I knew I had to have her. But that wasn't what she was really like at all, and it was quite a while before I found out."

Lymie remembered the tray of the high chair coming over his head and being lifted out of it when he choked. And later, when he was old enough to sit at the table in a chair with two big books on it. And taking iron through a glass straw. And sometimes having to take cod-liver oil. And the square glass shade that hung down over the round dining room table, with the red-and-green beaded fringe. And the fireplace with the tapestry screen in front of it during the summertime. And the Japanese garden with putty for the shores of the little lake, grass seed growing, and carrot tops sprouting with little green leaves, and a peculiar, unpleasant smell. And the real garden outside, beyond the grape arbor. And around in front the two palms in their wooden tubs on either side of the front walk. . . .

"Whatever she did and whatever she thought," Mr. Peters said, "turned out to be right."

When he talked like this it was largely to make himself suffer (he too had trouble remembering his wife's face, and the last years of his marriage had not been as happy as the first; there had been quarrels and misunder-standings, also that girl in the barber shop) and he did not expect Lymie to offer consolation. He took out his watch, glanced at it, and then put it back in his pocket.

The marble headstone of the small grave read:

Infant daughter of Lymon and Alma Peters
died March 14, 1919
aged 4 days

Looking at the inscription Lymie realized that he was not yet ready to go. He was suddenly filled with the remembrance of the sound of his mother's name: *Alma,* everyone called her. The richness and warmth of the sound. *Alma . . . Alma . . .* Like the comfort he got from leaning against her thigh.

When she was away there was the terrible slowness of time. Even when she was downtown shopping or at a card party. Though he knew she would be back at five o'clock, how could he be sure that five o'clock would ever come? And when his mother and father were away once on a visit to Cincinnati, that was really a long time. And they got home and she told him that she had a paint book for him in her trunk, and then that the trunks were lost.

But what he remembered most vividly of all as he turned away from the grave was the question that used to fill his mind whenever he opened the front door: *Where is she?* he used to cry. *Is she here? Has she come back yet?* And the rooms, the front hall where she had left her gloves, the living room where her pocketbook was (on the mahogany table), and the library beyond, where she had left a small round package wrapped in white paper, all answered him. *She's here,* they said. *Everything is all right. She's home.*

20

In April there was trouble over the fraternity house. It began on a rainy Monday afternoon. Six of them were there. Catanzano had a sprained ankle and was enthroned on the couch. The others were trying out his crutches. Lynch was about to play a medley of songs from "No, No, Nanette" on the victrola when the janitor, who was a Belgian, walked in. He had a couple with him—a very tall man whose wrist hung down out of the sleeves of his black overcoat and a woman in a purple suit with a cheap fur neckpiece, blondined hair, blue eyes, and very red skin. She looked around critically and then said, "Fourteen dollars?"

The janitor nodded.

"Well," the woman said, "I don't know." She crossed the room and would have tripped over Catanzano's bandaged foot if he hadn't drawn it hastily out of the way. The other boys stood still, like figures in some elaborate musical parlor game.

The man couldn't have been more than five years older than Mark Wheeler but life had already proved too much for him. There was no color in his long thin face. The skin was drawn tight over his cheekbones. His hair was receding from his temples, and something about him—the look in his eyes, mostly—suggested a conscious determination to shed his flesh at the earliest possible moment and take refuge in his dry skeleton.

The woman was almost old enough to be his mother but there was nothing maternal or gentle about her. She went into the bathroom and came out again, inspected the only closet, discovered that there were no wall plugs, and sniffed the air, which smelled strongly of wet wool. Still undecided, she wandered back to the door.

"I've never lived in a basement apartment before," she said, turning to the man, "and I'm kind of afraid of the dampness. On account of my asthma."

"Is not damp," the janitor said.

"Maybe not now with the heat on, but in summer I bet it's good and damp. . . . What about it, Fred?"

The young man was looking at the picture of the English bulldog. "It's up to you," he said. "I'll be away all day."

"Well I guess I'll have to think about it," the woman said, shifting her fur. The expression on her face was like a pout, but she wasn't pouting, actually; she was thinking. "I don't want to move in and unpack everything and then find out that I can't breathe," she said. And then, turning to the janitor, "We'll let you know."

She looked once more at the boys without seeing them and walked out. The janitor followed, and after him the young man, who had a sudden coughing fit in the area-way and left the door wide open behind him.

Lymie Peters was the first to recover. He was standing in a draft and he sneezed. Dede Sandstrom walked over to the door and slammed it. As if a spell had been lifted, the victrola needle came to rest on the opening bars of "I Want to Be Happy," and they all started talking at once. Their excitement, the pitch of their immature voices, the gestures which they made with their hands, and their uneasy profanity were all because of one thing which none of them dared say: Their house, their fraternity (which stood in the minds of all of them like a beautiful woman that they were too young to have) was as good as gone. If these people didn't take it, the next ones would.

The record came to an end and the turntable of the victrola went round and round slower and slower until at last it stopped. Mark Wheeler and Dede Sandstrom went out and called Bud Griesenauer, who wasn't home. His mother didn't know where they could reach him. On their way back to the apartment they met the janitor in the areaway. Mark Wheeler walked up to him and said, "What's the big idea?"

The janitor shrugged his shoulders. "I show the apartment, that's all."

"But it's our apartment," Dede Sandstrom said. "We pay rent on it."

"Maybe somebody else pay more rent on it," the janitor said, and disappeared into the boiler room.

The second indignation meeting lasted until almost dinnertime. On the way home Lymie Peters stopped in a drugstore and called Bud Griesenauer. This time he was at home. They'd all been calling him, he said. Wheeler and Hall and Carson and Lynch and everybody. And he'd called his uncle. It was probably a misunderstanding of some kind, his uncle said, and maybe the people wouldn't rent the apartment after all. But if they did decide to take it, there was nothing anybody could do. The boys didn't have a lease and the owner of the building naturally had a right to try to get as much money out of it as possible.

They held a special meeting the next afternoon, and it was decided that somebody should come down to the fraternity house every afternoon after school, in case the janitor showed the place to any more people; and that they should take turns staying there at night. The rest of the time they would lock the door with a padlock. They wrote days of the week on slips of paper and put them in Mark Wheeler's hat and passed the hat around. Lymie drew the following Friday, and Spud Latham offered to stay with him.

When they arrived Friday night, Lymie had three army blankets under one arm and a coffeepot under the other. Spud carried a knapsack containing all the equipment and food necessary for a large camp breakfast.

The apartment was very warm when they got there but they built a fire in the fireplace anyway. Lymie sat on the floor in front of the fire and took off his shoes, which were wet, and loosened his tie and unbuttoned his shirt collar. Spud took all his clothes off except his shorts. Then he emptied the knapsack out on the hearth, arranging the skillet, the coffeepot, the iron grill, the plates, knives, forks, salt, and pepper so that they would all be ready and convenient the next morning. The food he put in the bathroom, on the window sill, and the blankets he spread one by one, on the couch. Every movement of his body was graceful, easy, and controlled. Lymie, who was continually being surprised by what his own hands and feet were up to, enjoyed watching him. With the firelight shining on his skin and no other light in the room, Spud looked very much like the savage that he was playing at being.

When he had finished with the couch, he stretched out on top of the blankets and there was so much harmony in the room that he said, "This is the life. No school tomorrow. Nobody to tell you when to go to bed. Plenty to eat and a good fire. Why didn't we think of this before?"

"I don't know," Lymie said. "Why didn't we?"

"There's always something," Spud said. The full implications of this remark, in spite of its vagueness, were deeply felt by both of them. Spud picked up the volume of Balzac's stories and read for a while, lying on his back with his knees raised. Lymie continued to sit in front of the fire, facing him. The expression in his eyes was partly pride (he had never had a friend before) and partly envy, though he didn't recognize it as that. He was comparing his own wrists, which were so thin that he could put his thumb and forefinger around one of them and still see daylight, to Spud's, which were strong and square. The wish closest to Lymie's heart, if he could have had it for the asking, would have been to have a well-built body, a body as strong and as beautifully proportioned as Spud's. Then all his troubles would have been over.

When Spud turned and lay on his stomach, Lymie got up and sat down beside him on the edge of the couch, and began to read over Spud's shoulder: . . . *woman will heal thy wound, stop the waste hole in thy bag of tricks. Woman is thy wealth; have but one woman, dress, undress, and fondle that woman, make use of the woman—woman is everything—woman has an inkstand of her own; dip thy pen into that bottomless inkpot* . . . Without looking up, Spud rolled over on his back, so that Lymie could stretch out and read in comfort. But Lymie didn't move. His face was troubled. He started to say something and then, after a second's hesitation, he went on reading. *Woman makes love; make love to her with the pen only, tickle her fantasies, and sketch merrily for her a thousand pictures of love in a thousand pretty ways. Woman is generous and all for one, or one for all, must pay the painter, and furnish the hairs of the brush* . . . At the bottom of the page Spud looked up to see if Lymie was still reading. Lymie had been finished for some time. He was staring at Spud's chest.

"Let's do something else," he said.

"Why?" Spud asked. "This is interesting." He rolled over on his stomach again and was about to go on reading when Lymie surprised him by grabbing the book out of his hands. It sailed across the room into the blazing fire. Spud sat up and saw with a certain amount of regret that the flames were already licking at the open pages.

"What did you do that for?" he asked.

Instead of explaining, Lymie prodded at the book with the poker, so that the leaves burned faster. Pieces of charred paper detached themselves and were drawn, still glowing, up the chimney.

"You're going to have a hell of a time explaining to

Hall about his book," Spud said.

"I'm not going to explain about it," Lymie said. His jaw was set and Spud, realizing that Lymie was very close to tears, sank back on the couch as if nothing had happened.

After a week in which no one, so far as the boys knew, was shown through the apartment, they gave up staying there at night, and with the warm weather they stopped going to the fraternity house altogether. It took too long, and besides, they were suffering from spring fever. When they emerged from the school building at three o'clock with their ties loosened and their collars undone, they had no energy and no will. They stood around in the schoolyard watching baseball practice and leaning against each other for support. Any suggestion that anybody made always turned out to be too much trouble.

There is no telling how long it would have taken them to find out about the fraternity if Carson hadn't wanted suddenly to play his record of "I'll See You in My Dreams." The record was at the fraternity and he asked Lynch to ride down there with him. Lynch's last report card was unsatisfactory and he wasn't allowed out after supper on week nights, so Carson went alone. When he came around the corner of the apartment building and saw the furniture clogging the areaway, he stopped short, unable to believe his eyes.

The couch was soggy and stained from being rained on. The chairs were coming unglued. There were wrinkles in the picture of the collegian, where the water had got in behind the glass, and the grass rug gave off a musty odor. The English bulldog was missing, but Lynch was too upset to notice this. It was his victrola, the condition of his victrola, that upset him most. The felt pad on the turntable had spots of mildew, the oak veneer of the case peeled off in strips, and both the needle and the arm were rusted. When he tried to wind it, the victrola made such a horrible grinding sound that he gave up and went in search of the janitor. There was no one in the boiler room or in any of the various storerooms in the basement. He came back and tried the door of the apartment. The padlock that they had used was gone and in its place was a new Yale lock. No one came to the door.

The victrola records were warped and probably ruined, but he took them anyway and walked around to the front of the building, intending to peer in at the basement windows. They had net curtains across them and he could see nothing. He went off down the street with the records under his arm and his spirits held up by anger and the melancholy pleasure of spreading the news.

21

With school almost over for the year and summer vacation looming ahead, the loss of a meeting place made very little difference to any of them. Spud Latham and Lymie Peters met in the corridor by Spud's locker, after school, and went off together. Lymie had a malted milk and Spud had a milk shake and then they came out of the stale air of LeClerc's and separated. Or else Lymie went home with Spud. He never asked Spud to come home with him and Spud never suggested it. So far as he was concerned, Lymie belonged at his house, and had no other home.

No matter how often Lymie went there, Mrs. Latham always seemed glad to see him. She treated him casually and yet managed to watch over him. When she caught him helping himself out of the icebox as if he lived there, all she said was "Lymie, there's some fudge cake in the cakebox. Wouldn't you rather have a piece of that?"

At mealtime there was a place for him at the dining room table, next to Spud. From the other side of the table Helen teased him because he didn't like parsnips or because he needed a haircut, and Mr. Latham used him as an excuse to tell long stories about the heating business.

After supper Lymie and Spud studied together in Spud's room until their minds wandered from the page and they started yawning. Then they got up and went across the street to the park and lay on the grass and stared into the evening sky and thought out loud about what the future had in store for them. Spud's heart was fixed on a cabin in the North Woods where they (it was understood that Lymie was to be with him) could fish in the summertime and in winter set trap lines and then sit around and be warm and comfortable indoors, with the wind howling and the snow banked up higher than the windows of the cabin. Lymie chewed on a blade of grass and didn't commit himself. It all seemed possible. Something that would require arranging, perhaps (pleasant though such a life might be, there was obviously not going to be much money in it) but perfectly possible.

At nine-thirty or a quarter of ten he pulled Spud up off the grass and they went back across the street. Lymie gathered up his books and papers. As he passed by the living room door he said "Good night, everybody," and Helen and Mr. and Mrs. Latham looked up and nodded affectionately, as if he had told them that he was going down to the drugstore on the corner and would be right back.

One day Mrs. Latham discovered that there was a button missing from his shirt after he and Spud had been doing push-ups on the living room rug. They looked under all the furniture without being able to find it and then she made Lymie come into her bedroom with her while she hunted through her sewing box for another white button to sew on in place of the one he had lost.

Something in the tone of her voice caught Spud's attention. He stood still in the center of the living room and listened, with a troubled expression on his face. His mother was talking to Lymie in a scolding way that was not really scolding at all and that he had never heard her use with anybody but him. He felt a sharp stab of jealousy. It was one thing to have a friend, but another to . . . . He raised the sleeve of his coat and looked at it thoughtfully. A piece of brown thread dangled from the cuff where a button should have been.

"Speaking of buttons," he said quietly.

"Oh, all right," Mrs. Latham answered him from the bedroom. "I've been meaning to fix it but I just didn't get around to it, with all there is to do in this house. Leave it on your bed when you go to school tomorrow. . . . Stand still, Lymie. I don't want to stick you. . . . And next time remember to save the button, do you hear? It isn't always easy to——"

She didn't bother to finish the sentence, but Spud's face cleared. He was reassured. His mother still loved him the most. She had heard him two rooms away, even though he hadn't raised his voice; and she knew exactly what button he was talking about.

Another afternoon when they got home from school, Spud was restless and wanted to go walking in the rain. They walked a long way west until they came to the Northwestern Railway tracks, where further progress was blocked by an interminable freight train. They stood and counted boxcars and coal cars and oil tankers, and the train shuddered violently once or twice and came to a dead stop. By that time they were tired of waiting for it to pass and so they turned back. The soles of their shoes were soaked through and the bottoms of their trousers were wet and kept flapping about their ankles. When they got home they hung their yellow slickers on the back porch to dry, and retired to Spud's room with a quart of milk and a box of fig newtons. Noticing the hollows under Lymie's eyes, Spud decided that he ought to take a nap. There was plenty of time before dinner, and he began to undo Lymie's tie. Lymie refused, for no reason; or perhaps because Spud hadn't given him a chance to consider whether he was tired or not. Spud got the tie off but when he tried to unbutton Lymie's shirt, Lymie began to fight him off. He had never really fought anybody before and he fought with strength that he had no idea he possessed.

At first Spud was amused, and then suddenly it became a life-and-death matter. He wasn't quite sure how to come at Lymie because Lymie didn't know the rules. He fought with his hands and his feet and his knees. He gouged at and he grabbed anything that he could lay hands on. Each time that Spud managed to get his arms around Lymie he twisted and fought his way free. The noise they made, banging against the furniture, climbing up on the bed and down again, drew Mrs. Latham, who stood in the doorway for a while, trying to make them stop. Neither of them paid any attention to her. The expression on Lymie's tormented face was almost but not quite hate. Spud was calm and possessed, and merely bent on making Lymie lie still under the covers and take a nap before dinner. He pried one of Lymie's shoes off and then the other. His trousers took much longer and were harder to manage, but in the end they came off too, and one of Lymie's striped socks. With each loss, like a country defending itself against an invader, Lymie fought harder. He fought against being made to do something against his will, and he fought also against the unreasonable strength in Spud's arms. He butted. He kicked. All of a sudden, with no warning, the last defense gave way. Lymie quit struggling and lay still. As in a dream he let Spud cover him with a blanket. Something had burst inside of him, something more important than any organ, and there was a flowing which was like blood. Though he kept on breathing and his heart after a while pounded less violently, there it was all the same, an underground river which went on and on and was bound to keep on like that for years probably, never stopping, never once running dry.

He watched Spud pull the shades down and leave the room without having any idea of what he had done.

BOOK THREE

A Cold Country

22

"Alastor is not antisocial," Profesor Severance said, with a puckered expression about his mouth. Apparently there was something else he would have liked to add, something which was perhaps too flippant and would have destroyed (or come dangerously close to it) his hold on the class. "Alastor understands people rather better by getting away from them than by being buffeted by them." Heads bent over notebooks, fountain pens began to scratch. "In solitude only can we attune ourselves to the meaning of nature and the deep heart of man,"

Professor Severance said, teetering slightly, and with all traces of the flippant remark, whatever it was, gone from his rather tired, his definitely middle-aged, scholar's face. "So the poet turns from love to understand love."

This struck Mrs. Lieberman—the small, quiet-faced, prematurely white-haired woman sitting in the third row next to the window—as just nonsense. Her fountain pen remained idle in her hand. She was enrolled as a listener and so it didn't matter whether she took notes during the lecture or not. She wouldn't be called upon at some later date to fill two pages of an examination book with the house of cards that Professor Severance was now erecting, sentence by sentence.

"Alastor loves beyond the Arab maid," he continued, "and understands human nature beyond human inter-course." He spoke directly to Mrs. Lieberman, since she was the only person in the class who was looking at him. That he was well taken care of, there could be no doubt, she thought. But by whom? He was never without a fresh white handkerchief in his breast pocket, he never forgot his glasses. But on the other hand, Professor Severance didn't look like a married man. There was never a flicker of complacency, and also his lectures—always beautifully phrased, models of organization, style, and diction—from time to time showed a shocking (or so it seemed to her) lack of experience.

He picked up *The Complete Poetical Works of Shelley* in order to read from it, or perhaps in order to pretend to read from it, for his eyes only occasionally skimmed the page.

Earth, ocean, air, beloved brotherhood . . .

The voice in which Professor Severance read poetry was high and reedlike. The young man who sat on Mrs. Lieberman's right, the blond athlete with the block letter sewed on the front of his white pullover, thrust one long, muscular, football player's leg into the aisle and looked pained. In the row ahead of him, his exact human opposite —flat-chested with a long pointed face and straight dark hair that grew down on his forehead in a widow's peak— didn't seem to be listening either. His eyes were vacant. But when Professor Severance cleared his throat and said, "Mr. Peters, in what other English Romantic poet do we find these same 'incommunicable dreams,' these 'twilight phantasms' that invoke a greater responsiveness to 'the woven hymns of night and day'?" Lymie separated his legs, which were twisted together under the seat, and said, "Wordsworth?"

"Precisely!" Professor Severance exclaimed and Mrs. Lieberman decided that he must live with his mother.

It is always disturbing to pick up an acquaintance after several years. The person is bound to have changed, so that (in one way or another) you will have to deal with a stranger. Yet the change seldom turns out to be as great as one expects, or even hopes for. The summer that Lymie was seventeen, Mr. Peters found a place for him in a certified public accountant's office, downtown in the Loop. He wanted Lymie to learn the value of money by earning some. When Lymie went back to high school in September he saw that most of the boys his own age had put on weight. Some of them had put on as much as twenty-five or thirty pounds. That summer it seemed to happen to all of them. Their faces hadn't changed much, but they seemed to move differently. From being thin and gangly, they had spread out in the shoulders, their legs and arms had become solid, and they were beginning to be broad through the chest. Ford, who had never been heavy enough for anything but track, played football. So did Carson and Lynch. Lymie had grown slightly more round-shouldered from sitting all day on a high stool in front of a comptometer, but that was the only physical change in him. He tried doing setting-up exercises morn-

ing and night in front of the open window, but they didn't
help. And he had an uneasy feeling that he had somehow
missed his chance.

Perhaps he attached too much importance to physical development. It is, after all, a minor barrier in the
Grand Obstacle Race. The ordinary person manages it
successfully (or doesn't) and goes on to leap (or fall into)
the twenty-foot pit of shyness, to clear (or go around)
the eight-foot wall of money, to climb (or fall headlong
from) the swaying rope net of love, and so on and so on.
Some fail at one obstacle, some at another. The sensible
ones go on, if they fail, and try the next. Those with too
much imagination keep throwing themselves at the first
one they fail at, as if everything depended on that, and
so forgot the others which they might have managed
easily. When Lymie was in high school, not being able
to hold his own in games had serious consequences. Now
that he was a sophomore in college, it no longer mattered,
or at least nothing like so much. But he still clung loyally
to that one insurmountable barrier.

At nineteen he was almost painfully thin. The look of
adolescence was gone from his face, his hair was less unruly, and his hands had taken the shape they would have
for the rest of his life. His eyes still had a hesitant look,
even when Professor Severance called on him and he produced the right answer out of the air. Which may have
been the result of one failure after another on the high
school baseball field and in the swimming pool. Or this
hesitancy, this habitual lack of self-confidence, might well
have been the cause of those failures.

When Professor Severance went on with his lecture,
Lymie wrote something in his loose-leaf notebook which
couldn't have had anything to do with Wordsworth or
Shelley, because the two girls who sat on either side of
him read it surreptitiously and smiled. They were friends,
the three of them. They arrived at the classroom together,

and small folded pieces of paper often passed between them, sometimes to the annoyance of Professor Severance, who, as a gentleman, could only combat rudeness by ignoring it.

Sally Forbes, the girl who sat on Lymie's left, had on a red leather coat and a close-fitting gray felt hat with a clump of cock feathers over each ear. Her father was a full professor in the department of philosophy. The cock feathers were light green and bright blue, and the ends curled over the brim of the hat and lay flat against her tanned cheeks. Her hair was straight and almost black. Bangs covered her forehead, and her mouth was large and a little too prominent, but nothing could destroy or in any way diminish the effect of her very beautiful, eager, dark brown eyes. She had entered college when she was sixteen, and was now seventeen, and looked older than that. Her shoulders were square, her back as straight as a child's, and she hadn't yet outgrown the childish habit of biting her fingernails. Her hips were narrow, her legs were slender but strong. Her breasts were small and there was no suggestion of softness about her anywhere.

Lymie and Hope Davison had known each other in high school, but not very well. They didn't actually get to be friends until they came down to the university. Hope's tan coat and skirt, white sweater, and brown and white saddleback shoes all said *There is a right and a wrong way to dress*. Hope disliked bright colors, loud-voiced people, and any display of egotism. Her face was small, delicate, and sober. Her mouth was nicely shaped but obstinate, and her light blue eyes had an unnerving effect on young instructors who were not used to lecturing from a platform. They left no room anywhere for the mysterious or the irrational. If voices had spoken to her out of a burning bush, in all probability she would have stood waiting for some natural explanation to occur to her.

Professor Severance did not mind being stared at. He had been teaching for twenty-two years, and knew that the faces that looked up at him would shortly be replaced by other faces not unlike them. His own face, at that moment, was turned toward the windows. Seeing handfuls of leaves coming down in a sudden stirring of the air outside, he spoke with such intensity of the despair that dogs every hope, and the resurrection through scourging, that his words at last reached the minds of his students. They realized uneasily that he had stopped talking about Shelley and was referring in a veiled way to himself. The fountain pens stopped scratching.

"Through crucifixion," Professor Severance said, "one arises to a new life. Death is a mere incident, for Alastor dies daily, entering more and more into eternity, so that when death comes to him it is somewhat overdue."

There was a solemn pause when he finished speaking.

"On Wednesday," Professor Severance said, "I shall take up the relation between Shelley's ethical philosophy and the idiom of his art. Will you please be prepared to recite on—" The bell rang before he could complete his sentence, and with the ringing of the bell, his power went out of him. He was Samson without his hair. Voices broke out all over the classroom. His students, a moment before so docile and so determined to get into their loose-leaf notebooks all that he had to say about the life of solitude, rose up in their seats and filled the aisles to overflowing. Professor Severance put the works of Shelley away in his battered brief case and gathered up his hat, his gray gloves, and his cane. The aisles were emptied almost immediately. He bowed Mrs. Lieberman out of the door ahead of him, and then marched briskly down the corridor.

Outside it was the very peak of fall. The sky was clear and very blue. The air was warm, the leaves were coming down in showers. Mrs. Lieberman was right behind Lymie and the two girls as they descended the iron stairs at the back of the building, and then were forced off the sidewalk by the two streams of traffic—one leaving University Hall, the other coming toward it. They stood a moment, talking, until dust and leaves, caught up in a miniature cyclone, made them turn their backs.

Hope said, "Hang on, Lymie—we don't want to lose you."

"Okay," he said, and took hold of her arm lightly.

"In case you think that remark was funny, Davison," Sally said, "you're sadly mistaken."

"I suppose I am," Hope said, "but on the other hand, I didn't mean to—"

"You never do," Sally said. "Why don't you hit her, Lymie?"

"I can't," Lymie said. "I wasn't brought up that way."

"Well, I wasn't *either*," Sally said, "but I knocked a boy out cold when I was nine years old, and nobody taught me how to do it. I just picked up a brickbat and hit him with it. Johnny Mayberry, his name was. He was a very nice boy. I don't remember what he did to me that made me so irritated with him, but anyway they had to take five stitches in his head, and his mother wouldn't let me come over and play in their yard for a long time afterward."

While she was talking, she opened a book and took out a gray envelope, pressed between the pages. Then with a strange asking look on her face she said, "Lymie, will you do something for me? Will you give this to your stuck-up friend?"

Lymie took the envelope and thrust it in his coat pocket. "He's not really stuck-up," he said slowly. "It was just a misunderstanding."

"I know it was." Sally nodded. "I just said that. But

the thing is, a note probably won't be enough. And if it
isn't, will you?——"

Mrs. Lieberman realized suddenly that neither of
these girls was for Mr. Peters. Over a period of weeks she
had built up an elaborate speculation about the intimacy
in the row ahead of her and now in half a minute it was
demolished. This was always happening to her, and it
didn't really matter, except she was sorry for him. He
needed someone. He needed fussing over and caring for.
He needed lots of love. (She had two sons of her own,
both in college, but when they came klop-klopping down
the stairs in the morning, it sounded like horses, and they
slipped past her and out of the house and into a world of
their own making, where nothing she said ever penetrated.) And what grieved her as she started on down
the walk, under the high nave made by overarching elm
trees, was that she herself had no daughter to push at him
—for she would have liked very much to take him home,
fatten him, and keep him in the family.

23

The front corridor of the men's gymnasium was empty
except for a set of scales facing the door and a glass case
containing trophies. The prevailing odor was of chlorine,
from the swimming pool. At either end of the corridor, a
short flight of stairs went up and another flight went
down, the result being in either case the same: row on
row of metal lockers, long wooden benches, and shower
rooms. In this part of the building, which was always
overheated, the stale odor of male bodies met and grap-
pled with the dank odor of drains.

The third floor of the gymnasium was a single vast

room, light and sunny, with a narrow balcony running all the way around it and a high steel-ribbed roof. In the absence of partitions the floor space was divided by the equipment. Rings, parallel bars, ladders, tumbling mats, and a leather horse took up half the gymnasium. Most of the remaining area was required by the flying trapeze apparatus, but there was room under the balcony for several wrestling mats, and in the opposite corner a punching bag. Two sets of stairs led up to the balcony, which was an indoor running track steeply sloped at the curves and almost level on the straightaway. Three more sets of stairs went down to the locker rooms.

After four o'clock in the afternoon the gymnasium was like a men's club. The same undergraduates, the same faculty members came there day after day to work out and most of them knew each other, if not by name at least to speak to. Lymie came up from the locker rooms, in his street clothes, with his logic book under his arm, and his leather notebook, his anthology of nineteenth-century poetry. He stood for a moment at the head of the stairs. His eyes took in the little group around the high parallel bars, the tumblers doing double backflips, the mathematics instructor pulling at chest weights, and the two boys who were slowly swinging, head downward, from the iron rings. In a far corner he located the person he was looking for—a boxer who appeared at ten minutes after four every afternoon, in trunks and soft, leather boxing shoes, with his wrists taped, and on his hands a pair of pigskin gloves with the fingers cut out of them. The boxer was Spud Latham. There was no mistaking him, although in four years' time his face had grown much harder and leaner and his jaw more pronounced.

Spud was skipping rope when Lymie came up to him, and he acknowledged Lymie's presence with a curt nod. On the count of thirty-nine the rope caught on his heel.

His face relaxed and he said, "This is one hell of a place. Nobody will put the gloves on with me."

"Did you try Armstrong?" Lymie asked.

"He's still sore on account of what happened last time," Spud said.

"You shouldn't have hit him so hard, probably."

"I didn't mean to," Spud said. "I just got excited, I guess, and the first thing I knew he was sitting on his can."

"Well," Lymie said, "you can't blame him for not wanting to do it again."

"I didn't hurt him," Spud said. "It just shook him up. You'd think with a whole gymnasium to choose from, somebody would be interested in something besides walking on their hands."

"What about Maguire?" Lymie asked.

"Same thing." Spud tossed the skipping rope aside and jabbed at the punching bag, making it *ka-slap, ka-slap* in whatever direction he wanted it to. His movements were quick, controlled, and certain, and there was a cruel look in his eye.

Lymie took off his shoes in order to practice skipping rope. His performance was not expert like Spud's. He was too tense. He missed on the count of thirteen and had to start over.

Spud was a year older than Lymie and his body showed it. His body was finished. It was the body of a man, slender, well-proportioned, compact, and beautiful. He had been a life guard all summer long at one of the street-end beaches in Chicago and his hair and eyebrows were still bleached from the sun. His skin was so tanned from the constant exposure that it looked permanent. He could have been a Polynesian. Though Lymie had seen him dress and undress hundreds of times, there is a kind of amazement that does not wear off. Very often, looking at Spud, he felt the desire which he sometimes had looking at statues—to put out his hand and touch some part of Spud, the intricate interlaced muscles of his side, or his shoulder blades, or his back, or his flat stomach, or the veins at his wrists, or his small pointed ears.

Spud turned away from the punching bag and went up on the balcony where the rowing machines were. While he was gone, a thickset boy with red hair picked up the boxing gloves which Spud had tossed aside, and started punching the bag. Spud came downstairs immediately and stood close by, watching him. When the redheaded boy turned aside to rest, Spud said, "You wouldn't like to show me something about boxing, would you?"

The redheaded boy looked at him suspiciously and said, "Get somebody that knows something about it."

"There isn't anybody," Spud said. "They're all acrobats and like that. I can tell from watching you that you know a lot more than I do. And if you don't mind showing me a few things——"

The other boy pulled his sweat shirt off, over his head. "Okay," he said. "If you're that crazy to box, I'd just as soon."

Lymie tied Spud's boxing gloves on for him and then went over to the redheaded boy, who had finished tying one glove and was trying to manage the knot in the other. When Lymie took over, the redheaded boy said, "Much obliged," and looked past him at Spud.

"Three minute rounds," Spud said, "and no slugging."

"Better make it two," the redheaded boy said.

With Spud's pocket Ingersoll in his right hand, Lymie backed away and called "Time!" The two boxers closed in cautiously. The redheaded boy had at least twenty pounds advantage in weight, but he moved slowly. Spud walked round and round him, jabbing at him, blocking with his shoulder or his elbows, and breathing in through his mouth and out through his nose. Lymie looked down at the watch and then his eyes flew back to Spud. Once as Spud ducked, Lymie's head also moved sidewise. The movement was very slight, almost as if Lymie were asleep and dreaming that he was fighting.

At first the boxing was scientific and careful, but toward the end of the second round, Spud let go of one. He apologized and they went on fighting. In the third round the same thing happened again and this time he didn't apologize. Neither did the redheaded boy when he broke through Spud's guard a minute later and sent him sprawling.

Lymie called "Time!" sharply but nobody paid any attention to him. Spud got to his feet and resumed his shuffling and dancing, but he didn't box as well as he had before. The redheaded boy got through to him again and again—on the chin, on the side of the head, above his eye. Spud began to lose ground and eventually the two of them, still flailing at each other, ended up between the high parallel bars, to the annoyance of the boy named Armstrong, who jumped down and separated them.

"Why don't you stay over there where you belong, Latham?" he asked.

"Oh, don't be a sorehead," Spud said and turned his back on him. Lymie, who had followed the fighting anxiously all the way across the gymnasium, now untied the strings of their boxing gloves. Spud and the redheaded boy pulled their gloves off, shook hands, and went off to the showers together.

Left to himself, Lymie put his shoes on and picked up his coat, his books, the boxing gloves, and Spud's skipping rope. As he started down the stairs he saw by the big clock on the wall that it was now five-twenty-five. The trapeze performers had also decided to call it a day. They were dropping one after another into the net, like ripe pears.

24

When Sally left Lymie and Hope, she hurried home. It was her mother's "day" and she was expected to help. The Forbeses lived in a two-story bungalow a little over a mile from the university campus, in a quiet neighborhood. The outside of their house was white stucco covered with a thick, three-pointed ivy. Mrs. Forbes had grown it from a slip that she had carried away from Kenilworth Castle in her purse. Between the Forbeses' house and the Albrechts' house on the right, there was barely room for a narrow cement driveway. The apple tree in the Forbeses' back yard also shaded the flower garden of the economics professor and his wife whose house was on the left. The economics professor claimed the fruit that he could reach from his property, and a coolness had developed between the two families, partly as a result of this and partly because Professor Forbes, on summer evenings when the lawn needed sprinkling, very often placed the sprinkler so that most of the water went on the sidewalk, and passersby had to make a detour through the wet grass or walk in the street.

Mrs. Forbes was "at home" the second Thursday of every month. On these occasions Professor Forbes was on duty at the front door, where he shook hands with the arriving guests, and took their hats and coats from them, and if it was raining, their umbrellas and rubbers. During the fall and winter months there was always a wood fire burning in the living room fireplace. The curtains were drawn, the lamps were lit. In the dining room there were tall lighted candles in silver candlesticks, and the table was covered with a lace tablecloth and that in turn by stacks of hand-painted plates, rows of shining teaspoons,

and platters of fancy sandwiches. Sometimes the woman
pouring tea at the copper samovar was Mrs. Somers, the
wife of the dean of the Graduate School. Sometimes it
was Mrs. Severance, Professor Severance's mother. Or
Mrs. Clark, whose husband was head of the English department. This afternoon it was Mrs. Philosophy Mathews, so-called to distinguish her from the Mrs. Mathews
whose husband taught animal husbandry.

Mrs. Forbes herself, always serene, always handsome,
stood in the living room receiving. Her guests presented
a grand panoramic picture of the Liberal Arts faculty and
the Graduate School. As with all such pictures (the
"Coronation of Napoleon," for example, and "Men and
Women of Letters of the Nineteenth Century") you
have to have a key. A stranger would have seen a room
full of middle-aged and elderly people in groups of twos,
threes, and fours, with teacups in their hands, talking a
little too loudly in each other's faces. Mrs. Wentworth,
whose husband was in the psychology department, and
Mary Mountjoy, who taught Italian, were arguing about
the best time to transplant dahlias. The head of the classics department and a young biology instructor were listening to a businessman who had married into the faculty.
The world and his office, he was saying, could develop no
trouble that two Manhattans wouldn't cure. After ad-
vancing this contention cheerfully and without opposition, he went on to assert that most people are enor-
mously improved by liquor. The Althoffs and Helen
Glover were twitting the head of the English department
on his 8 A.M. broadcasts. Mrs. Baker, who taught the modern novel (with special emphasis on Henry James) and
Alice Rawlings were standing in a corner trying to get
away from the fireplace. They were discussing Mrs. Baker's Minnie, who was colored and who, after seven years
of faithful service had had a major operation in August
and then had declared that her boy friend was going to

finance a whole year's vacation for her. Alice Rawlings said that she had given up and was going it alone with a superb houseman-yardman Fred, on Fridays. It was his one slum day, she said. He came straight from the Wilsons and the McAvoys, and was doing his best to make her back yard resemble their estates. Kathryn Shortall was saying what a blessing it was that her husband enjoyed eating out sometimes, and Sally's father, out in the hall, was talking to an exchange professor from the Sorbonne about Montaigne. Everyone knew everyone else and it was a good deal like progressive whist, or some game like that, since it involved a frequent change of partners. You went up to any group you felt like talking to. They opened automatically and amiably, and there you were, allowed to pick up the threads of the old conversation or start a new one.

There were several young girls, Sally among them, who came and went, bearing cups of tea and platters of sandwiches. Though Sally had known some of her mother's guests since childhood and was privileged to call many full professors by their nicknames, today she looked on everybody with the eyes of a stranger. There was no place for her in this world. She liked dogs, horses, sail-boats, airplanes, climbing apple trees, staying up late at night, walking in the rain, driving round and round in an open car on a summer afternoon, sitting by a beach fire at night, lying on the ground and looking up at the under-sides of leaves and at lightning bugs and falling stars, di-viding her attention between a book that she had read many times and an apple, watching the sun go down and the moon come up, wondering what the boy she was go-ing to marry would look like and where he was at that moment, and how long it would take him to find her. . . . The list was endless and made up entirely of normal hu-man pleasures. If it had only included an appreciation of respectability, she would have been happier. Or at least she would have been spared a great many bitter arguments with her mother. The words "nice" and "proper" seemed to inflame Sally, and an attempt to consider her conduct in the light of conventional standards made her start talking furiously in a loud voice without much logic.

She loved her mother and father but she didn't love the things they lived by—professorial dignity, scholarship, old books, old furniture, old china, and brand new amusing gossip. She liked storms, lightning and thunder, excitement; and the climate of her home was unfortunately a temperate one.

When there were too many arguments in too short a time, she took a few clothes and moved into the sorority house, where she ran into similar difficulties. She was expected to be careful of her appearance and of her friends, and to remember at all times that she belonged to the best sorority on the campus. She didn't try to do any of these things and so there were more arguments, especially in chapter meetings. She moved around the house in a cloud of disapproval, which had the curious effect of making her clumsy. She tripped over rugs, her feet slid out from under her on the stairs. The girls that she wanted to have like her did, actually, but they also laughed at her, because she was so enthusiastic and so like an overgrown puppy; and this hurt her pride.

The girls who were not amused by her behavior were appalled by it. No room that she walked into was ever quite large enough, nothing was safe in her apologetic hands. She didn't mean to drop Emily Noyes' bottle of Chanel No. 5 or split open the seams of Joyce Brenner's white evening dress which she had asked to try on, but the result in each case was disastrous. The girls snatched fragile things from her if she showed any sign of picking them up, and the girl she bumped into hurrying around a corner of the upstairs hall took to her bed, with cold compresses on her head. It seemed to her that all girls were made of glass and she alone was of flesh and blood and constantly cutting herself on them. She gave up trying to please them.

Though she was undeniably a tomboy, there was nothing masculine about her appearance. She was a recognizable feminine type which the Greeks represented as a huntress with a crescent moon in the center of her forehead, a silver bow in her left hand, a quiver of arrows slung over one shoulder, and her skirts caught up so that her long thighs would be free and unhampered. During the annual festival which the Romans held in her honor, hunting dogs were crowned with garlands and wild beasts were not molested. Wine was brought forth and there was a feast consisting of roasted kid, cakes served piping hot on plates of leaves, and apples still hanging in clusters on the bough. It was not a type generally admired or often found in the university in the year 1927.

The one girl whom she made friends with, Hope Davison, was also a nonconformist, though of a different kind. She did nothing to call attention to herself, she had no sneak dates, and she never broke house rules. But she had a way of looking at people as if she saw through them, and didn't think too much of what was there. Her stare was, more often than not, unconscious, but the other girls in the sorority suffered from it, and from her remarks, which were more candid sometimes than there was any need for. After a year they had devised no adequate way of dealing with her or with Sally.

When Sally's nose was shiny, well it was shiny. Anybody who didn't like shiny noses could look the other way. The belt of Sally's red coat was sometimes missing for days. The left pocket had been ripped and not very expertly sewed up again. The lining was moth-eaten, and the coat itself had, on at least one occasion, been fished out of the waste basket where Mrs. Forbes had put it. Sally went on wearing it, partly because she loved it and partly because it was an offense to every self-respecting member of her sorority. Some of the girls threatened to burn the coat if she didn't stop wearing it, but this threat was never carried out. It would have been dangerous, and they knew it.

Sally and Hope had appeared together in Lymie Peters' freshman rhetoric class, the beginning day of the spring semester. The girls took the two empty seats beside him, and when the instructor didn't bother to alphabetize the class, they stayed there. By the end of the first week they were borrowing theme paper from Lymie. After the second week Sally and Lymie changed seats so that he was in the middle. Often when the class was over, all three of them would retire to a confectionery called the Ship's Lantern, which was long and narrow and pitch dark when they walked into it out of the sunlight. Sometimes they studied, but more often they sat and exposed their minds to each other while they made a mess out of melted ice cream and paper straws, cigarette ashes, and the dregs of Coca-Cola.

One afternoon soon after the semester had started, Spud and Lymie met Sally coming out of the campus bookstore. She spoke to Lymie and he would have said "Hi" in return and walked on, but a sharp poke in the small of his back stopped him. After the introduction had been managed there was an awkward silence and Spud suggested that they go somewhere and have a Coke. This seemed to Lymie a very silly idea, since it was almost twenty minutes of six. Sally accepted the invitation, to his surprise, and all three of them went to the Ship's Lantern. Spud found an empty booth in the back and maneuvered Sally into the seat beside him. Lymie sat across from them. Lymie had never seen Spud in such a state of foolish excitement. He gave his imitation of an overstimulated horse, and of the flew-flew bird that swims backward to keep the water out of its eyes. He also found an occasion to exclaim: "*O grim-look'd night! O night with hue so black!*" and to demonstrate that it is possible to swallow a lighted cigarette without pain or even discomfort.

Sally was amused and delighted by everything he said. She was also very quiet, for her. Occasionally her eyes met Spud's for a second, but then she looked away immediately at his tie, or at the handkerchief folded and tucked so carefully in his coat pocket, or at his broad-knuckled hands. Her own, with their chewed-off fingernails, she kept out of sight under the table.

At six o'clock when Sally got up to go, Spud told her that if she cared to come down to the gym with him some afternoon he'd show her how to box.

"Oh, I'd love to," she said. Her eyes flew wide with pleasure at the prospect, and then she looked crestfallen. "You're just making fun of me," she said sadly.

"I'm not either," Spud exclaimed. Although he had been kidding, now that she spoke about it in this way, the whole idea seemed to take on a different aspect. "I mean it," he said.

"I'd love to," Sally repeated. "More than anything in the whole world."

"All right," Spud said. "I'll show you all I know about boxing. Here, put your hands up. Might as well give you the first lesson right now." He took hold of both her arms, by the wrists, and moved them into position. "There," he said. "The rest is easy."

Whether it was or not, she didn't have a chance to find out, for there were no more lessons. The next day Spud met her on the steps of University Hall and she looked right at him without speaking. He came home to the rooming house where he and Lymie were living, slammed his books around in a fury, and said the hell with her, the hell with all women.

Lymie asked Sally about it, the next time he saw her, and she had no idea what he was talking about. She hadn't seen Spud, she said. Really she hadn't! It was just that she was so nearsighted. She couldn't recognize her own grandmother six feet away, without glasses on. And that was why she hadn't spoken to him.

Spud wouldn't believe this at first, and after he did believe it he couldn't seem to get over his feeling that somehow (even though Sally hadn't recognized him) he had been snubbed. He refused to see or have anything more to do with her.

25

Lymie went down two flights of stairs, turned left, and went on until he came to Spud's locker. He put down the things he was carrying and turned the dial padlock until it fell open. Then he reached inside and brought out a clean towel. Farther down the row of lockers two boys were dressing. Lymie laid the towel across the bench and walked over to a door that opened into the swimming pool. There were half a dozen swimmers still in the pool. One of them was swimming back and forth, churning the water with his feet and ankles. The others were waiting their turn at the diving board. A boy with close-cropped curly blond hair did a high jackknife and then a tall freckle-faced boy tried a half gainer, which was not a success. He came up slowly and shook the water out of his eyes. The next boy placed both hands on the board, out at the very end, and then up went his naked legs, slowly and easily. He balanced himself for fifteen seconds, wavered, regained his balance, and dropped head first into the water. The tall diver returned to the board and Lymie could tell by the way he braced himself that he was going to try the half gainer again.

The two boys farther down the row of lockers finished dressing and slammed their locker doors shut. They saw the clean towel on the bench and their eyes turned from it to Lymie, standing with his nose pressed to the glass pane in the door. Once the towel was in their possession, no one could prove that it wasn't theirs. As they walked toward it, Lymie glanced at them, over his shoulder. They left the towel where it was.

The diver took a running jump from the end of the springboard. A moment later, Lymie turned away from the swimming pool and went back and sat down in front of the open locker. From his coat pocket he produced the gray envelope. *For Spud Latham* it said in Sally's round legible handwriting. The flap was unsealed. For a second Lymie was tempted to read it; he put both the temptation and the envelope aside.

Spud came up shining from his shower, found the towel Lymie had laid out for him, and dried himself. His eyes were clear and bright and full of happiness. "That was a good scrap," he said. "I enjoyed it. The guy was really mean, once he got started."

Lymie reached into the locker, found Spud's shorts, and handed them to him. "Didn't you hear me calling time?" he asked.

Spud shook his head. "I didn't hear anything," he said. "I was busy keeping from getting killed."

He sat down on the bench to dry his feet. When he had finished, his shoes and socks were waiting on the floor beside him, and the boxing trunks and jock strap that he had brought up from the shower room in his hand were hanging on a hook in the locker. It was not callousness that let him accept these attentions simply and without thinking about them. He wouldn't have allowed anyone else to do for him the things that Lymie did. And besides, he recognized that it gave Lymie pleasure to bend over and pick up the towel where he had dropped it, and to go off to the towel room and exchange it for a clean one.

When Lymie came back, Spud was dressed and tying his tie in front of a small mirror which hung at the end of the row of lockers. "I feel wonderful," Spud said. "What do you think we'll have for supper?"

"Wednesday, veal birds."

"I could eat a steer," Spud said, "without half trying."

Lymie buried his head in the locker, searching for Spud's big black notebook, and heard him say, "What's this, a communication from the dean's office?" and realized that he had discovered the gray envelope.

"It's for you," Lymie said.

Spud tore the envelope open and glanced at the note inside. "Here," he said, and tossed the note at Lymie. *Dear Spud*, it said, *We're having an informal house dance on the Saturday after Homecoming. Would you care to come? Sincerely yours, Sally Forbes.* Lymie folded the note, slipped it back in the torn envelope, and laid it on the bench. Homecoming was the twenty-fifth. The dance would be the second of November.

"What do you think?" Spud asked. "Do you figure I ought to go?"

"If it were me," Lymie said slowly (for he would have liked to be asked to the dance himself) "I'd go. You'll probably have a good time."

"Has Hope asked you yet?"

Lymie shook his head.

"Why hasn't she?" Spud asked.

"Maybe she's got somebody else in mind that she wants to ask," Lymie said. "Or she may be waiting to see whether you decide to come or not."

"We'll go together," Spud said suddenly. "And we'll tear the place down, shall we?"

"All right," Lymie said. "Anything you say."

He tossed the towel into the locker and closed it. On their way out of the gymnasium they stopped at the drinking fountain. Lymie held the lever down for Spud, who drank and drank. "Aah," he said as he straightened up. "That's better. I was dry as a bone."

"You're always dry as a bone," Lymie said. He bent down to the stream of water for a second only, and then wiped his mouth with the back of his hand.

In the front corridor they swerved from their path and went over to the scales. Lymie put his own books on the tile floor and took Spud's leather notebook from him. Spud planted himself firmly on the scales. The needle flew up to a hundred and fifty-seven pounds. He stepped down and Lymie took his place. This time the needle rose more slowly and wavered at a hundred and nine.

"Would you look at that!" Lymie exclaimed. "I've gained a pound and a quarter. It must be from skipping rope. It must be the exercise."

"Give me my notebook," Spud said. "You're cheating."

Without the notebook the scales declined to a hundred and seven and three-quarters. Lymie stepped down, his face shadowed by disappointment.

He and Spud were outside, almost at the front walk, when he remembered his own books. He ran back into the building for them, though he knew that Spud would wait. And when he had picked up the books, he hurried out again.

There were very few moments in the day when Lymie had Spud all to himself, and the last two summers they had been separated six days out of the week by their summer jobs in Chicago. Even on Sundays, when Lymie went to the beach to be with Spud, he had to share him with other people and pretend that he didn't mind when Spud rowed off in a boat with six other life guards, or lorded it over everybody on the beach from a high

wooden perch where Lymie (although occasional marks
of favor were bestowed on him) couldn't sit. There were
so many things Spud liked to do that Lymie couldn't do
with him, such as boxing, or playing football, or learning
to fly an airplane, and Lymie spent a good deal of time
watching from the sidelines, and waiting for Spud to
come back to him. Oddly enough, Spud always did.

Before they went off to college, Lymie assumed that
they would both belong to a fraternity, as a matter of
course, but Mr. Latham put his foot down. It would take
all the money he could scrape together, he said, if Spud
was going to have four more years of schooling. For him
to live in a fraternity and pay dues and have a lot of extra expenses, unless he could find some way to make the
money himself, was out of the question. Lymie didn't
want to belong to a fraternity if Spud couldn't and so
when Bob Edwards, who had graduated the year before
and was a Sigma Chi at the university, invited them both
to stay at his fraternity house during Rushing Week, they
wrote and declined the invitation.

The following September Lymie and Spud, Frenchie
deFresne, and Ford all sat together on the train going
down to the university, which was located in a small town
something over a hundred miles from Chicago. Frenchie
had been captain of the football team in his senior year,
and he was staying at the Sigma Chi house. Ford had in-
vitations from the Sigma Chi's, the Delts, and the Phi
Gams, and he was staying at the Psi U house. Mr. Ford
had been a Psi U, and so his son was prepared to be one
too.

One of the Psi U's met him on the station platform
and took his bag. Frenchie was surrounded by five
upperclassmen, three of them letter men in football.
Lymie and Spud saw him a few minutes later riding off in
a rattletrap open car without fenders or top, and with
signs painted all over it.

They checked their suitcases in the station and took a tiny streetcar which bounced and jounced and eventually went right through the heart of the campus. Lymie and Spud got off there and looked around. The buildings seemed very large, the stretch of green lawn interminable. Before they found a place to live that they liked, they walked up and down several of the streets bordering on the campus. Even without the sign ROOMS FOR BOYS in the front window, it was easy to tell which houses had rooms for students and which were private homes. The rooming houses invariably needed a coat of paint. There were no shrubs or flower beds around them, and the grass, when there was any, was sickly from too much overhanging shade.

Spud would have turned in at the first one they came to, but Lymie stopped him. They kept on walking until they found themselves in a slightly better neighborhood. At the first sight of the house with the mansard roof, Lymie said, "There's the place we're going to live!" It was painted white, and set well back from the street; and it had fretwork porches which ran around the front and sides of the house, on two stories, like the decks of a river steamboat.

They went up on the porch and twisted the Victorian doorbell, which gave out a hollow peal. Inside the house a dog started barking. Through the frosted glass landscape in the front door they could make out the shapes of furniture crowded into the front hall, as if the people who lived here were just moving in. They heard the dog quite plainly then, and a man's voice saying, "Pooh-Bah, for pity's sake, it's only the doorbell!"

The door swung open and they were confronted by a middle-aged man with gray hair and horn-rimmed glasses which hung on a black ribbon.

"Yes?" he said.

"We're looking for a room," Lymie explained.

The words were drowned out by the barking of the dog, a black and white spaniel trying frantically to work his way between the man's legs.

"Excuse me, just a moment," he said, and grabbed the dog by the collar. "Pooh-Bah, *will* you be quiet? I'll have to get a switch and whip you, do you hear? I'll whip you good!" Then with an expression of extreme agitation on his face, the man turned back to Lymie and Spud. "He must have thought you were the postman. Two separate rooms, did you say? Or do you want a room together?"

"We want to room together," Lymie said.

"Well," the man said, backing away from the door, "come in and let me show you what I. . . . Stop it, Pooh-Bah. I won't have this continual yiping and carrying on. These are two young gentlemen who are interested in a room, do you understand? Now one more bark out of you and I'll shut you up in the kitchen."

Single file they threaded their way through the spinning wheels and drop-leaf tables, the marble-topped washstands, the Boston rockers, andirons, horsehair sofas, chairs, and what-nots that cluttered the front hall.

"I hope you don't mind all this," the man said, waving at a collection of glass hats, hens, and hands. "My sign is being repainted just now so there's no way, probably, that you'd know it from the outside, but I'm in the antique business. The first floor is my shop, as you can see. I try to keep it tidy but people bring me things and suddenly there isn't room to breathe."

By the time they reached the foot of the stairs, the dog had stopped sniffing at Spud's trousers and was making overtures of friendship. Spud bent down and scratched his ear.

The rooms on the second floor opened one out of another, and no two of them seemed to be on the same level. The windows were large and the ceilings high, but the rooms themselves were cut up into odd unnatural shapes, apparently after the house was built.

"I have only two vacancies at the moment," the man said, "and one of them is too small for you, I feel sure. It's hardly more than a cubbyhole. But this one—" He threw open a door "—if you don't object to a north exposure and that Chinese gas station across the street, is quite respectable."

The room had two large windows and was furnished with two study tables, two unsightly wooden chairs, two cheap dressers, a Morris chair with a cigarette burn in the upholstery, and a small empty bookcase. The curtains were limp, and the rag rug was much too small for the floor; it was also coming unsewed in several places. Lymie looked from the pink and blue flowered wallpaper to the shades, which were green and had cracks in them. It was not the room they had imagined for themselves. It was not at all like the college room in the picture of the young collegian smoking a long-stemmed clay pipe. Spud looked inquiringly at Lymie, and then walked over to the closet with the dog following at his heels. The closet was a fair-sized one.

"Suits me," he said.

"How much is it?" Lymie asked.

"Well, I tell you," the man said thoughtfully, "I've been getting fifteen for it, for one person, a charming young man who graduated last spring. But it's really worth more than that: It's a good-sized room, as you can see, and I don't know that I can afford to rent it for any less than—my coal bills are really outlandish, you know, and so is the electric light. And of course you get hot water and all. Suppose I say eighteen dollars for the two of you?"

"A week?" Lymie asked anxiously.

"Oh dear no. I wouldn't dream of asking eighteen

dollars a week. Not for a room like this. Not with all this dreadful furniture in it anyway. Eighteen dollars a month. Nine dollars apiece for each of you. I think you'll find, if you look around, that that's as good as you'll do any place. A room this size, and with a decent light and all. There's nothing the matter with it really. The only thing you may not like is living with so many people. There are eleven people living on this floor now—all of them students, of course—and somehow, I don't know what it is exactly, but whenever you get too many people under one roof, it always seems to lead to violence."

They decided to take the room.

That night after they had finished unpacking, they went out for a walk. There was a full moon, the biggest they could ever remember seeing. They were both aware that the world had grown larger, and that they had money to spend (though not a great deal) and that no one would inquire how they spent it. They had escaped from their families, from the tyranny of home. Feeling a need to celebrate all this they turned into a drugstore and ordered vanilla ice cream with hot fudge sauce. It was so wonderful when it came that they made up their minds to have ice cream with fudge sauce every night of the school year.

26

The antique dealer's name was Alfred Dehner. He occupied a large bedroom on the first floor, next to the kitchen, and slept in a four-poster bed with a soiled white canopy. There was no bathroom downstairs, so he used the one on the second floor and kept his toothbrush and tooth powder, his Victorian shaving mug, brush, and straight-edged razor, a cake of castile soap, iodine, and bicarbonate of soda in the medicine chest over the wash-stand. Although the boys stole from each other continually, they never touched his toilet articles.

Within a week after Lymie and Spud had moved in, they discovered that Mr. Dehner had jacked up the price of their room—two boys had occupied it the year before, not one, and they had only paid fifteen dollars a month. What Mr. Dehner had said about violence, however, proved to be true. The genteel atmosphere created by the antique furniture ended at the foot of the stairs. On the second floor the boys came and went from the shower naked or with a towel around their hips, and anybody who felt like singing did, at the top of his lungs. The boys seldom stayed in their own rooms but wandered aimlessly all evening long, looking for somebody who would let them copy his rhetoric theme, somebody who would loan them four bits till Friday, somebody to practice ju-jitsu, somebody to pester. Six or seven of them would crowd into a single room and sit around on the floor, talking about football or baseball or girls. Occasionally when the racket was louder than usual, one of the boys would look up from the serial in *Collier's* that he was reading and yell "Study hours!" but it never had the slightest effect. It was not intended to. It was just a remark, or perhaps even an excuse to start a fight.

Fights developed all the time, out of nothing at all—over a fountain pen that had been borrowed and then returned without any ink in it, over how many yards had been gained by a certain end run against the University of Illinois two years before, over who broke a string in the house tennis racquet. It was nothing to come home and find two figures in the upstairs hall, rolling over and over, grunting, gouging at each other, and kicking the floor with their heels. Mostly the fighting was good-natured but sometimes it was in earnest. If you wanted to stay and watch, you could. If you didn't, you stepped over the bodies and went on to your own room.

In the wintertime there was no heat in the radiators after ten o'clock. As the study rooms got colder the boys put on more clothes—sweaters, bathrobes, overcoats, and mufflers, until finally they had to go to bed to get warm. The dormitory was on the top floor, under the mansard roof. There was no heat in it, and the windows were left wide open from September until late in June.

At night, in the deepest quiet, bare feet would pad across the floor and a conversation started downstairs would go on gathering momentum until everyone in the dorm was awake and taking part in it. Sometimes two or three people in a row would stop when they came to Lymie's bed and shake him gently and say, "Want to pee, Lymie? . . . Do you have to pee?" Sometimes the door would fly open and a voice would cry "Fire! Fire! Steve Rush is on fire!" and ten or eleven boys would leap from their beds and rush to the second floor bathroom for water. If the fire spread, Freeman or Pownell also had to be put out. Usually Rush's bed was the only one that got soaked. He was a sound sleeper and also he had a mean streak in him and could be counted on to emerge from the dorm screaming and cursing and ready to kill anybody he could lay his hands on.

The noise and the confusion bothered Spud, who was used to quiet when he studied, but Lymie felt at home in the rooming house as soon as he sat down at his desk and wrote "Lymon Peters Jr., 302 South Street," in all his books. His desk faced one window, Spud's faced the other. When Lymie was studying, he seldom saw the boys who walked through continually on their way to some other room. When they tripped over the sill and started swearing, he looked up sometimes and smiled.

If there was no other sound, if peace descended on the second floor for five minutes, somebody was sure to start making faces at the dog and the dog would whine and bark and race around wildly until Mr. Dehner came running to the foot of the stairs.

"Are you teasing that poor animal again?" he would shriek up at them with his hand on the banister. "Really, such cruelty, such lack of any decent human feeling! If you don't stop it I'm going to call the dean's office! I give you my word! I'm going to call the dean's office and I'm going to ask to speak to the dean!"

Mr. Dehner's voice was shrill and penetrating, and his accent was not Middle Western. The *r*'s were slurred. The *a*'s were broad and for some reason they seemed to carry better than the flat kind. Whenever Mr. Dehner started talking loudly, Lymie put down his book and listened. Mr. Dehner was nearly always agitated about something—or, as it turned out nine times out of ten, about nothing. His voice would rise higher and higher, as if he were at last in real trouble, and Lymie would tiptoe to the head of the stairs, lean over, and discover that Mr. Dehner was talking to a couple of faculty wives about Paul Revere silver, or telling them how to take alcohol rings off the tops of tables with spirits of camphor.

The boys called him "Maggie" behind his back, but they liked him. They liked anything that was odd or extreme. They thought it was fine that Colter knew how to call pigs; that Fred Howard was a Christer and spent all his spare time at the Wesley Foundation; that Amsler's mother drove over from Evansville once a week just to see that he was getting enough to eat; and that Freeman every now and then at dinner took out six of his upper front teeth and tossed them into the water pitcher.

Far from holding it against Lymie that he was so thin, they bragged about him to strangers. Geraghty, who was a premedic, used to come into Lymie's room at night and make him take off his shirt. It was as good as having

a skeleton, he said; he could find and name every bone in
Lymie's body.

The boys took a brief dislike for Spud until he persuaded Reinhart and Pownell to go to the gym with him
one afternoon and box. They nicknamed him "The Killer"
and from that time on, he had his place in the gallery of
freaks; he belonged.

Most of the boys ate at a mixed boarding club which
was three blocks from the rooming house. The weekly
meal tickets were five dollars and if you wanted a date of
a certain kind, the boarding club was an easy place to get
it. The boys from "302" ate at the same two tables breakfast, lunch, and dinner. Sometimes Lymie and Spud were
separated when there was only one chair vacant at each
table but usually they ate together.

In a fraternity house this would have been spotted
almost instantly. One of the brothers would have said,
"It's time to break that up." Spud and Lymie would not
have been allowed even to walk to the campus together
without someone stepping between them. At "302" nobody cared.

Sometimes, while Lymie sat at his desk with a book
open in front of him, Spud got himself into trouble (the
crime was unspecified) and Lymie took the blame for it
and gladly and willingly spent the rest of his life in prison
so that Spud could go free. Then they were in a lifeboat,
with only enough food and water for one person, and
Lymie, waiting until Spud was asleep, slipped noiselessly
over the side into the cold sea. Then they were fighting,
back to back, with swords, forcing the ring of their enemies slowly toward the little door through which one of
them could escape if the other went on fighting. . . .

Spud spent at least an hour every evening tidying up
the room. He lined up his shoes and Lymie's in a straight
row on the floor of the closet. Then he rehung several
pairs of trousers so that the creases were straight, and

made sure that Lymie hadn't concealed the vest of one suit inside the coat of another. The objects on top of his desk—his pencils, his blotter, his fountain pen, ruler, and bottle of ink—had to be in an exact arrangement, and the desk and bureau drawers in order. Otherwise there was no use in his trying to concentrate on calculus or German grammar.

Not all of this tidying was love of order. Spud's conscience wouldn't let him go to a movie on a week night or read detective story magazines; that wasn't what he had come down to college for. But he managed to put off studying until he had done everything else he could think of, and what with visitors and playing with the dog and other unforeseen interruptions, very often he would read two or three pages, yawn, and discover that it was ten o'clock, time to put the book down and get ready for bed.

He and Lymie were always the first ones to go up to the dorm. In the big icy-cold bed they clung to each other, shivering like puppies, until the heat of their bodies began to penetrate through the outing flannel of their pajamas and their heavy woolen bathrobes. Lymie slept on his right side and Spud curled against him, with his fists in the hollow of Lymie's back. In five minutes the whole bed was warmed and Spud was sound asleep. It took Lymie longer, as a rule. He lay there, relaxed and drowsy, aware of the cold outside the covers, and of the warmth coming to him from Spud, and Spud's odor, which was not stale or sweaty or like the odor of any other person. Then he moved his right foot until the outer part of the instep came in contact with Spud's bare toes, and from this one point of reality he swung out safely into darkness, into no sharing whatever.

27

The first afternoon that Sally brought Lymie home with
her, she led him upstairs to Professor Forbes's study,
where her father and mother were sitting with Professor
Severance. Mrs. Forbes was darning socks. A pair of tor-
toise-shell glasses rested insecurely on the bridge of her
nose. She had Sally's eyes, hair, and coloring but she was
more self-contained. Her hair was parted in the middle
and came down over her temples in two raven's wings.
Her smile was charming but also rather ambiguous.

"I'm glad you decided to put in an appearance,
Lymie," she said. "I was beginning to wonder about you.
Some of the people Sally talks about don't exist, I'm sure.
They couldn't. . . . This is Mr. Severance."

"Mr. Peters and I are already acquainted," Professor
Severance said, nodding. "We see each other every Monday, Wednesday, and Friday at two."

"And that's my Pop," Sally said.

Professor Forbes rose and held out his hand. He was
a tall, black-haired, black-eyed man with thick lips showing through his beard. He offered a box containing cigarettes and Lymie shook his head.

"Did you notice the tree as you came in?" Mrs.
Forbes asked.

"Which tree?" Sally asked.

"The one between the curbing and the walk."

"No," Sally said, "what about it?"

"Your father ran into it today."

"No!" Sally exclaimed. "How could he? It's at least
four feet from the driveway."

"He did it," Mrs. Forbes said triumphantly. "Don't
ask me how. . . . My husband is learning to drive," she

explained for Lymie's benefit. "He's had several lessons and today he took the car out alone, after lunch, and as he was coming back he turned into the driveway and knocked almost all the bark off one side of that huge tree!"

"You're exaggerating," Professor Forbes said, without removing his cigarette from between his lips. "The whole story is a gross exaggeration." The cigarette ashes drifted down on the front of his smoking jacket.

"I'm not exaggerating," Mrs. Forbes said. "I went out and looked at it."

"What about the Albrechts' bay window?" Sally asked.

"The Albrechts' bay window is still intact," Mrs. Forbes said.

Professor Severance shook with laughter.

"Couldn't we change the subject?" Professor Forbes asked irritably.

Mrs. Forbes looked at him over her glasses. "Maybe we'd better," she said, raising her eyebrows.

"How's Mrs. Sevvy?" Sally asked.

"Better, thank you." Professor Severance abruptly regained his composure. "She's still in bed though. The doctor said another day or two wouldn't hurt her."

"Mr. Severance's mother is a most remarkable woman," Mrs. Forbes said, turning to Lymie. "She's seventy-three and serves the best food and gives the gayest parties of any woman in town. I hope you meet her sometime."

"When my mother's feeling better you must come and have dinner with us," Professor Severance said. "I've been wanting to tell you, Mr. Peters, how much I enjoyed reading your examination paper."

Lymie blushed.

"It's so discouraging to get your own words thrown back at you twenty or thirty times," Professor Severance went on. "I feel as if I were lecturing to a class of parrots. It's all on account of those miserable notebooks, of course. Some day I'm going to collect them all and throw them out of the window."

"You might as well throw the students with them," Professor Forbes said.

"Some of them are too large," Professor Severance said, "and too athletic."

"What about *my* examination paper?" Sally said, leering at him. "Wasn't it original, Sevvy?"

Professor Severance cleared his throat and then beamed at her affectionately. "Yes, my dear," he said, "almost wholly original. My one—ah—hesitation about it was that there seemed to be an insufficient acquaintance with the subject matter of the course."

"There," Sally said, turning to her mother, "you see?"

"Only too plainly, I'm afraid," Mrs. Forbes said. She excused herself and left the room.

A heavy silence descended. Sally was embarrassed by her mother's remark, and Professor Forbes had come to depend so on his wife's small talk that he had none of his own to offer. Politeness prevented Professor Severance from continuing the subject they had been discussing when Sally and Lymie appeared—Spenser's indebtedness to the *Orlando Furioso*—since it would probably have no interest for them.

Lymie's eyes wandered around the room. The ceiling was low and sloped down to the long bookcases on two sides. There were Holbein prints on the walls and a colored map of Paris. Professor Forbes's desk was placed near two small front windows. Next to it was a large table with a lamp on it, and more books piled helter-skelter, some of them in danger of sliding off onto the floor. Lymie's glance came to rest on a large Chinese lacquer screen.

"That's a beautiful thing, isn't it?" Professor Severance said. "It's all very well about not coveting your neighbor's wife and his she-asses and his camels but when it comes to *objets d'art*, I find myself wavering sometimes." He got up and crossed the room so that he could examine the screen more closely. "Modern?" he inquired, over his shoulder.

"My brother-in-law sent it to us," Professor Forbes said noncommittally.

"The one who travels so much?" Professor Severance asked.

Professor Forbes nodded. "He got it in a hock shop in Manila."

"It's very beautiful," Professor Severance said.

The lacquer screen had three panels. On one side, the side facing the room, were white flowers which were like roses but larger and stiffer. Peonies, Lymie decided. The flowers were in square blue vases and the vases rested on carved teakwood stands, against a yellow background. Professor Severance folded the screen, turned it around, and opened it. On the reverse was a company of Chinese horsemen charging at an angle across all three panels.

The fat-rumped horsemen rode over pink flames and blue curlicues representing smoke. Their long, loose sleeves whipped from their elbows. Their tunics divided, revealing mail leggings and bare feet. The air was thick with arrows. Some of the horsemen rode with their lances set, their shoulders braced for the shock; others with daggers upraised, knees digging into their horses' sides. Here and there a rider twisted or rose in the saddle, and one of them hung from the stirrups with a spear coming out through the center of his back. Their faces were brick-red or deathly pale. All had identical thinly drawn mustaches and chin tufts, and expressions denoting fierceness or cruelty or cunning. The only calm face belonged to a severed head that had rolled under the feet of the horses and was gazing upward serenely toward heaven. The galloping horses shared in the frenzy of the riders. There were fat white horses, dappled horses, gold horses with the heads of dragons, ivory horses with gold manes and hoofs and tails, blue horses, pink horses, horses with scales and frantic, fishlike faces.

"I'd like to have known the man who made this," Professor Severance said. "The one who had the idea of putting still life on one side—those wonderfully placid white flowers—and warriors on the other."

"I assume it is a traditional juxtaposition," Professor Forbes said.

"No doubt, but somebody must have thought of it for the first time. The mutual attraction of gentleness and violence, don't you see, Mr. Peters? The brutal body and the calm philosophic mind."

"Don't talk to me about philosophic minds," Mrs. Forbes said. She came in carrying a tray with a silver teapot on it, teacups, a silver sugar and creamer, slices of lemon, and bread and butter cut paper-thin. "If I ever marry again it's going to be to a plumber. I've been trying for two days to get a man to come look at the hot water heater in the basement."

"Plumbing," Professor Severance said reproachfully, "is pure deductive reasoning."

"With a leak in it," Mrs. Forbes said.

He turned the screen around so that the flowers were showing as before. Then he sat down and with a curious intentness watched Mrs. Forbes arranging the cups and saucers on the tray.

"Sugar?" she asked, turning to Lymie. "Lemon?"

"No thank you," he said, both times.

"A purist," Mrs. Forbes said. She poured Professor Severance's tea without asking him how he liked it.

28

The night of the sorority dance it took Spud over an hour to dress. He and Lymie stood under the shower by turns, soaping themselves all over and washing the soap off again time after time, as if by this symbolical means they were getting rid of certain adolescent fears which had to do with women. Spud handed Lymie the soap and the nailbrush, and bent over with his hands braced against his knees. Lymie understood what was expected of him. He scrubbed until the skin from the base of Spud's neck to the end of his spine was red and glowing, and then turned around and submitted his own back to the same rough treatment.

When they were partly dressed, Spud got out the shoe polish and a rag and made Lymie stand with one foot on a chair, and then the other. Spud's shoes, already polished, were waiting with wooden shoe trees in them on the closet floor. He put them on, after he had finished with Lymie's, and tied the laces in a double knot. Then he attempted to cut his fingernails, which were thick and very tough. He could manage the fingers of his left hand without much difficulty but when he switched over, the nail scissors felt awkward and wrong. He made an impatient face, and Lymie took the scissors from him and finished the job.

Five whole minutes were consumed in picking out a tie for Spud, who had any number of them that he was especially fond of. The choice narrowed down finally to a blue bow tie with white polka dots and a knitted four-in-hand. Spud forced Lymie to pick out the one he thought Spud ought to wear, and Lymie chose the four-in-hand. Spud wore the bow tie, after explaining to Lymie all the reasons why it was better for this occasion, for a dance, than Lymie's choice. The bow tie had to be tied three times before the result was acceptable, and between the second and third attempt Spud decided that his collar was wrinkled, and changed to another white shirt. At nine o'clock he finished arranging the handkerchief in his breast pocket and was satisfied, or nearly satisfied, with what he saw in the mildewed mirror over his dresser. Lymie, who had been waiting for twenty minutes, said "Come on, let's go." A sudden wave of excitement carried both of them down the stairs, through the clutter in the front hall, and outside. The night air was crisp and cool, the November sky was blossoming with stars.

The sorority house was on the other side of the campus. From "302" the shortest way was through the university forestry, a narrow strip of woods which had sidewalks running through it and which at night was lighted at frequent intervals by street lamps. When the two boys emerged from the wood they were on the campus. The walk led them toward a series of new red brick Georgian buildings, each with dozens of false chimneys outlined against the starry sky. On the other side of the campus they passed a large unfinished building that was still under scaffolding—the new dormitory for men. As they came near the sorority house, they heard music.

"In Wisconsin," Spud said, "my sister used to go to dances at the lake club. She was fifteen and I was only nine or ten. They had dances every Saturday night. Sometimes my mother and father drove over in the car and watched, but I had to be in bed, because the dances didn't start until after nine o'clock. And I used to lie there on the screen porch and listen to the dance music. I used to wish I was older so I could be over there across the lake, like my sister. I used to wonder sometimes if I was ever going to be old enough to go to the lake club dances. Time seemed too slow then. One day lasted a lot longer than a week seems to now." Lymie put his right hand inside the pocket of Spud's coat, a thing he often did when they were walking together. Spud's fingers interlaced with his.

"Just when I was almost old enough to start going to the lake club dances," Spud continued, "we moved to Chicago. I don't know whether they still have them any more or not. I guess they probably do. They were nice. You could see the clubhouse through the trees, all lighted up with Japanese lanterns. And the music came over the water, the dance music. It was very plain. I used to lie awake listening to it."

Curtains were drawn across every window of the sorority house, upstairs and down. The two small lights on either side of the front door seemed brighter than usual. As Lymie and Spud turned in at the front walk, they could hear the orchestra playing "Oh, Katarina" rapturously. While they stood by the front door trying to make up their minds whether, since this was not like any ordinary evening, they ought to ring the bell, a boy came up the walk whistling, opened the door, and walked in. They went in after him.

There were a dozen boys standing in the front hall. Armstrong was among them. Lymie had never seen him anywhere except at the gymnasium and he wondered what would happen now if Armstrong, in his double-breasted dark blue suit, were to brace himself and do a handstand on the polished floor. He showed no signs of wanting to. He looked detached, very much at ease, very sure of himself. He recognized Spud with a slight flicker of surprise and spoke to him. Spud nodded coldly and went on to the coatroom, with Lymie in his wake.

All the hooks in the coatroom were taken and there were piles of coats on the floor. Spud took two of the coats off their hooks, dropped them on the floor, and hung his coat and Lymie's where they had been hanging. Then he combed his hair in front of the mirror in the lavatory, straightened his butterfly bow tie, and squared his shoulders until his coat collar came to rest against his neck. With his hand in the small of Lymie's back, pushing him, he came out into the hall once more.

On the opposite side of the stairs from the coatroom was another closet, the same size, where the house telephone was, and a set of electric bells which rang in the study rooms upstairs. Lymie pressed the ones marked *Davison: two long, one short* and *Forbes: one short, one long.* Then he came out into the hall again and stood next to Spud at the foot of the stairs. He had managed, during the walk across the campus, to mar the polish on his shoes. His long thin wrists hung down out of his sleeves, and his cowlick, that he had spent so much time plastering down with water, was sticking straight up. He stood stiffly with his back to the wide gilt mirror and didn't discover any of these flaws in his appearance.

Armstrong had gone now. His girl had come down the stairs in a white dress and he was dancing with her in the long living room, which was swept bare of rugs and furniture. The light everywhere downstairs was softened. There were yellow chrysanthemums on the white mantelpiece, and lighted candles. Oak leaves concealed the chandeliers. The dancers swung past each other performing intricate steps, their eyes half closed, their heads sometimes touching.

To pass the time while they were waiting, the boys in the front hall drew handkerchiefs out of their hip pockets and mopped their foreheads, or produced silver cigarette cases with an air of boredom, of disdain.

Lymie was expecting Hope and Sally to come down the stairs together, but Hope came first and alone. She was wearing a brown flowered chiffon dress that Lymie, who knew nothing about women's clothes, realized in-

stantly was not right for her. It was not at all like the
dresses the other girls were wearing.

Spud pulled Lymie's pants leg up a couple of inches
in order to embarrass him, and although the effort suc-
ceeded, Hope didn't notice. She handed Lymie a small
enamel compact, a lipstick, a tiny lace handkerchief, and
said gravely, "Put these in your pocket." As they moved
toward the entrance to the living room, the music ended.
The couples stopped dancing and waited, in the subdued
light. The girls were smiling with their eyes, or chatter-
ing. The boys reached inside their coats and drew their
shirt sleeves up. Then, remembering where they were,
they looked bored. The chaperons were in an alcove off
the living room, playing bridge. The orchestra—a piano
player, a drummer, saxophone, clarinet, trumpet, and
slide trombone—was in another alcove partially concealed
by potted palms. They made tentative noises with their
instruments and then were silent. The dancers moved
across the floor toward the dining room, toward the
punch bowl, which was under the eye of Mrs. Sisson, the
housemother. So far it had not been spiked. Lymie and
Hope moved into a corner where they would not be noticed.

"People ought to dress up oftener," Hope said. "I've
just decided that. It makes them nicer to live with. I stood
in the upstairs hall and watched the girls go down." The
girls whose fathers had not retired from business, she
meant; the girls who could have new clothes whenever
they wanted them. Aloud she said, "They looked so
lovely, so unlike themselves," and raised her chin slightly,
for she knew how she looked. She had seen herself in a
full-length mirror in Bernice Crawford's room. Bernice
had said, "You can't wear that, Davison. It doesn't look
right on you!" and had offered to loan her a black dress
with gold clips and a narrow gold belt, but the black dress

was too tight. As Hope drew it off over her head she prayed that Lymie, who was always absent-minded anyway, would forget to come; that she herself would have an attack of appendicitis and be rushed to the hospital; that something, some merciful intervention would save her from having to go down the stairs. She decided to leave a note for Lymie and sneak out the back way, down the fire escape, and spend the rest of the evening in the Ship's Lantern, but it was already too late. Her bell rang, two longs and one short, as she was reaching into her closet for a coat.

"*You* look very nice tonight," she said to Lymie and before he had to answer her, the orchestra swung into the beginning of "Blue Skies." He put his arm around her and they started dancing. They were soon surrounded by other couples and in a moment Spud and Sally danced by. Spud danced very well and he looked smooth on the floor, Lymie thought. Spud didn't see them. His face when he danced was an unseeing mask. But Sally turned her head and called "Hello, Lymie, old socks!" She was wearing a peach-colored satin dress and her dark hair was piled on top of her head in a way that changed the shape of her face, made her look older, and emphasized her cheekbones and her wonderful dark brown velvet eyes. Lymie stepped on Hope's foot and apologized.

"Isn't Forbes *something!*" Hope exclaimed.

Lymie nodded without hearing what she had said. Here in this long dimly lighted room, where everyone had a price mark attached to him, he recognized Sally's value for the first time.

29

Lymie got home before Spud and passed through Dick Reinhart's room on the way to his own. Reinhart was in a sagging overstuffed chair and his feet, braced against his study table, were higher than his head. He looked up from Steve Rush's copy of *Psychopathia Sexualis* and said, "Well, Don Juan, did you have yourself a time?"

"I guess so," Lymie said. His mind was churning with images and excitement, and he wanted to talk to someone but not to Reinhart. "How late is it?" he asked.

"Quarter to one," Reinhart said. "Time all Phi Betes were in bed." His eyes were already searching for the place where he had stopped reading: *CASE 138. Z., age thirty-six, wholesale merchant; parents were said to have been healthy; physical and mental development normal; irrelevant children's diseases; at fourteen onanism of his own accord; began to. . . .*

Reinhart looked up from the page and saw that Lymie was still standing there. "You ought to read this book sometime," he said. "It's very interesting. I used to think I was a regular heller but compared to some of these guys I'm not so bad I guess. I could teach Sunday school if I wanted to."

Lymie went on to his own room and undressed. Then with his bathrobe pulled around him and his winter overcoat over his knees, he sat down in Spud's Morris chair and tried to read *The Eve of St. Agnes*, which Professor Severance had assigned for Monday. He got as far as the owl that for all his feathers was a-cold and then the page blurred, the words ran together like water. When his eyes focused again, he was looking at the row of suits, his and Spud's, hanging from the pole in the closet.

Lymie got up and went over to the closet and reached for the two victrola records which he kept on the shelf, under Spud's R.O.T.C. hat and spurs. He turned out the light and went into Pownell's room, which was also dark, and put one of the records on Pownell's victrola. The record was "Tales from the Vienna Woods" played by the Philadelphia Orchestra. As a rule he only played his records on Sunday morning early, when there was nobody around who might object to classical music. Now he drew a chair up and sat with his head between the doors of the machine. The room filled with waltzers, with girls turning and turning to the music, and he was in love with all of them, with their soft white arms, their small breasts, their dark eyes and their shadowy hair, which became Sally's hair, her coal-black bangs. She turned and smiled at him deliriously, and the peach-colored skirt flared out like the petals of a flower.

Lymie played the record twice and then turned the victrola off and sat with his forehead resting on the hard arm of the chair. There was a strange ache in his chest which he seemed to remember from a long time before, from when he was a child maybe. He sighed and then a few minutes later he sighed again.

Colter and Howard came in and passed through the room without turning the light on and without discovering him. Spud came home. Lymie recognized his step on the stairs and raised his head to listen. Spud stopped in Reinhart's room and Lymie heard them talking in low voices. A shoe dropped. Lymie was about to get up and go join them when he heard Spud say quite distinctly, almost as if he were complaining: "I've seen it happen to a lot of guys but I somehow never thought it would happen to me."

"Yeah, I know," Reinhart said.

"The funny thing is," Spud said, "I don't know what to do about it."

"You don't have to do anything," Reinhart said. "You're hooked."

Lymie, listening, felt a double twinge of jealousy. The words could only mean one thing, no matter how you twisted them. And since it had to be that way, the least Spud could have done was to tell him about it first, not Dick Reinhart.

While Spud was in the bathroom brushing his teeth, Lymie crept up the stairs. He was, to all appearances, sound asleep when Spud crawled in beside him.

30

Dick Reinhart was from South Chicago. He had been raised a Catholic and wore around his neck a small silver scapular medal in the shape of a cross. It had been blessed by Father Ahrens of Hammond, Indiana, and was the equivalent of five holy and miraculous medals. At the top of the cross, in relief, were the head and shoulders of Our Lord, with the right hand raised in benediction and the left hand pointing to the Sacred Heart. This same symbol appeared again, larger, in the center of the cross. On the left arm were St. Joseph and the Infant Jesus. On the right was St. Christopher with his staff and the Infant Jesus on his shoulder. At the bottom of the cross was a full-length figure of the Blessed Virgin Mary, who was also on the reverse of the medal, supported by clouds, with the Infant Jesus in her arms and around her head a ring of seven stars.

When Dick was two years old his father died and about a year later his mother married again. Dick's step-father didn't like children and so he was sent to live with his grandmother, a devout German woman, who used to sit beside him at the kitchen table and feed him

from a big spoon, long after he was old enough to manage for himself. Although she had been dead for years
now, whenever he wanted to he could still hear her voice
saying, *Mund auf . . . Mund zu . . . kauen. . . .* The
year he was seventeen he fell in with a gang of hoodlums
who were caught breaking into a freight car one winter
night. The other boys took to their heels and got away,
but Dick didn't run fast enough, and the judge sentenced
him to six months in the state reformatory at St. Charles,
Illinois. He made no effort to cover up the fact that he
had been there, but when the boys at "302" tried to find
out what it was like in the reformatory, he wouldn't tell
them. He didn't seem to want to talk about it.

After he finished high school he got a job with a construction company in Cicero, Illinois, and was made fore-
man of a sewer gang. The men worked in continual danger of being buried under a cave-in. They were sullen and
hard to handle. He never dared turn his back on them, for
fear he would be hit over the head with a shovel, but he
liked his job, even so, and he made friends with an Italian
family who lived in the neighborhood. After the day was
over he would sit in their kitchen drinking homemade
wine with them.

When he had been working about six months, a man
named Warner, who was in the office of the construction
company, took a liking to him and taught him how to do
elementary surveying. Warner was in his late forties and
had been divorced twice. His second wife had been a para-
chute jumper and Warner was in love with her, he told
Reinhart, but she tried two-timing him, so he walked out
on her. When Warner found out that Reinhart liked to
drink, he started taking Reinhart around with him at
night. Warner could hold any amount of liquor without
showing it, and he knew all the speakeasies in and around
Chicago, and the women were crazy about him. No matter where they went, there were always three of them—

Reinhart on one side of Warner and a woman on the other. He used to introduce Reinhart as his son, and he even talked about adopting him, but Reinhart never thought he would actually do it.

All this part of his life Reinhart told Spud one night when they were both staying up late in order to study for exams. Spud didn't get much studying done, but he didn't mind; he was finding out about life.

One day, Reinhart said, Warner called him into his office and asked him if he wouldn't like to go back to school. Unless he did, Warner said, there was no real future ahead of him in the construction business. He needed mathematics and a general background in engineering. Warner offered to give him the money for his books, tuition and room rent. The rest Reinhart would have to do for himself. The money was to be in the form of a loan, without interest. Reinhart could pay it back after he was out of college.

That fall he came down to the university and got a job in a drugstore, behind the soda fountain. There was no money in it; he worked five hours a day in exchange for his meals. Within a week he was pledged to a fraternity. It had a name like Beta Theta Pi, only one of the letters was wrong. The house was new and built of red brick with two-story white columns along the front of it, the architect having arrived at a compromise between the new Georgian architecture of the south campus and a Mississippi mansion. The house was out near the stadium, where land was cheaper. That meant a ten-minute walk to and from the buildings on the campus. The older fraternity houses were all within three or four blocks of the university. They had been built twenty years before, and they were not very impressive from the outside, but then they didn't have to be.

Reinhart had had no intention of joining a fraternity. What happened was that a kid who worked with him be-

hind the soda fountain asked him to his fraternity house
for a meal. The food was good and it was a beautiful
warm night and that week there happened to be a full
moon. After dinner a boy from Terre Haute played the
banjo, somebody else played the piano, and the brothers
stood around on the terrace outside the fraternity house,
singing. It was exactly what Reinhart had always thought
college would be like, and after three days of working
behind a soda fountain, it made his eyes fill with tears.

A group of the boys took him indoors later and led
him to a leather sofa in front of the big fireplace, where
he could get a good look at the trophies on the mantel.
When they produced a pledge button and asked him if
he'd like to be one of them, he said he would, right away.
He was afraid that if he hesitated, they'd change their
minds about wanting him. Afterwards he realized that he
ought to have asked Warner about it first. The trouble
was, Warner had been a Phi Gam when he was in school
and without seeing this beautiful new house or having a
chance to get acquainted with the brothers, he was almost certain to think that Reinhart had made a mistake.

As soon as Rushing Week was over, the boy with the
banjo cleared out. So did several others. They had graduated the year before, it seemed, but that fact wasn't
made clear until now. The brothers who were left were
not the ones Reinhart had liked especially. They were
athletes, most of them, who had done well enough in
high school to get their names and sometimes their pictures in the papers, but after they came to college they
pulled a tendon or got water on the knee or became ineligible because of their grades. They stayed ineligible year
after year and the greater part of the time they slept.
Whenever Reinhart passed through the living room he
found at least one of them stretched out on a leather
couch, sound asleep with the radio going full blast in his
ear.

Reinhart roomed with a senior who needed two and a half hours to graduate and was out tomcatting every night. Reinhart never saw anything of him; only his clothes strewn from one end of the study room to the other when Reinhart came down in the morning. The clothes, of course, had to be picked up, and there were pledge duties. Even though Reinhart was working and didn't have as much free time as the other freshmen, he had to sweep the front walk one week and the next week he had to see that the grate fire in the living room didn't go out, or to take the mail down to the railroad station at eleven-thirty at night, or to get up at six and go through the dorm waking the others at fifteen-minute intervals until seven-thirty. On Saturdays he had to wash windows and wax floors and clean study rooms with the other freshmen. The owner of the drugstore made him work longer hours than they had originally agreed upon, and he got so little sleep that the moment he opened a book his eyelids grew heavy. He began to fall behind in his engineering subjects.

Also, there was one sophomore who made trouble for all the pledges. They'd be in their study rooms after dinner and the sophomore would stick his head in, hoping that they'd gone out of the room and left the light on; or he'd want them to go on errands for him. He thought up more errands and gave more black marks than any other upperclassman in the fraternity. He seemed to have a particular dislike for Reinhart. One night he came into Reinhart's room, backed him up against the wall, and gave him a lecture on his attitude: "Reinhart, you're one hell of a good guy, or could be if you weren't so goddam lazy. You're the laziest human being—I guess you're a human—that I've ever seen or heard of. You're so lazy. . . ." There was a great deal more of this, and Reinhart stood it all patiently. When the sophomore got through talking he pulled Reinhart across the hall into his own room and said to get busy and clean it up. Reinhart saw, in a bloody rage, that it was at least a two hours' job. The sophomore's room had been cleaned on Saturday and now you could hardly wade through it. He told the sophomore that he couldn't clean the room up; that he had to study. The sophomore gave him five more black marks for disobedience. When Reinhart said, "You dirty son of a bitch, clean it up yourself!" the sophomore took a poke at him and Reinhart laid him flat.

At this point in the story, Spud rolled his eyes and rocked with pleasure.

Half an hour later, Reinhart said, the upperclassmen held a special meeting in the chapter room, which was in the basement. When it was over, two of them came into his room and told him to be downstairs in front of the fireplace at quarter of eleven, for a paddling party. He took the pledge button out of his lapel and handed it to them, and the next day he moved into Mr. Dehner's rooming house, where there were no pledge duties, and where a sophomore was no better than anybody else.

Warner continued to send him money regularly all through his freshman year, and when summer vacation came around, Reinhart went back to his old job. Warner got married, very suddenly, on the Fourth of July, and his wife, a thin, rather nervous blonde, didn't like Reinhart. She thought he was a bad influence on Warner. In a moment of confidence he told Reinhart, but it would have been better if he hadn't, because Reinhart didn't like Warner's new wife very much either, and the more he saw of her the less he liked her. When Warner wanted him to go out drinking with them, on a Saturday night, Reinhart made excuses and finally Warner stopped asking him.

Toward the end of the summer Reinhart noticed, or thought he noticed, a change in the way Warner acted toward him. He made a very slight mistake on the job, something that was easily corrected and that ordinarily

Warner wouldn't have paid any attention to. They had an argument about it, and Reinhart lost his temper. He apologized the next day, and Warner told him to forget it, but there was a speculative gleam in his eye which Reinhart saw several times after that. Apparently he thought Reinhart was trying to put something over on him.

Before Reinhart went back to school, Warner told him that his wife was going to have a baby. The baby was born early in April. It was a boy and Reinhart was very happy about it. He sent Warner a telegram, which Warner didn't answer for about ten days. The letter was typewritten and had been dictated to one of the stenographers in the office. At the bottom of the page, Warner had added a postscript in ink: he was very sorry but he had had a good many extra expenses lately and he wouldn't be able to send any more money.

It was very hot that April and the third floor was like an oven. The boys dragged their mattresses down to the second-story porch and slept there, until one night Reinhart, full of liquor, rolled off the porch and broke his arm. He had his scapular on when he fell, but then he could so easily have broken his neck. The next day the news of the accident was all over the campus and cars kept driving by with people hanging out to look. The other boys were proud, naturally. It gave their rooming house prestige. The first time Reinhart left for the campus with his arm in a sling, five of the boys just happened to be leaving at that moment and they surrounded him like a military escort of honor. For a long time afterward, people walking by "302" would say, "That's the place where the boy fell off the roof."

Without help from Warner, and unable to work in the drugstore with his arm in a cast, Reinhart was ready to drop out of school, but Mr. Dehner made an arrangement with him, apparently out of the kindness of his heart. Reinhart didn't inquire too closely into it. When

his arm was well he washed windows and polished furniture for Mr. Dehner, made the beds in the dorm, and
was general handy man for the place. In return for this,
he was given his room free and enough money to eat on.

The work didn't take much time, but he was obliged
to listen politely to Mr. Dehner, who lay in wait for him,
in the front hall among the spinning wheels and the glass
hens.

"Dick," he would begin, in a piercing whisper, "could
I have a word with you? Steve Rush is—I know I've
spoken to you about this before but he's two whole
months behind now in his rent and something's got to be
done. You know how fond I am of him and I don't want
him to get thrown out of school or anything like that, but
on the other hand there are certain fixed charges—light,
heat, food for me, dog biscuit for Pooh-Bah, and the
money I have to pay the bank every month—because
they own this house, you know; I don't. I wouldn't take
it if you gave it to me. It's too big and it's altogether too
much of a responsibility. When I was younger perhaps but
not now. Not at my age. I don't suppose the bank could
sell it either, but then they don't want to, I'm sure. It's
more profitable to rent it to some gullible person like me.
You know the bank I mean? Not the bank across from
the Co-op. The other one, the bank downtown. All they
do there is sit around and clip coupons and give people
two per cent interest on money they loan out for four and
a half and five. It's shocking, I must say, and not like the
antique business, but what can I do? I have to have a roof
over my head, no matter what happens, and I have to eat.
. . . What was I talking about? Dear me, I don't remember. Well, anyway, I don't want to keep you. You're sure
you're dressed warmly enough? Because it's quite cold
out. Much colder than it looks. You ought to have a
sweater on, under your coat, in weather like this. It's

strong healthy young creatures like you who die of pleurisy and pneumonia. . . ."

For two and a half years Reinhart had been listening to Mr. Dehner, who liked to talk to him because he was older than the other boys, and more patient. Dick was twenty-three now, and his hair was already getting thin. When he combed it, leaning over the washbowl, he would look down sometimes and count the hairs in the basin and shake his head sadly, but he never put oil on his scalp or did anything about it.

He went to Mass every Sunday but he also, from time to time, visited a house on South Maple Street. The eye of God must relax occasionally, and Dick seemed to know when this was about to happen. Once when he was waiting for a streetcar downtown a woman came along in a maroon-colored roadster and picked him up. They drove to a town thirty miles away, and spent the night there in the hotel. The woman was married and Dick knew that he had committed a sin with her, but after he had been to confession his sins no longer weighed on him.

Every so often he came home roaring drunk and sat up in bed and held an inquisition on himself and all the others. "You, Geraghty," he would say, "who do you think you're fooling? I saw you come in last night with that sly, satisfied look on your face. I know what you were up to. The first thing you know you'll get that poor girl in trouble, and then what'll you do? Where'll you get the money to have her taken care of? . . . And you, Howard, you Christer, isn't it about time you began sleeping with your hands outside the covers? . . . You needn't laugh, Colter. Don't think I don't know how you got through that physics course . . . Peters, what you need is a secret vice . . . And you, Latham, you're going to kill somebody some day, do you hear? You're going to kill somebody with your bare hands and you'll burn in

hell for it . . . And you, Amsler, why don't you tell
your mother to stay home? Because you don't dare, that's
why. Because you're afraid of her, you damn, damn, dou-
ble-damn fucking little coward. . . . I'm sorry, boys. I'm
very sorry. I guess I've had a little too much to drink.
Drink . . . Reinhart, you're drunk, you're pissyass drunk.
You're so drunk the bed's going around. And whether
you realize it or not . . . but it's so nice sometimes, it's
such a wonderful, wonderful relief. . . ."

The boys didn't hold anything that he said against
him afterwards, possibly because he sat around all the next
day with his head in his hands and looked so gray and his
misery was so acute that they could only feel sorry for
him. But also because when Reinhart came home drunk,
nobody escaped damnation and it cleared the air for a
while.

31

It didn't seem to bother Spud or Sally that Lymie was
with them a great deal of the time. They felt that in a
way he was responsible for their happiness, and out of
gratitude they included him in it. He accepted the role of
the faithful friend, the devoted, unselfish intermediary.
As such he was useful in many ways. When Sally met him
on the Broad Walk between classes, she took all his books
from him and shook them. If nothing fell out, it was
Lymie's fault; he had lost the note somewhere, or left it
in the wrong book, or was hiding it. When Spud had to
ease his congested feelings by talking to somebody about
Sally, there was Lymie, always at hand, always willing to
listen, to encourage, and even (to a certain extent) sharing his delight, his wonder at what had happened to him
and at the extraordinary change which had come over
the world.

Sometimes all three of them sat in a booth in the back of the Ship's Lantern, and Spud and Sally talked about the house they were going to build as soon as they got married. Spud wanted a two-story sunken living room with a balcony. Sally agreed to the balcony but she was more concerned with the fireplace. It was to be stone, and very big. In addition to the dining room, kitchen, and usual number of upstairs bedrooms, there was also to be a library, a gun room, a billiard room, and a five-car garage. And the house was to be near the water, so that they could keep a sailboat. They drew plans and elevations on paper napkins or in Spud's loose-leaf notebook. So far as Lymie could make out, looking at these plans upside down, the house was of no recognizable style but merely enormous.

When they grew tired of arranging the future, Spud measured his hand against Sally's (she had stopped biting her nails) and was amazed each time at how much bigger a boy's hand is than a girl's. Or they sat and looked at each other and smiled and were sometimes pleased with the silence, or drove it away by talking a silly, meaningless language that they had invented between them. Because they felt free to say anything they wanted to in front of Lymie, they didn't realize that he was there, much of the time. But if he got up to go, they would get up too and go with him.

When the weather was bright they sometimes went walking along the Styx, a small creek that ran through the campus and across the town and out past the country club and then, a thin strip of woods along either side of it, into open farm land, the corn and wheat fields. Eventually they settled in some sunny spot and Spud would put his head in Sally's lap. Lymie lay on the ground near them, with his hands or his forearm cushioning his head, and looked up into the sky. If Sally wanted to kiss Spud, she went ahead and did it. And once when she was feeling particularly happy she leaned over and kissed Lymie. He took his handkerchief out and wiped his mouth with mock fastidiousness.

Sally made a face at him. "Lymie's an old woman-hater," she said. "He's the world's worst. But how could we ever get along without him?"

"Dandy," Spud said, rolling over. "We wouldn't have a bit of trouble. We need Lymie the way a cat needs two tails." He sat up then and picked a burr from his trousers and poked at Lymie and said, "Old friend, tell us a story."

"I don't know any stories," Lymie said.

"Yes, you do," Spud said. "Tell us that story you told me last summer on the beach. The one about the kid that fastened his sled on behind a big sleigh and couldn't get it loose."

"You mean 'The Snow Queen'," Lymie said. "That's too long. And anyway I don't remember all of it any more." He shielded his eyes from the sun with one hand. "I found a story in the library the other day. It was in a book of German legends but it's not a fairy story. It's about a man who had a coat that he liked very much. It made me think of you, Sally. But it wasn't the same kind of a coat, of course."

"Never mind what kind of a coat it was," Spud said. "Let's hear the story."

Lymie waited a moment before he began: "There was a man who had a coat which was woven in the design of a snakeskin but softer than velvet. He lived in a cold country but when he wore the coat he did not know whether it was winter or summer out, and at night when he fell asleep, it was with the coat spread over his blanket, so that he was as warm in his unheated balcony as his neighbors were who had tiled stoves to sleep on. And he still was not happy. He was perpetually examining his elbows to see whether they were beginning to wear out. He was haunted night and day by the thought that not this year perhaps or the next but certainly some day his beautiful snakeskin coat would wear out, and then he would be cold again."

Lymie turned his head slightly without taking his hand away, and saw that Spud had picked up a stick and was writing something with it on the bare ground. Sally was watching him. When they realized that he had stopped talking, Spud tossed the stick away and took Sally's hand instead. "Go on," he said. "We're listening."

"One night in a dream," Lymie continued, "the man saw himself giving the coat away to a beggar, and the light and the happiness from the dream lasted just long enough, after he had awakened, for him to see that that was what he must do with the coat—give it away. He sat all day with the coat across his knees, just inside the front door of his house, waiting. And although it was a part of town where many beggars lived and although seldom a day passed that one of them didn't come to his door asking for something, this day there wasn't a one.

"Toward nightfall, as he was about to give up his search, there were steps outside and he rushed out and found that a very rich man, with his horse and his two servants, was about to enter his house. He knew that the man was rich because he had fur on his collar and silver on his bridle and silver spurs on his heels. Without waiting to find out what had brought the rich man there, he pressed the coat on him and ran back into the house and locked the door. Almost immediately he realized that something was wrong, that he had acted in confusion, but by that time the rich man and his two servants were almost out of sight and he was ashamed to run through the streets after them.

"Instead of a coat to keep him warm that night, a coat which was woven in the design of a snakeskin but softer than velvet, he had only a slight hope that the rich man, in spite of the fur on his collar and the silver on his bridle and spurs, would understand the value of what had been given to him and find some use for it. And even so, he slept better than he had slept in a long time."

When Lymie finished, he took his hand away from his eyes. There was a silence and then Sally said, "I don't think I like that story very much. It's too sad. And besides, I don't know what it means exactly."

"It was just a story I read in that book I was telling you about. I read several of them. Do you want to hear any more?"

"No," Spud said. "One's plenty. I'm going to turn my attention, my undivided attention, to Miss Forbes. Are you happy, Miss Forbes?"

"About as happy as I ever expect to be," Sally said. "And you, Mr. Latham?"

"Tolerably happy," Spud said. "Just tolerably." He made a clucking noise with his tongue, and heaved a sigh as Sally pulled his head back into her lap.

After a time, Lymie grew restless and wandered off, but they soon came and found him. There is a species of cat that needs two tails.

32

One afternoon when Sally and Spud were sitting in a booth in the Ship's Lantern, Armstrong and his girl walked in. The girl's name was Eunice. She had fluffy light-brown hair and hazel eyes and at nineteen she was pretty in a sly, selfish way. She saw Sally and Spud, and without waiting to be asked, sat down with them. Armstrong moved in beside her. There was no room for Lymie when he appeared. Spud wanted to move over, so that he could squeeze in next to them, but Lymie insisted that he had a conference with his German instructor and fled.

Armstrong's girl was wearing his jeweled fraternity pin on her coral-pink cashmere sweater. She unpinned it for Sally to admire and Sally, turning it over to examine the safety clasp, dropped it.

"Oh, that's just like you, Forbes!" the other girl exclaimed.

"Well I didn't *go* to drop it," Sally said, trying to peer under the table. "It just slipped through my—"

"Don't step on it, anybody," Armstrong said. "Don't move your feet for a second while we look for it."

He and Spud slid out of their seats and got down on their knees in front of the booth and began searching.

"If that pin meant as much to you, Sally Forbes, as it does to me—" the girl said bitterly. Spud's head rose above the table. "Did you find it?" she asked anxiously.

He had the fraternity pin in his hand and put it on the edge of the table. As if the pin exercised a kind of foolish fascination for her, Sally started to pick it up again. The other girl snatched it from her and pinned it on the front of her sweater, above her heart. In her gratification at getting the pin back, she forgot to thank Spud.

Both boys got up, dusted the knees of their trousers, and then sat down again. The palms of Spud's hands were black from the dirt that he had been fingering, under the table. He tried to clean them off with his handkerchief. Armstrong's hands were still immaculate. He offered a package of Camels around. Spud shook his head but the girls each took one. Armstrong lit a match with his thumbnail and cupped his large hand around it as he held the match toward Eunice first and then for Sally. It was the gesture of a full-grown man, not a boy, and must have required practice.

Armstrong was a senior and a good campus politician. He had just missed out on being class president, in one of the off semesters. He looked well in his clothes and under all ordinary circumstances (that brief unpleasantness in the gymnasium hardly counted) he was easy and sure of himself. When people are too obviously and too variously blessed there is always a natural desire to find some flaw in them. The only thing that one could object to in Armstrong was that his full, heavy face, although handsome, had no character. Any number of boys in the university at that time could, from a distance, have been mistaken for him. And those qualities which made him outstanding in college probably meant that he would be a mediocrity later in life; though that didn't necessarily follow. He knew hundreds of people and had no trouble in keeping them straight. Boys kept nodding to him, on their way in or out of the Ship's Lantern with their dates, and he spoke to them by name. He spoke to the girls as well.

A tall thin boy with a crew haircut let his girl walk on ahead while he stopped and asked, "How are you, fella?"

"Not bad," Armstrong said.

"What did you get in that psychology exam Friday?"

"B minus," Armstrong said. "What did you get?"

"You're lying. You didn't get a B minus out of Lovat. He never gives higher than a C. No kidding, Army, what did you get?"

"I got a B minus, no kidding."

The tall boy put out his hand. "Let me feel you. I just want to touch a guy that got a B minus from Lovat."

"I got an A," Armstrong's girl said.

"That doesn't mean a thing," the tall boy said. "If you're a girl all you have to do is sit in the front row and cross your legs once in a while."

"You know Spud Latham?" Armstrong asked. "This is Bill Shearer."

"Glad to know you, Latham," the tall boy said and held out his hand. "I've seen you around."

There was no way that Spud could shake hands without revealing the dirt on the palm of his right hand. He nodded stiffly, and kept both hands under the table, making an easy enemy for the rest of his college life. The tall boy, flushing slightly, turned back to Armstrong.

"What about that accountancy problem for tomorrow?" he asked. "Have you done it yet? We could do it together."

"Okay," Armstrong said.

"Come over right after dinner."

"I can't," Armstrong said. "We've got a volley ball game with the A.T.O.'s."

"Who've they got?"

"Short and Harrigan and—"

"Harrigan's good."

"You're telling me. They've also got Safford, Rains—"

"Is Rains an A.T.O.? I thought he was a Delt?"

"That's his brother you're thinking of. His brother is a Delt. This guy's an A.T.O."

"I wonder why he didn't pledge Delta Tau Delta?"

"He could have, I guess," Armstrong said. "But you know how brothers are with each other. He probably wanted to show his independence so he came down to school and pledged A.T.O. But anyway, he's good."

"He's damn good," the tall boy said. "Herb Porter was talking about him. You know Porter, don't you?"

"Delta Chi?"

"Chi Psi."

"I meant Chi Psi. Yeah, I know him."

"Well, good luck anyway."

"Oh, we'll beat 'em," Armstrong said.

The tall boy shook his head admiringly. "You boys aren't overmodest, I'll say that for you."

Armstrong smiled. "Why don't you go bag your head, Shearer," he said.

"My girl's making motions. She'll give me hell if I don't. . . . Okay, fella. Be seeing you."

"Okay, fella," Armstrong said.

There were three of these conversations, all within fifteen minutes. Spud took no part in them. The girls talked to each other, but he sat back with a stiff expression on his face—the expression his mother put on sometimes when she found herself among women whose husbands were more successful than Mr. Latham, and whose diamond rings were more showy than hers. At four o'clock when Spud got up to go, Armstrong took the check and left with him. As soon as they had gone, Armstrong's girl leaned forward, as if she had something to say which must not be overheard. "Army noticed Spud at our house dance."

"Is that so?" Sally said.

"He likes Spud. He told me so. He thinks Spud is a very good guy. I do too, Sally. Only I think it's too bad that he doesn't belong to a fraternity. For your sake, I mean."

"I'll manage," Sally said.

"I don't mean that. Of course you'll manage. All I'm trying to say is that Spud *ought* to belong to a fraternity. I think it would be very good for him."

With her lips curling slightly, Sally said, "And very good for the fraternity."

When Lymie appeared on the top floor of the gymnasium later that afternoon, Spud and Armstrong were boxing. They went at it easy, and after a few minutes Army said that he had had enough, and pulled the gloves off and went back to the iron rings. Spud turned to the punching bag for a while and then he walked up to Lymie, took the rope away from him, and held out the pair of gloves that Armstrong had been using. "Here," he said, "put these on."

"Are you out of your mind?" Lymie asked.

"Go on." Spud unlaced one of the gloves. "Put your hand in here and shut up."

"I don't want to box with you."

"Why not?"

"Because I don't."

When the glove was on Lymie's hand, Spud wrapped the strings twice around Lymie's thin wrist and then tied them. "Hold out your other hand," he said.

"You'll forget," Lymie said, "and the first thing you know they'll be sending for the pulmotor."

"No, I won't, Lymie. Honestly. I'll take it easy. I promise. I just need somebody to practice with."

"Well, keep off my feet, whatever you do," Lymie said, and looked down at the gloves with distaste. Spud put on another pair and walked across the floor to the low parallel bars and held out his gloves for a sophomore named Hughes to tie.

"Now," he said, when he came back. "You want to fight with one foot flat, see? And your weight on the ball of the other foot. Or you can shuffle—the idea being that you always stand so that you can move somewhere else in a hurry."

"I see," Lymie said earnestly, and stood with one stockinged foot flat and his weight on the ball of the other.

"Watch me," Spud said. "Hold your arms like this and remember you've got to cover yourself no matter what happens." He stepped out of position and shifted Lymie's tense arms so that the elbows were in close to his sides and the gloves one in front of the other.

"Something tells me I'm going to get killed," Lymie said.

"Nothing's going to happen to you. Stop worrying."

"Okay," Lymie said, and led with his right and followed with his left and caught Spud almost but not quite unprepared.

"That's fine. Always get the first punch, if you can, for the psychological effect. . . . No, cover yourself. . . .

That's it . . . there. . . . No . . . you're wide open, Lymie. . . . See, I could have taken your head off if I'd really wanted to. I could have knocked you cold. Keep covered . . . that's it . . . that's it. . . ."

Stepping backward, and then backward again, trying vainly to defend himself from the incessant rain of blows, Lymie tripped over his own feet and sat down.

"Did you hurt yourself?" Spud asked.

Lymie shook his head and got up again.

"You forgot what I told you about keeping on the balls of your feet. Keep moving, as if you were dancing almost."

When they stopped to rest, Lymie leaned against the wall, panting, his face red from the exertion. Spud turned away to the punching bag, and let fly all the energy he had been so carefully restraining. For a moment it seemed likely that the bag would break from its moorings and go flying across the gymnasium.

"Time," Spud said.

Lymie advanced from the wall to meet him. In the second round Spud tapped him on the nose harder than he had meant to. He dropped his arms immediately and said, "Oh God, Lymie, did I hurt you?"

Instead of stopping to feel the injury, Lymie lost his head and sailed into Spud with such a sudden and unexpected fury that he backed Spud against the brick wall. In Lymie's eyes was the clear light of murder. Spud made no effort to defend himself and after a few seconds Lymie stopped, confused by the lack of opposition. "What's the matter?" he asked.

Spud turned and leaned against the wall and laughed until he was weak. When he had gathered himself together again he saw that it was not Lymie's nose but his feelings that had been hurt. Spud put his arms around him and said, "There, Lymie, old socks, I didn't mean to laugh at you, honestly. I just couldn't help myself. The look on your face was so funny. You were doing right well, though. Fine, in fact. If you keep on like that, you'll be the next featherweight champion of the world. All you need is a few lessons."

But Lymie wouldn't box any more. He pulled the gloves off without bothering to untie them, and returned to the skipping rope. Later, after Spud was dressed and as they were leaving the gymnasium, Armstrong, whose locker was on the other side of the swimming pool, caught up with them and began talking about Christmas vacation, which was three weeks off. His remarks were addressed exclusively to Spud, although he had seen Lymie just as often upstairs and knew that they roomed together. Spud answered in monosyllables, and Lymie walked along with his hands in his pockets and his eyes off to the side—the nearest he could come to deafness, dumbness, blindness, and utter nonexistence.

He had to wait two days for Spud's reaction to these rather pointed attentions. The reference, when it came, was oblique, but Lymie was used to that. They were in their room studying, after supper, and although Spud's head was bent over his German reader, he had not turned a page for some time. When he was actually studying, you could always tell it. His eyes went back and forth continually between the day's assignment and the vocabulary at the back of the book.

"Do you think," he began, in a faraway voice, "—do you think Sally would like me better if I belonged to a fraternity?"

33

During Christmas vacation Mr. Peters' cousin, Miss Georgiana Binkerd, who was a very wealthy woman, came through Chicago. She had agreed to pay half the expense of Lymie's college education (Mr. Peters paid the other half) and now felt a proprietary interest in him. The three and a half hours that she allowed for having lunch with Mr. Peters and Lymie was ample, but it did not allow her to find out very much about them. From the fact that she had her hat on and was waiting when the taxi driver rang the bell in the vestibule of the apartment building, one might gather that Miss Binkerd had arrived in Chicago with her conclusions already formed (Mr. Peters was the black sheep of the family) and wished to leave with them intact.

Miss Binkerd was in her late forties and there was nothing about her to suggest that she had ever been any younger, but Mr. Peters could remember her when she was nine and had a brace on her right leg. Georgiana Binkerd's mother and his mother were half sisters, and as a boy he had been taken to visit the Ohio relatives every summer. His two little cousins used to tease him because he stuttered, and since they were both older than he was and both girls (so he couldn't hit them when he felt like it), they always got the best of every argument. At that time they lived outside of Cincinnati in a big square yellow brick farmhouse with a cupola on it and a double row of Scotch pine trees leading from the road to the front porch. What Mr. Peters remembered best about this place was the long room which took up half of the downstairs and had parquet floors. It was intended as a formal drawing room but his uncle used it as a place to store feed. At night the rats ran all over the house, inside the walls. As a boy Mr. Peters used to lie awake listening to them and imagining that he had a shotgun in his hands.

He liked his aunt but he was afraid of his uncle, who had a beard and wore a gold collar button in his shirt on Sundays and didn't like children. During those years his uncle was a farmer. Later he made a fortune in railroad stock, lost it, and made another fortune in a patent medicine which was still on sale in drugstores, with his uncle's name and picture on it. They lived now—his aunt and Georgiana and her sister Carrie—in a big ugly house in the best residential section of Cincinnati. Mr. Peters had visited them there also, after he was grown. By that time the old man was stripped of his authority. No matter what he said, his wife and daughters corrected him. Under the guise of caring for his health, they had taken complete charge of his mind, his habits, the way he dressed, what he ate, his very life. When it finally dawned on the old man that he was never going to get any of these things back, he died. The women were still flourishing.

Georgiana Binkerd looked like her father except that he had been a large rawboned man and she was a small thin woman with pale selfish blue eyes that bulged slightly behind her rimless glasses. She had had infantile paralysis as a child and one leg was several inches shorter than the other and had no flesh on it. She was thrown off balance at every step and she walked with a nervous lurching which both Mr. Peters and Lymie, as they held the vestibule doors open for her, ignored. When they reached the cab, she turned to Lymie and put her claw-like hands on his shoulders and kissed him.

"Good-by, my dear! I wish you were my own child," she said, and with some awkwardness got her crippled body into the taxi.

Mr. Peters stepped in after her and closed the door from the inside. "The Union Station," he said, leaning forward and addressing the driver. From the tone of his voice one would have thought that it was he who had a train to make, not Miss Binkerd. She let it pass.

"Good-by, God bless you!" she called to Lymie, and he called back "Good-by, Cousin Georgiana," from the curbing. Though he continued to wave until the cab turned the corner, his mind was not on her but on her

baum marten neckpiece, which was very lifelike. The cab
turned south on Sheridan Road, then east for two blocks
at Devon Avenue, then south again. Mr. Peters' mind was
on the thick roll of American Express traveler's checks
which he knew to be in Miss Binkerd's black leather purse.

"I can't tell you how much I've enjoyed this visit
with you, Lymon," she said, swaying with the movement
of the cab.

"It's been mighty nice having you," Mr. Peters said.
His hand went toward the pocket where he kept his cigarettes, but he checked himself in time. "I've enjoyed every
minute of it," he said. "And Lymie has too."

"He looks like his mother," Miss Binkerd said.

Mr. Peters nodded.

"I never saw Alma but the once, when I came for
your mother's funeral," Miss Binkerd said. "But I remember her. She was a fine woman."

"She was indeed," Mr. Peters said. "Do you mind if
I smoke?"

"It makes me cough," Miss Binkerd said.

Mr. Peters' hand withdrew from his pocket.

"There's one thing I'd like to say to you," Miss
Binkerd announced impressively. "And that is, you de-
serve a great deal of credit for the way you've brought
up your son all alone without any help."

"Thank you," Mr. Peters said.

"I watched him all through luncheon. He has very
good manners. He could go among people anywhere and
know what to do. The only thing that isn't as all right as
it might be is his posture."

"I know," Mr. Peters said gloomily. "I nag him about
it but it doesn't seem to do any good. He just won't stand
up straight. Also, he's not strong, as you can see. He needs
to be outdoors more. I've thought some lately of joining
a country club if I can lay my hands on the money to do
it. Golf is very good exercise and I could probably man-

age to play with him every week end during the summer months. It would do him a world of good, if I could only arrange it."

The sudden hard light that came into Miss Binkerd's eyes was not a reflection from her glasses. She had had a great deal of experience with remarks which could, if followed up, lead to a direct request for financial assistance.

"Lymie's a very nice boy the way he is," she said. "I wouldn't try to change him if I were you."

"Oh I don't," Mr. Peters said hastily. "I just meant that—"

"I've never been sold on country clubs. Cousin Will Binkerd belongs to one and I hear that the men drink in the locker rooms."

"Lymie wouldn't be likely to do that," Mr. Peters said. "He's not the type."

"No, I can see he isn't," Miss Binkerd said. "But even so. With boys you can't ever be sure. The quiet, well-behaved ones often cause their parents the most misery and heartache before they're through."

Mr. Peters suspected that this remark was directed obliquely at him, although as a boy he had not been conspicuously quiet or well-behaved.

"When Lymie was little," he said, "he used to have a terrible temper, and also he was very jealous. Especially of his mother. If he thought she was paying too much attention to some other child, he'd fly into a rage and she couldn't do a thing with him. Now that he's grown he never gives me the slightest trouble, except that I can't teach him the value of money. Slips right through his fingers."

"He comes by it honestly," Miss Binkerd said. This time there was no doubt whom the remark was directed toward. She peered out of the window of the taxi and said, "Is that the Edgewater Beach Hotel?"

Mr. Peters said that it was.

There was a silence which lasted for perhaps a minute and a half, and didn't seem to bother Miss Binkerd in the least. Mr. Peters, casting around uneasily in his mind for some way of ending it, said, "I wish we could have seen more of you—not just between trains."

"I know," she said. "Next time I'll pay you a real visit, Lymon. But it's a long trip and I'm not as young as I once was, and it's hard for me to get around. I could have taken the sleeper from Kansas City to St. Louis, and not had to change stations. But I haven't seen Lymie since he was a year old, and Mother was curious to know how you were getting along."

"Well, you tell her we're getting along just fine," Mr. Peters said.

"I will," Miss Binkerd said, nodding. "I'll tell her. And she'll probably ask if you're still as handsome as you used to be. In that case I can fib a little."

She laughed and leaned back, happy that she had at last repaid him for calling her a spider when they were children, thirty-five years before.

34

The faces Spud saw around him were healthy, handsome, and intelligent but not too intelligent. There were no freaks in Armstrong's fraternity, nobody that you would ever need to be ashamed of.

The dining room walls were of solid oak paneling. The drapes were a plain dark red. There were six tables, and Armstrong sat at the head of one of them, with Spud on his right. Two boys from Chicago, a boy from Bloomington, another from Gallup, New Mexico, and a boy from Marietta, Ohio, filled out the table. The Chicago boys were talking about the new dance band at the Drake

Hotel, where they had celebrated New Year's Eve. They may have been bragging when they talked about how drunk they had got, but in any case they weren't ashamed of it. They spoke with the natural, easy assurance of people who know that they are, socially speaking, the best; and that everywhere they go the best of everything will be reserved as a matter of course for them. Their attitude toward Spud could be gauged by the fact that they remembered to use his name each time that they spoke to him, by their polite interest in his description of the winter carnival at his home town in Wisconsin, and even by the way they offered him the rolls before they helped themselves. It was clear that he also belonged among the best people, otherwise Armstrong would never have asked him to dinner.

While the four student waiters cleared the tables after the main course, there was singing. First the university anthem, then a football song, then the fraternity sweetheart song, which was full of romantic feeling and required humming in places. Spud would have liked to join in but he didn't know the words and he also felt that, being a guest, he ought not to. He sat stiffly with his hands in his lap.

Between the salad and the dessert they sang again. They sang a long drawn-out dirty ballad which began:

Oh the old black bull came down from the mountain . . .
Houston . . . John Houston . . .

and ended with the old black bull, all tired out, going slowly back up the mountain. And then a song that somebody had put to the tune of "The Battle Hymn of the Republic:"

Mary Ann McCarthy she . . . went out to gather clams
Mary Ann McCarthy she . . . went out to gather clams
Mary Ann McCarthy SHE . . . went out to gather clams
But she didn't get a . . .

Forty-one spoons struck forty-one glass tumblers in uni-
son, twice.

                                                    . . . *clam*

> *GLO-ry, glo-ry, hal-le-lu-jah*

The voices soared out the refrain.

> *Glo-ry, glo-ry, hal-le-lu-jah*
> *Glo-ry, glo-ry, hal-le-lu-jah*
> *For she didn't get a . . .*
>   (clink, clink)

                                                    . . . *clam*

The dessert was peach ice cream with chocolate cake
on the side. It looked to Spud like the cake his mother
made, and he bit into it hopefully. He was disappointed,
but he ate it anyway.

A signal from Armstrong produced the simultaneous
scraping of forty-two chairs. The boys hung back, hugging the wall until he and Spud were out of the dining
room, and then closed in behind. Instead of going back
into the living room, Armstrong took Spud on a tour of
the two upper floors of the house. Spud was favorably im-
pressed by the two bathrooms, each with a long row of
washbowls, which made it unlikely that anybody would
have to wait in line to shave; and by the study rooms.
They opened off the long upstairs hallway, instead of one
out of the other; there wouldn't be a steady traffic
through them, the way there was through the rooms at
"302." Each study room door had a padlock on it. At the
rooming house Spud's favorite ties had a way of disap-
pearing. They were not always in good condition when
he found them, and two or three he had never been able
to locate, though he suspected Howard. Padlocks were
the only solution to the problem, obviously, and they
were not, in Spud's mind, incompatible with brotherly
love.

He was also struck by the fact that the dormitory, which was on the third floor, was the same temperature, or nearly so, as the rest of the house. In the daytime, Armstrong explained, the windows were kept closed, and there was heat from a couple of long radiators. At night when the windows were open, it was cold but not freezing. Spud nodded approvingly at the double-decker single beds, each with its cocoon of covers. He preferred sleeping by himself.

Study hours began at seven-thirty. The freshmen left the living room and many upperclassmen followed them. The dart game in the basement and the ping-pong table on the sun porch were deserted. There was no more shouting in the upstairs hall. In five minutes the house quieted down in a way that "302" seldom did before midnight.

Spud and Armstrong and two upperclassmen sat in front of the grate fire in the living room and talked. It was the time of year for arguing about basketball. Spud pretended that he was interested, but actually he was busy installing himself on the second floor, in a large corner room, with Lymie's desk next to his. He was wondering if it wouldn't work out better to put Lymie somewhere near by—down the hall, say, with another roommate for a change (better for Lymie, that is)—when the clock on the mantel struck eight. He got up to go, slipped his overcoat on in the front hall, tied his scarf correctly, shook hands all around, and left, very pleased with the house and the fraternal atmosphere, and rather pleased with himself.

A week later he was asked to dinner again and this time the conversation in the living room was not about basketball but moved in a straight line. At the end of five minutes Armstrong produced a triangular pledge pin. Although Spud had been expecting it, he colored with embarrassment. It was not easy to explain, with four people looking at him, that he didn't have the money to join a fraternity.

"We can get around that difficulty," Armstrong said, "if you're willing to take a dishwasher's job or wait table." Then, correctly reading the look on Spud's face, he added, "It won't make any difference so far as your standing in the house is concerned. Also, it won't take much time from your studies. You'd naturally spend a certain amount of time sitting around after dinner, chewing the fat. The only thing you have to worry about is the hundred dollar initiation fee."

Spud nodded.

"Do you think you can manage that?" Armstrong asked.

"I'll have to think about it," Spud said.

Armstrong tried to press him, but he refused to commit himself, and his refusal was so firm that Armstrong gave way before it. "We're not in the habit of making open bids," he said. "And although in your case we're willing to make an exception, I think you ought to realize that there are plenty of guys—big men on campus—who would jump at the chance."

Spud did realize this, but he wasn't jumping, even so. He left, without a pledge button in his lapel, and went to the Ship's Lantern, where Sally and Lymie were waiting for him. They sat smiling while he described his evening, and once or twice a look passed between them which Spud intercepted. It meant nothing but that they were pleased with him for being so much like himself and so unlike anybody else, probably, who had ever lived. He began to suspect that there was some kind of a secret understanding between them, from which he was excluded.

"If you want to join it," Sally said, "go ahead. It's a good enough fraternity. The best there is, I guess. But of course they change. What's good one year isn't necessarily good the next. And I'm not sure I know what they mean by 'good' anyway."

"Wouldn't you be proud of me?" Spud asked.

"I am already," Sally said. "I won't love you any more because you've got a piece of fancy jewelry on your vest."

"You could wear it," Spud suggested.

"I don't need to," Sally said. "Everybody knows I've got you just where I want you."

"Humph," Spud said. What he wanted was for Lymie, who had everything to lose by the arrangement, or Sally, who had nothing to gain, to decide that it was to his best interest to join a fraternity. Then he would have been sure that he didn't want to. When Lymie said, "It's entirely up to you," Spud was thoroughly exasperated with both of them.

"It isn't entirely up to me," he exclaimed. "I don't know why you keep saying that. I can't walk off and leave you with that double room on your hands. If I go, you have to go too."

"So far," Lymie said, "nobody has asked me to join a fraternity."

"They will ask you," Spud said.

Sally said nothing. She had not said anything for a minute or so, but now Lymie was aware of her silence. It had changed its quality somehow. He smiled at her, by way of conveying that she didn't have to be tactful. He had known all along they were not going to ask him to join the fraternity. To Spud he said, "It doesn't really matter to me where I live, and it does to you, so you'd better decide."

"In the first place—" Spud began.

Lymie interrupted him. "I move this meeting be adjourned. All in favor say 'Aye.'"

"Aye," Sally said, peering into her compact.

"Motion carried," Lymie said, and picked up the check. "Forbes, it appears that you owe me a nickel. . . . Latham, twenty cents, please."

"Fifteen," Spud said. "Chocolate sundae is only fifteen."

"Twenty with nuts on it," Lymie said.

Spud put his right hand over his pants' pocket and then said, "How'd you like to treat me?"

"What would be the use of doing that?" Lymie asked.

"Well, I don't know," Spud said. "I thought you might enjoy it."

"Fork over," Lymie said.

"You're the tightest guy I ever knew," Spud said indignantly. "Barring none." He began systematically emptying all his pockets. There was no money in any of them.

35

When Reinhart offered to loan Spud a hundred dollars, he was so surprised that it didn't occur to him to ask questions. Even so, Reinhart felt that some explanation was necessary. "My aunt sent it to me," he said. "She does that once in a while. I don't happen to need it just now and I thought maybe you could use it." Reinhart who hadn't had a new suit in three years, who had no aunt, whose debts were as numerous as the sands of the sea.

"As a matter of fact I *could* use it," Spud said, and thought how wonderful it was that, just when you needed something very much (like a hundred dollars) along it came. For no reason. The exact amount. He was on the point of explaining to Reinhart about the fraternity, but then he remembered that Reinhart had had a bad experience with fraternities and would probably judge them all by the one he had been pledged to. "It's really damn nice of you," he said, letting gratitude take the place of explanations.

Reinhart shrugged. "I'm not giving it to you. It's a loan," he said, twisting a lock of hair between his thumb and forefinger.

"Even so," Spud said. He saw the rooming house, which he had for so long been ashamed of, and Reinhart slouched down in his overstuffed chair, with new eyes. It is foolish to contend that money doesn't make any difference. With a hundred dollars, the means of escape, in crisp clean bills in his right hand, Spud was no longer anxious to leave. After all, he had lived here for a year and a half, and these guys were his friends. When he needed help, they came across, without his even asking. Guys who did that were worth hanging on to.

Out of a sense of obligation Spud stayed and talked to Reinhart a few minutes longer and then walked across the campus to Sally's sorority house. She had told him that she was going home that afternoon, to get some clothes that she needed; but the hundred dollars had driven everything else out of Spud's mind. He had no intention of telling Sally about the loan, for that would have involved matters he didn't care to go into, such as how and when he was going to pay the money back. But he wanted to pin her down about the fraternity. He felt sure, although she had refused to influence his decision one way or the other, that she would be pleased if he were a fraternity man. After she had admitted this, he would tell her why he was going to turn the offer down.

He walked into the sorority house and pressed her bell, in the telephone closet. There was no answer. He pressed it a second time: *one short, one long.*

"Not in," a voice called down from upstairs.

Spud came out of the closet and stood at the foot of the stairs. "Know where she went?" he asked.

Hope Davison, with her hair in brown kid curlers,

leaned over the banister. "Oh, hello, Spud. Don't I look a
sight? Forbes has gone out. I think I heard her bell ring a
little while ago, and then I guess she went out. Anyway
she isn't here now."

"Was she with Lymie?" Spud asked up the stair well.

"I don't know," Hope said. "If she wasn't with you,
she must have been with him. She's always with one or
the other of you."

"Thanks," Spud said, and a second later she heard the
front door slam.

During the first block, while he was calmly walking
along, he beat Lymie to a pulp three times. With his bare
hands he smashed Lymie's nose and closed his eyes and
knocked his teeth in and made him spit blood. In the second block he hit Lymie in the stomach and knocked the
wind out of him. Lymie crumpled, gasping, and Spud hit
him again, on the way down. Lymie cried for mercy,
begged for it, but Spud lifted him to his feet again and
stood there a minute looking at him, at the guy that he
had trusted, the guy that he had always thought was, of
all the people he knew, his friend. He hit Lymie square on
the chin with his bare knuckles, but he didn't feel a thing.
All that he was conscious of was the change in Lymie's
face. Lymie's eyes seemed to become glazed and then he
seemed to wilt. In the following block Lymie came to,
groaning. Spud knocked him down four more times and
after that he made Lymie train with him every day. He
made him drink lots of milk and fruit juices and eat fresh
vegetables and get plenty of sleep and take exercise, and
pretty soon Lymie began to put on weight. His chest
filled out and his arms began to have some muscle and the
first thing anybody knew, Lymie was a good boxer, quick
and intelligent. He got to be a little better still, and soon
he was the same size Spud was. Then Spud took him on
one day and beat the piss out of him. . . .

When Spud appeared on the top floor of the gymnasium Lymie was there, waiting for him. At the first sight of Lymie, Spud realized that it was no use. No matter how long Lymie trained, he would never be big enough for anybody to haul off and hit.

36

Professor Severance lived with his mother in a large white clapboard house which had been built in the 'eighties and was not far from the Forbeses' house. When Lymie rang the bell at six-thirty that same evening, a colored woman in a maid's uniform opened the door to him and took his coat and muffler. Then Professor Severance appeared and shook hands with him warmly. For the first few seconds Lymie missed the wooden desk and the low lecture platform. Being able to look straight into Professor Severance's eyes made him feel shy, and in the presence of a stranger. Through the double doorway he could see into a long brightly lighted living room, where an old woman sat waiting on a high-backed horsehair sofa.

It was a beautiful room, furnished with taste and with the help of money. The antique sofas and chairs, the little rosewood tables had been polished to a satiny texture. Against one wall was a square concert grand piano with the lid down, and on it were dozens of tiny painted clay figures—a Chinese wedding procession with men carrying banners, men bearing lanterns and spears, and horsemen riding behind the two palanquins of the bride and groom. Japanese prints hung at intervals around the room: a Hiroshige snow scene, the Hokusai great blue-and-white frothy wave on the point of breaking, two portraits of eighteenth century Japanese actors, a girl wading in blue water with her skirts tucked up to her knees; a group of women seated in a fragile black boat. In the bay window a card table had been set up with a bridge lamp shining on it, and cards laid out in rows, for solitaire.

For all its calm and elegance, the room was a battle-field. The card table, where Professor Severance had been sitting when Lymie arrived, and the copy of *Mansfield Park*, lying now on the table next to the sofa with a carved wooden paper knife in it, were sometimes the weapons with which Professor Severance and his mother attacked each other, sometimes the fortifications behind which they retired, when one or the other was momentarily victorious. The smoke of stale quarrels hung on the air. Professor Severance led Lymie over to the horsehair sofa and said, "Mother, this is Mr. Peters."

"How do you do?" the old woman said, in a voice that was clearer and stronger than Lymie had expected. Looking down at her, at the massive head and yellowish white hair and the colorless lips, Lymie thought how much like a St. Bernard she looked, except that the eyes were not only sad but sick as well. Even so, they managed a sudden yellow gleam that charmed him. Mrs. Severance sat, large and shapeless, in a gray silk dress with her long-fringed silk shawl slipping from her shoulders. A carved cane leaned against the corner of the sofa.

"Sit here beside me," the old woman said, patting the horsehair seat. "I want to talk to you. My son tells me you're a friend of Sally Forbes. You're in love with her, aren't you? It's all right. You don't have to blush like that. She's a darling girl. I've known her ever since she was born. She'll make you a good wife, I'm sure, though she's not as pretty as her mother was. Her mother was a real beauty. I always wanted her to marry William. I've never forgiven her for marrying Professor Forbes instead."

"My mother is of the opinion that everybody should get married," Professor Severance explained with a crisp smile. "The sooner the better."

"The sooner the better," Mrs. Severance said, nodding. "Look at William. He'll be forty-three next June and he gets more trying to live with every day of his life."

"I don't believe that's true," Professor Severance said mildly. "I should have said that I'm probably quite considerate, even-tempered, and in fact very little trouble to anybody."

Instead of answering him, Mrs. Severance asked Lymie how old he was, and he told her.

"Nineteen . . . Think of it!" she exclaimed. "I would have said he was fifteen at the most, wouldn't you, William?"

"No, I think he looks somewhere between eighteen and nineteen."

"At the most, fifteen," Mrs. Severance repeated. Then to her son, as if Lymie had suddenly vanished from the room, "Your students get younger and younger. When we first moved here, there weren't any that were fifteen years old. Or if there were, I don't remember them."

"But Mr. Peters isn't that young, Mother," Professor Severance said patiently. "He's just told you that he was nineteen."

"You're too young to be away from home," Mrs. Severance said, shaking her head at Lymie. "I feel quite certain of it. I dare say your mother feels the same way."

"My mother is dead," Lymie said.

The old woman's face took on a look of almost total blankness, as if she were listening to footsteps in the upstairs hall, or in some empty corridor of her mind. Then she looked at Lymie and smiled. "What a pity!" she exclaimed, reaching out toward him. "I'm so sorry!" Her clasp was warm and friendly. "What thin hands he has," she said, turning to her son. "They're as small and thin as a girl's."

Professor Severance rested his head on the back of his chair and half closing his eyes, said, "I've been trying most of my life to convince my mother, or to suggest, rather—for the suggestion by itself, adequately conveyed, would probably be enough—that it isn't polite to make personal remarks."

"Oh, pshaw!" Mrs. Severance exclaimed. "Mr. Peters is not offended, are you, Mr. Peters?"

Lymie shook his head.

"Besides," the old woman said, "I only say what I think, which is a compliment."

Professor Severance cleared his throat. The sound was noncommittal.

"William also tells me that you like poetry," she said. "Why don't you become a professor? It's a very pleasant life. So safe. Nothing to worry about as long as you live. You don't make any money, of course, but I can tell just by looking at you that you'll never make much money anyway. You're not the type. If I were you I wouldn't try. Settle down here and teach. William will tell you just how to go about it."

"Yes," Professor Severance said, nodding. "It's very simple. And I'm sure Mr. Peters would make an excellent, perhaps even an inspired, teacher, but he may prefer to be a poet instead."

"What nonsense," Mrs. Severance said. Twisting in irritation, she gathered the fringes of her shawl into a rope which she laid across her knees. "You can't starve in a garret these days. There aren't any. They've all been converted into apartments that cost thirty-five or forty dollars a month. Besides, you mustn't pay any attention to what William says. His students probably have a certain amount of respect for him, because he's read so much, but he's only a child, I assure you, in spite of all those books in his study. I'm sure that in many ways you are older than he is, Mr. Peters. Far older." She looked down at the large pink cameo which was pinned on the front of her dress and straightened it. "If this attachment between you and Sally Forbes doesn't work out," she said suddenly, "I wish you'd let me know. Because I have a grand-daughter coming along, a dear sweet girl, and you might like her even better. She's fifteen now—just your age."

Professor Severance's eyebrows flew upwards and then settled again, into their usual repose.

"My niece lives in Virginia," he said. "I think you're safe enough, Mr. Peters. For the time being."

"Let me show you her picture," Mrs. Severance said. She reached across *Mansfield Park* and took a small framed photograph and handed it to Lymie. The photo-graph was tinted slightly, and he saw by the head and shoulders that Mrs. Severance's granddaughter had been even younger, probably about thirteen when the picture was taken. Compared to Sally she was not very interest-ing.

"It's very nice," he said, rather as if he had been asked to admire an antique gold bracelet or an amethyst ring.

"She lives just outside of Charlottesville in a beautiful old house that William's brother has bought there, with box hedges and holly trees and I don't know—I can't re-member how many rooms with fireplaces in them. But anyway, she's coming for a visit in the spring. I'll see that you meet her."

The colored woman appeared in the doorway to the dining room and said, "Dinner is served."

"All right, Hattie," Professor Severance said, nod-ding.

Mrs. Severance placed the picture on the table and reached for her cane. With some difficulty she lifted her heavy bulk from the sofa. Then, leaning on the cane and with one hand through Lymie's arm, she stalked slowly toward the dining room.

The dining room table was large enough for eight people. Only three places were set, far apart, on a white damask cloth, the corners of which almost touched the floor. Between the two silver candlesticks in the center of the table was a crystal bowl filled with yellow and lavender stock. The air was heavy from the odor of the flowers, and Lymie had an uneasy feeling as he held Mrs. Severance's chair out for her and helped her dispose of the cane, that there were more people in the room than just the three of them. Even after he sat down, the feeling persisted (The fear of death, could it have been, standing patiently behind Mrs. Severance's chair? And behind her son's, the fear of being left alone with his decks of cards, his never-finished game of solitaire?) until the swinging door to the pantry flew open and the colored woman reappeared with a fourteen-pound turkey on an enormous blue china platter.

"I hope you're hungry," Mrs. Severance said. "It always exasperates me so when people don't eat."

No one saw or was conscious of the figure behind Lymie's chair.

37

When Spud appeared at "302" that night there was a pledge button in his lapel. Freeman and Amsler noticed it and withdrew from him as if he had contracted some fatal disease. They told Reinhart, who came into Spud's room with a puzzled expression on his face and stood watching Spud pack. He had emptied out his dresser drawers and his clothes covered the tops of both desks. Reinhart handed him a pile of shirts, when he saw that Spud was ready for them, and then a handful of socks, rolled up tight in the shape of an egg. There was absolutely no reason for Spud to avoid Reinhart's eyes. Unless he was drunk, Reinhart never made any comment, never offered advice. Nevertheless Spud took the things without looking at him.

A big suitcase and a canvas duffelbag held all of Spud's earthly possessions. When he had finished packing, the room was tidy but it had a disturbed air and seemed larger than usual. Reinhart took the suitcase, Spud the duffelbag, which was full of books and soiled clothes, and very heavy. They passed by several open doors but no one spoke to them, no head was raised. At the front porch of the fraternity house Reinhart stopped and put the suitcase down. When Spud asked him to come in, he shook his head. "I'll be seeing you," he said, and went off down the walk.

The brothers were expecting Spud and gathered around him in a cluster at the front door and said, "Congratulations, boy. We're glad to have you with us!" One after another gave him (their little fingers interlocking) the pledge grip.

Armstrong wasn't there. He had taken his girl to a movie, and one of the other boys led Spud upstairs to his room. It was not the corner one, as he had hoped, but it was a large square room, with three windows, a comfortable chair for reading, two study tables, two dressers, green curtains, and plain cream-colored walls. His roommate turned out to be a boy named Shorty Stevenson, who was majoring in economics and wore glasses.

By ten o'clock Spud had finished putting his clothes away and he sat down at his new desk. His pencils, blotter, fountain pen, ruler, and ink were in their usual exact arrangement. His chemistry book was open before him, at the next day's assignment. The only thing that disturbed his sense of order was the boy who sat studying quietly, four feet away. Shorty Stevenson had on a maroon-colored bathrobe over green and orange striped pajamas. Lymie's bathrobe was blue and he always wore white pajamas.

In a sudden reversal of feeling Spud wanted to empty

all the bureau drawers and start packing again. This isn't right, any of it, he said to himself.

He began to think about Lymie coming home to the bare ugly room on the other side of town. He saw the boys meeting him—Reinhart or Colter or Howard, maybe, or Freeman—at the head of the stairs, and telling him what had happened. Spud saw Lymie trying to pretend that it didn't matter, that he wasn't upset by it; and then a few minutes later, undressing and getting ready for bed and going up the stairs alone.

For the first time it crossed Spud's mind that he could have waited. He should have stayed there until Lymie got home from Professor Severance's. Or at least left a note for Lymie. It was that, he decided, that was causing him all this uneasiness. And in the next second he recognized that it had nothing to do with Lymie but only with himself; that he was frightened. He didn't like strangers and never had liked them.

All he had to do was to repack his things. But what would Shorty Stevenson think if he got up now and started taking shirts and socks and underwear out of the dresser and putting them back in an empty suitcase?

In a kind of slow panic Spud took his watch off, wound it, and placed it on the desk next to his chemistry book. Then he switched the goosenecked student lamp on and began to read. Sometimes his lips moved, shaping words and formulae. And sometimes his mind veered off toward things that had nothing to do with chemistry: *Why was he here where he didn't want to be? Who made him do it?*

They were both reasonable questions.

38

When Lymie managed through Reinhart to loan Spud a hundred dollars, so that he could join the fraternity if he wanted to, Lymie believed that he was acting under a wholly unselfish impulse. But if that was true, why wasn't Spud happy afterward? Why didn't the unselfish act (it had taken Lymie two long dreary summers to save that hundred dollars) lead to some good? From that which is genuinely good, good only ought to flow; not misery and misunderstanding.

The next morning when Spud awoke he was still lost, still unsure what he wanted to do. He was afraid to tell Armstrong that he had changed his mind. Armstrong would think he was crazy. They had given him all the time in the world to decide, and there was no way for them to know that he had done it all in a rush. The best thing to do, he decided finally, was to get Lymie into the fraternity as soon as possible.

He asked Lymie to dinner on guest night and Lymie came. He was all dressed up but with his shoes scuffed as usual, and the shirt he was wearing was not entirely clean. Lymie would never understand, Spud thought sadly looking across the table at him, how things like that counted against you. Lymie's feelings were deeply hurt, from the look in his eyes, and from the care that he took to make everything seem natural between them. But that, Spud decided, they could straighten out later, after Lymie had moved into the fraternity house. Spud didn't know quite how to suggest this to Armstrong but he figured that as soon as Armstrong and the rest of the brothers saw how bright Lymie was, they'd take him into the living room and pledge him.

After dinner Spud showed Lymie over the house. Lymie admired Spud's room and asked to be shown where he slept in the dorm. When Spud pressed him for his approval he said reluctantly that the house was very nice and that he liked the fellows very much. Spud revealed his plans, and Lymie shook his head. It was a fine idea, he said, but he was sure that they wouldn't ask him to join the fraternity.

He was invited for two guest nights in a row, and then he came and went casually. Sometimes he was at the fraternity house for a meal when the boys were on their ordinary behavior. They came down to the dining room helter-skelter, some of them without ties and their shirt collars open, and fought over second helpings and sang off key deliberately. Sometimes he and Spud studied together in Spud's room, of an evening. The boys in the fraternity were friendly toward Lymie, and accepted him, but as an outsider, a foreigner with all the proper credentials. Their attitude was a good enough indication of what he could expect, socially, the rest of his life. If he had been the kind of person who mixes easily and makes a good first impression, he wouldn't have walked past the plate glass window of LeClerc's pastry shop, years before, when he was in high school. Nor would he have felt the need of a special entrance to the iron fence that surrounded the yard outside his own house, when he was a child. He would have used the front gate, like other people.

39

As soon as Spud moved out of "302" the closet in his and Lymie's room, which had always seemed ample, contracted. It was too small even for Lymie's clothes. It was also very disorderly. Lymie made an effort to straighten it occasionally, though his idea of order was not Spud's. He didn't really mind confusion, but he was afraid that Spud might come over to see him and be upset because the closet wasn't the way he had always kept it. Day after day passed and Spud didn't show up. The closet became a catchall. Shoes, bedroom slippers, rubbers, a battered felt hat that belonged to nobody, wire coat hangers, a box of stale Nabiscos, shirts, underwear, socks, handkerchiefs, a suitcase, a crinkled necktie . . . all this and more was in the pile on the closet floor. The closet became indistinguishable from all the others on the second floor of the rooming house. When Lymie undressed at night, he hung his trousers upside down, by the cuffs in a dresser drawer. In the morning he left his pajamas where he stepped out of them.

He saw Spud every afternoon at the gymnasium. One day when Spud found somebody to box with, he brought his gloves over for Lymie to tie, as usual, but he stood looking past Lymie at the trapeze net. Lymie observed that his eyes had a cold glitter in them. When he finished tying the gloves, Spud walked away. At first Lymie thought that Spud must be sore at somebody else, since he himself had done nothing. But from that moment, Spud avoided looking at Lymie or speaking to him. Although Lymie was bewildered, he kept on coming to the gymnasium, day after day. The fact that he still had access to Spud's hands was a comfort to him. It was at least something. Afterward, while Spud was below in the shower room, he waited by the open locker. When Spud had finished dressing he managed, without either looking at Lymie or speaking to him, to indicate that he was ready to go. It would have been easy for him to hunt up Armstrong and walk home with him, instead of with Lymie, but he didn't. They weighed themselves in the front hall, and then, as they walked away from the gymnasium,

Lymie usually made some careful, almost natural remark, to which Spud didn't reply.

Lymie went to bed every night at ten o'clock, as usual, but he had trouble getting to sleep. He was conscious of the cold all around the edges of the bed. Wherever he put out a hand or a bare foot, it was icy cold and it remained that way.

If you take a puppy away from the litter you can keep it from whimpering at night by bedding it down with an alarm clock and a hot water bottle. Deceived by the warmth, it will accept the ticking of the clock for the beating of its mother's heart. Lymie learned to make similar sad substitutions. The other pillow, the one Spud had slept on, at Lymie's back warmed him almost as quickly as a living body. By an effort of the imagination, his own arm, thrown lightly across his chest, became Spud's arm, and then he could sleep.

But it was sleep of a different kind, restless and uneasy. The dreams that came to him were troubled, even the ones that began in happiness and security. Usually when he awoke he could remember only certain threads —fragments of what had frightened him. But there was one dream that remained intact in his mind. He was standing on a street corner with Mrs. Latham. They were looking at a circus parade and they just had time, after the calliope had passed, to run to the next corner and see the parade all over again, coming back. Only this time the circus animals swerved and marched up onto the sidewalk, so that he was crowded back against a high wire netting which stretched between the sidewalk and the street. He left Mrs. Latham standing there and went into a large hotel, and downstairs to the men's room, where he urinated. When he came back the parade was over and Mrs. Latham was gone. He asked several people about her and one man pointed to a railway trestle, which was enclosed, with five stories built on top of the level where

the trains ran. She was up there. Somebody, a man, a man
with an evil face, had grabbed hold of her, while he was
in the hotel, and had taken her away and now she was in
trouble and it was his fault. He should never have left
her alone on the street corner while the parade was passing by.

He thought he saw her at one of the windows high
up on the trestle but it might not have been Mrs. Latham.
There were many windows and people kept appearing at
them, sinister people. The woman he saw, the one who
appeared to be in such distress, might have been somebody else. The woman he saw in the street, later, *was*
Mrs. Latham. She had disguised herself with a red wig, so
that she looked much younger and like the women who
used to come to see his father, the women whose voices
were too loud and whose dresses kept coming up over
their knees. He knew her, even so, but he couldn't go to
her. She went up to an elderly man who was walking
with his wife and put her arms around him and begged
him to save her, but the man didn't understand, and his
wife interfered, and people gathered around them in the
street, so that there was no hope, even before the man
with the evil face came down once more from the high
trestle.

Whether the man took her away or what happened
to her, Lymie didn't know because he found himself in a
stony field. The field stretched as far as the eye could
see, and he was still there, walking and walking, when
the morning light awakened him.

40

During the last days of February, after a heavy snow, the
thermometer went down to zero at night and rose only
a few degrees in the daytime. The wind was from the

north and nothing, not even a coonskin coat, was adequate protection against it.

The boys at "302" slept with their overcoats spread over the foot of their beds, and woke in the night and complained bitterly of the cold. Amsler, who had been sleeping alone, moved into Lymie's bed. Though Lymie had every reason to be grateful for human warmth, he waited until Amsler was asleep and then withdrew shivering to the farthest edge of the bed. For an hour and a half he lay there, not daring to move. Then he slipped out of bed and crept downstairs and spent the rest of the night in Reinhart's big chair, with two coats spread over him. At six o'clock, stiff with cold, and lightheaded from lack of sleep, he went into his own room and sat down at the desk. *Whatever it is that keeps you away*, he wrote, *so that we aren't able to talk to each other like we used to, I think it's time we did something about it. If I've done anything to offend you, I'm sorry. You haven't done anything to me. And even if you had it wouldn't make any difference. Since my mother died you're the only person who has meant very much to me . . .*

That afternoon, when Professor Severance started writing questions on the blackboard, the two seats on either side of Lymie were still vacant. Twenty minutes after the examination had begun, the classroom door opened and Sally tiptoed in and took her seat in the second row, next to Lymie. Her cheeks were red with cold. She looked at the questions on the board and then, in a slightly dazed way, at the blank examination book on the arm of her seat.

She barely nodded to Lymie. "The old English madrigal," she wrote, "was an amatory poem to be sung by three or more voices." The musical implications, Professor Severance had once said, were not to be lost sight of. Fortunately, she hadn't lost sight of them.

It was some time before Sally discovered the large question mark on Lymie's blotter. She shook her silver fountain pen, which had become clogged, and wrote "Hope" on the edge of her own blotter. Lymie had to wait until they emerged from the room where the examination was being held, for further enlightenment.

"The weirdest thing," Sally exclaimed as she closed the door behind her. "Hope had an exam in botany this morning, and she wasn't prepared for it—I was over at the house for supper last night, but I've been living at home. She told me she was going to tell Mrs. Sisson that she had appendicitis, and spend the morning in bed. And this noon I met Bernice Crawford and she said that Mrs. Sisson had called Dr. Rogers—you know that bald-headed little man with the goatee, the one that's always pinching people. Girls, I mean. I don't think he pinches boys. But anyway, he rushed Hope off to the hospital and took her appendix out before lunch. That's why I was late. I went to see her. She was still under the anesthetic, but they said she was coming along all right. Only there was nothing wrong with her, and she can't afford an operation. My God, Lymie, the things people get themselves into!"

"Maybe she really did have appendicitis," Lymie said.

"In a pig's ear!"

The door opened and Lymie moved to one side, so that two girls could get past.

"What are you looking so bedraggled about?" Sally asked.

"Who, me?" Lymie asked. "I feel fine."

"You don't look it. Maybe you'd better have your appendix out too."

"I can't," Lymie said. "I forgot to join the Hospital Association."

"Well then, you'd better not," Sally said.

He brought out the note and said, "Would you mind giving this to Spud?"

"Won't you be seeing him at the gym?"

Lymie hesitated and then shook his head. "Not this afternoon," he said. "I've got some work to do. I have to study for an hour exam."

"You aren't sore at each other?"

"No," Lymie said.

She sighed and put the envelope in her pocket. "I won't be seeing him until after supper probably. Do you know, Lymie, when I first knew you, you were different from the way you are now."

"In what way?"

"Well," she said slowly, "for one thing, you didn't tell lies."

41

Lymie went up to the dorm early that night, knowing that if Spud were coming it would have been before this, because pledges were not allowed out of the fraternity house on a week night after seven-thirty. He was hoping that he could fall asleep immediately and not know when Amsler came, but he turned and turned in the cold bed, without making a place for himself, and after awhile, he heard steps on the stairs. The door swung open and Howard and Geraghty came in.

"It's the whining," Geraghty said, as the door swung shut behind him. "If it wasn't for the whining I wouldn't care so much one way or the other. But this always wanting to know where you've been and who you were with and why you didn't call her up. It's enough to drive a guy nuts."

A bed creaked and Howard said, "Jesus, it's cold!"

"Somebody must have told her about Louise," Geraghty said mournfully. "She didn't say so but I'm pretty sure that's what must have happened."

Howard yawned. "Go to sleep," he said.

So Geraghty had a new girl, Lymie thought. And he hadn't got the old one in trouble after all, in spite of Reinhart's prophecies. Or maybe because of them. But why should Geraghty get tired of a girl who was so pretty and loving? Did he just want a change? And what would happen when Geraghty got tired of his new girl?

Lymie was not really interested in Geraghty or Geraghty's girls; he pulled the other pillow around to his back and waited. In a few minutes the door swung open again. It was Steve Rush this time. Freeman came shortly afterward. Then Pownell marched in, and Reinhart after him. Their beds creaked, and there was a soft rustling of covers as they settled down under the weight of coats and comforters. The wind tore at the corners of the house as if it had some personal spite against it and against all the people lying awake and asleep under the mansard roof. A floor board contracted. Lymie thought of Hope over in the university hospital. He heard the chimes in the Law Building strike midnight and wondered where Amsler was.

Lymie was hanging on the edge of sleep when he heard a step on the stairs, and it was something that he had imagined so many times the last few weeks that he didn't believe in it; not until the door swung wide open and the step (which couldn't be anyone else's) came nearer and nearer. Lymie waited. He felt the covers being raised, and then the bed sinking down on the other side, exactly as he had imagined it. Then, lifted on a great wave of unbelieving happiness, he turned suddenly and found Spud there beside him.

Spud was in his underwear and he was shivering.

"My God, it's cold," he said. He pushed the pillow aside, and dug his chin in Lymie's shoulder.

Anybody else in the world, Lymie thought, anybody but Spud would have said something, would at least have explained that he was sorry. But Spud hated explanations and besides there was no need for them. It was enough that Spud was here, whether for good or just for this once; that it was Spud's arm he felt now across his chest.

Lymie lay back on the wave of happiness and was supported by it. The bed had grown warm all around him. Spud's breathing deepened and became slower. His chest rose and fell more quietly, rose and fell in the breathing of sleep. Lymie, stretched out beside him, wished that it were possible to die, with this fullness in his heart for which there were no words and couldn't ever be. All that he had ever wanted, he had now. All that was lost had come back to him, just because he had been patient.

He heard Amsler come in and go to his own bed. Then, managing to keep Spud's warm foot against his, Lymie turned and lay on his back, so that Spud's arm would go farther around him. He made no effort to go to sleep, and sleep when it came to him was sudden. One minute he was wide awake thinking, and the next he was lying unconscious, on his back, as if he had been felled by a heavy blow.

BOOK FOUR

A Reflection from the Sky

42

Though it came from human throats the roar was animal.
Certain voices rose above it screaming
    Come on, colored boy
but the two fighters exchanging blow for blow didn't
hear. Except when the referee came between them saying
    Break it up, break it up
they were alone, under the smoky white light from the
reflectors. They were in a world of silence and one of
them was tired.

*Uppercut, Francis . . . Old Man Uppercut . . . the
head . . . up . . . up*

He's tired too, Rudy

*The head, not down there . . . up . . . up . . .
throw it in his face*

Oooh, that dirty nigger

The ice cream man moved in a world of noise, looking for upraised hands, for the quick turn of a head. At
that moment all heads were turned away from him, all
eyes were on the ring. The crowd moaned and moaned
again as the white boy sank from the ropes to the canvas.
In the back of the balcony a baby started crying. The referee waved the Negro to a neutral corner. On the count
of seven the white boy rose to his knees. At the count of
nine he was on his feet again but groggy.

Finish him off, Francis

*Not there . . . up . . . up . . . atsa baby . . . a
little higher and he's through*

*Come on, Francis . . . bring it up . . . up . . .
that's it . . . cute . . . more*

Good-by, Rudy

What hit him

Fall down, Rudy, you're through

Stop the fight

Come on, Francis . . . finish up fast

In the belly

That's it . . . downstairs, Rudy

*He don't know where it came from . . . he still
don't know*

In the belly, Francis

It's all yours, Francis

The fight was not, as it turned out, all Francis's. At
the end of the third round, the fighters broke apart. The
Negro went on dancing until the decision was announced. Then the handlers stepped through the ropes,
bringing robes and towels. Rudy's handlers congratulated

him. There were several voices from the balcony assuring Francis that he had been robbed, but nothing was done about it. He and the white boy faded into the darkness, into the thick fog of cigar smoke, and two other fighters took their places.

The announcer moved up to the microphone.

Ladies and . . . gentlemen . . . this contest three rounds

One of the fighters was towheaded, with very white skin. His weight was distributed in chunks over his body, giving a look of boxlike squareness to his back and shoulders, his thighs, and the calves of his rather short legs.

From Chicago's West Side . . . wearing black trunks . . . weighing one-forty-seven . . . Larry Brannigan Junior

At the first sound of applause the towheaded fighter doubled up, as if from a stomach cramp, and with one arm held out stiffly he wheeled around backward in a complete circle—the favorite accepting homage from his admirers.

From the University of . . . wearing purple trunks . . . weighing a hundred forty-six and three quarters pounds . . . Spud Latham

Again applause. Spud raised his glove to his father, who was watching from the door to the dressing rooms. Mr. Latham saw the gesture, but didn't realize that it was for him. The past four nights, taking on all comers, Spud had wiped out his father's failures, one after another. Mr. Latham was no longer the same man.

The two fighters, their seconds, and the referee stood in the center of the ring under the glaring white light. The referee was heavy-set and had bushy black eyebrows. He was wearing gray trousers, a white shirt, a black bow tie, a black leather belt, and boxing shoes. His face suggested no particular nationality. Neither Brannigan nor Spud heard his instructions. They were sizing each other up. There was a cut over Spud's left eye which had three clamps in it. This caught Brannigan's fancy and he smiled. Hit properly, the clamps could be driven straight into Spud's head. The referee looked at the cut before he checked their hands and wrappings.

In his corner, waiting for the fight to begin, Spud suddenly felt limp. His handlers were hovering over him, telling him to feel Brannigan out in the first round. Spud nodded, wondering what they would say if he leaned forward now and confessed to them that he didn't have any stomach. His knees were moving all by themselves, and his hands, inside all of that tape, felt soft as putty. The whistle blew. He got up and scraped the soles of his shoes in the resin box. Then he stood with his gloves on the ropes, waiting. The rubber mouthpiece was forced between his lips. It was wet and it tasted wonderful. At the sound of the bell he swung around and saw Brannigan coming toward him fast. Spud crouched and let Brannigan have one—a left hook that caught him under the heart. The crowd moaned. Brannigan missed a wild left swing and took a left and right to the jaw. They went into a clinch and the referee separated them.

Atta boy, Brannigan, give it to him . . . open up that eye

Left, Latham

Keep punching that eye

There . . . that hit him

That's all right . . . Junior's taking it easy . . . he's not getting excited

Jab it . . . keep your left hand up, Latham, lead with your left hand, not the right . . . the left hand . . . keep the left hand in his face

Look out for your chin, dear friend

Go way from that

Keep your head, Junior . . . take it easy . . . three rounds

Ooh

That hit him . . . that's the only one that hit him

What a headache

What happened . . . what happened

Come on, Latham . . . let's go

Keep that left hand out there . . . left in his face will knock him out

He needs more than a left . . . he needs a left and a right for that boy

What happened . . . nothing happened . . . don't worry, Brannigan

He's a murderer

Hit him with a wet glove . . . a good one . . . a wet one

Spud backed Brannigan against the ropes and slugged him twice before the referee, for what reason it was not clear, came between them. There were boos and hisses from the crowd.

Go on . . . get out

Go way from there

He had no right to stop him . . . they were both on their feet

Right . . . right . . . so what

So he should leave him alone . . . the fellow was on the ropes

Maybe the referee has got bets on him

Use the left hand

Off the ropes, Junior

All of a sudden the referee they got him from Halsted Street

Keep away from those ropes, you fool

Shut up

Why should I shut up? I paid my admission . . . didn't I? . . . The guy had the fight in the first round and the referee steps between them

Keep it in his face, Latham . . . the left

Eh, Brannigan . . . what happened?

Between the first and second rounds Spud leaned back with his legs sprawled out in front of him and tried to relax. He felt the cold water being poured over his head and spilling down his chest. His gloved hands were taken from the ropes and placed on his knees. One of the handlers held the elastic away from his belly and massaged his chest and solar plexus. The other bent over him, talking earnestly. Spud was too keyed up to pay any attention. All he wanted was to get back in the center of the ring. This fight and one more and he'd have the Golden Gloves. The whistle blew. Spud pushed the mouthpiece back in, with his glove, and got to his feet. The stool was removed. The handlers crawled out through the ropes and went on talking to him, from outside the ring. Then the bell. Then he was fighting.

Apparently it made no difference to the referee that he was unpopular with the crowd. He continued to move quickly in wide circles around the fighters, coming between them frequently and forcing them apart with his hands. His face was extraordinarily serene, as if he knew the outcome of each fight before it began. He saw Brannigan graze Spud's chin with the lacing of his glove, and warned him about it, but most of the time he was looking at Spud and the expression in his eyes was sad.

Spud was certain that the first two rounds were his. He went into the third determined to win by a knockout. He could see that Brannigan's arms were so tired that it was all he could do to lift them. He himself felt fresh as a daisy. When Brannigan finally left himself wide open, Spud had the knockout blow all aimed and ready. Brannigan fell on his knees and Spud, in his excitement and haste, before he could stop himself, hit him again.

Standing there alone in the center of the ring, after the referee had stopped the fight, Spud heard the crowd for the first time. It took him several seconds to realize that they were booing at him.

43

Two figures rose up from where they had been sitting, their view of the ring partly cut off by a large pillar, and made their way through the aisles. One of them was a girl. Her coat was thrown open and she was wearing a bunch of purple violets pinned to the collar. The young man with her was about nineteen. He carried his overcoat and a Scotch plaid muffler over one arm, and the same distress that was in the girl's face was also in his, like a reflection from the sky.

To get from the arena to the dressing rooms it was necessary to go through a lounge which had orange wicker furniture in it. Around the green walls were framed autographed pictures of boxers and wrestlers. From the door of this room Mr. Latham had watched Spud making his way to the ring. He was there waiting when Spud came back, his blue bathrobe tied around him and the sleeves hanging empty at his sides.

Disaster was something that Mr. Latham had had to contend with all his life. It didn't astonish him any more. But he was sorry, standing there in the doorway with a dead cigar in his mouth—that the run of bad luck was beginning now for Spud. When Spud's eyes met his father's for a second, Mr. Latham shook his head in sympathy and understanding.

Spud sat down on a wicker settee. His hair was soaking wet. The sweat was running down his forehead, down his chest, down the insides of his arms and legs. He had a headache and his mouth felt as if it were filled with cotton. He sat with his shoulders hunched, his wrists crossed under the folds of his bathrobe, handcuffed together by what had happened to him. The clumsy boxing gloves were resting on his bare knees. Another fight had already started in the arena, but Spud was involved in the last one. He couldn't get out of that moment when Brannigan had left himself wide open. From there things could have gone quite differently. *He slugged Brannigan and then he waited.* That was how it should have been, and how he kept making it be, over and over.

Although Mr. Latham seemed to be watching the fight, his look was inward. Lymie and Sally were almost close enough to speak to him before he saw them and stepped back from the doorway, so they could pass through it. When Spud saw them coming toward him across the room, he rose to his feet, ready to defend himself against both of them with his life's blood. *They were there. They had seen it.* But then he felt Sally's arms around him, hugging him, and he looked into her eyes and after that it was all right. That he had lost the fight with Brannigan didn't matter in the least.

It mattered to Lymie, though. "That dirty, double-crossing referee," he said. "You had the fight won in the first round."

Spud turned to him and smiled. "Pulled a fast one, didn't you?"

"We didn't know we were coming," Sally said. "I just couldn't stand it any more. You don't know what it was like having to wait for the next day's paper, and not being able to concentrate on anything for more than two minutes. I thought I was going crazy. So this morning Lymie and I looked up the train schedule and cut all our classes and came."

"What did your mother say?"

"She didn't say anything. She didn't know we were coming. I told Hope to call her after the train left."

Spud glanced uneasily at his father, while she was talking. When she finished he said, "Dad, this is Sally Forbes."

Sally took her hand away from Spud and put it in his. They smiled at each other and were, from that moment, friends.

"What happened to your eye?" Lymie asked.

"I got a bad cut," Spud said.

"When?"

"Last night. It bled all through the last round. After it was over they put some clamps in it."

"I'm glad I wasn't here," Sally said.

"I would just as soon have been somewhere else myself," Spud said. "That guy Brannigan, he kept trying to open it up but he didn't touch it once." His face lengthened. He was back in that moment when Brannigan left himself wide open. There was no hurry now.

"Don't worry," Sally said, with her cheek against his. "Don't even think about it."

Spud brought his arms out from under the bathrobe, and folded them around her.

"It seems as if you'd been away for years," she said sadly.

"Five days," Spud said. "It seemed like a long time to me too." He felt something soft and drew away from her. It was the violets. They had touched his bare chest. "Where'd you get the flowers?"

"Lymie bought them for me," Sally said. "He thought I ought to have some violets. I said this wasn't any symphony concert we were going to but he bought them anyway. And then we had dinner at a place called the Tip-Top Inn, where they have pictures of nursery rhymes on the walls, and an orchestra—all for eighty cents."

"It's across from the Art Institute," Lymie explained.

Spud took his arms away from Sally and appeared to

be concerned with the lacing of his gloves. "I have to go back in there," he said, jerking his head toward the arena. "As soon as this fight is over."

Sally looked at him in bewilderment but he avoided her eyes.

"I'll get something out of it anyway," he said, "even if it's only third place. You better go back to your seats." His tone was harsh. He might have been speaking to strangers.

"We'll stay here," Sally said quietly.

Lymie, who from long habit should have been sensitive to the changes in Spud's mood, had no idea that anything was wrong. The person who is both intelligent and observing cannot at the same time be innocent. He can only pretend to be; to others sometimes, sometimes to himself. Since Lymie didn't notice that anything was wrong with Spud, one is forced to conclude that he didn't wish to notice it. Some impulse that he was not willing to admit even to himself must have prompted him to buy violets for Sally. They reopened an old wound that was far more serious than the cut over Spud's eye, and one that it wasn't possible to put clamps in.

At the sound of the bell Spud left them and disappeared into the crowd. A moment or two later he and another fighter emerged under the white light of the reflectors. All that had happened before happened again, like a movie film being run through a second time, but it didn't last as long. In the first round Spud did something so stupid that Lymie, watching him from the doorway, contracted his shoulders and turned away in despair.

Spud's opponent was an Italian boy with black hair and eyes and soft muscles. Spud was having everything his own way. The referee had just pried them apart and when the Italian boy came toward Spud again, Spud doubled up, caught the Italian boy in the pit of the stomach with his shoulder and then straightened up with a quick jerk. As if the rules had been changed suddenly and this was now a wrestling match, the Italian boy flew clear over Spud and landed flat on his back.

The silence lasted several seconds, during which a single voice could be heard saying:

Ice cream . . .

The referee blew his whistle. Then the catcalls began, and the screaming. Pop bottles flew through the air, and the booing was like the waves of the sea.

44

After the radio had been turned off there was an unnatural quiet in the Lathams' living room. Mrs. Latham was sitting on the sofa in the full glare of the overhead light. Her face was gray and blotched with suffering, and her eyes, wide open, saw only what was in her mind—terrible fantasies in which her son, her beautiful son, was brought home to her, bruised and bleeding.

Helen crossed the room and knelt beside her. "Mother darling," she said, "listen to me. He's all right. It's over now, and you mustn't think about it, you mustn't grieve about it any more. The cut over his eye isn't serious. It will heal in a week's time and nobody will ever know it was there." She took her mother's hands between her own and chafed them, as if they were cold.

"He's got a taste of it," Mrs. Latham said quietly. "And there's nothing anybody can do to stop him. He'll ruin his life."

"Well, let him," Helen said bitterly.

Mrs. Latham made a slight gesture which her daughter saw and understood. The gesture meant that she was not to say anything against Spud. Jealousy welled up in her. There was no way that she could keep herself from knowing that her mother loved Spud more than she did her, and always had, and always would. But that didn't make any difference. She would go right on looking after her mother, and making her life easier for her, and maybe some day. . . .

"Let him go ahead and ruin his life," she said aloud. "Let him go on boxing until he gets his nose broken and ends up with cauliflower ears, and looking like a thug. That's what he is anyway, so he might as well look like one."

Mrs. Latham shook her head.

"If he can come home the way he did Monday night and see you in the condition you were in then," Helen said, "and go right back and fight the next night, and the night after that, and again tonight, regardless of what it is doing to you, then I don't care what happens to him. Almost any stranger that walked in off the street I could have more feeling for than I have for him right now. It's a terrible thing to say but it's true."

Mrs. Latham was searching for her handkerchief in the folds of her dress. Before she found it, the tears had begun to slide down her cheeks.

"Oh, I'm sorry," Helen exclaimed. "Really I am. You know I don't mean it." She took her own handkerchief and dried her mother's cheeks, but there was no stopping the flow of tears, now that they had started. "Why do you wait up?" she said. "You're exhausted and you ought to be in bed this minute. Come on. Come take your clothes off. I'll turn the covers down for you and you can slip into bed. I'll wait up for them."

Mrs. Latham took the handkerchief and put it to her face and then, turning her head slightly, shook with sobbing. Helen put her arms around her and clung to her, weeping too. She thought of her mother always as a tower of strength, and to see her this way now, so stricken, so helpless, was more than she could bear. It also frightened her.

"I'm going to make you some coffee," she said. "You stay here and be quiet."

She went into the bathroom and held a washcloth under the cold water faucet, wrung it out, and then came back into the living room and laid it on her mother's face, on her eyes and her hot forehead. She did this several times before she finally went out to the kitchen and took the coffee down from the shelf of the cupboard, and began measuring it into the percolator with a big spoon.

All *they* ever saw in her mother was somebody who administered to their comfort, kept their clothes picked up and in order, fed them, and made a home for them to come to, when it suited their convenience.

When Spud was a child she had loved him, but now that he was grown, it was impossible. Nobody could love him. He was an entirely different person, ungrateful, unmanageable, ill-tempered and surly. There was no use trying to get her mother to stop caring for Spud, because she always would, but sooner or later her mother would have to realize that nothing could be done for him, and then she would give up trying.

If anything happened to her father, they'd have to give up the apartment, probably, and she and her mother could take a smaller place. It needn't be very luxurious. Just a couple of rooms, large enough so that they wouldn't get under each other's feet, and she'd work and make enough money to support them, and they could live together quietly and in peace.

This idea had been in the back of Helen's mind ever since the letters had stopped coming from Wisconsin. Mrs. Latham saw Helen always as a little girl, a very good, obedient child, and so, if she had known what her daughter was thinking, she would have been surprised, as one is now and then by what children do and say. The plan itself would not have appealed to her. She had every intention of keeping her family together and intact forever. But she couldn't drink the coffee after Helen made it and brought it to her, and Helen put the cup and saucer on the table next to the sofa. There the coffee gradually grew cold.

It was after midnight when the car drove up in front of the apartment. The windows on the second floor were still lighted but no face peered out from behind the living room curtains, and the street lamps strung at intervals through the park served only to show how deserted it was at this time of night.

Mr. Latham turned the motor off and said, "Well, here we are, home again."

Reluctantly, as if they had expected to spend the night in the back seat of the car with the robe over their knees, first Lymie, then Sally, and then Spud piled out. Sally pulled at her skirt and pushed her hair back under her hat. "Do I look all right?" she asked.

"You look fine," Spud said. The yawn that he was trying to suppress came out in his voice. She saw that he hadn't even been looking at her, that he was too tired to care how she looked. The elm trees at the edge of the park were rocking in the damp March wind. The sky was clouded over.

"I don't feel the least bit sleepy," she remarked, as she followed the two boys up the walk.

Spud had forgotten his key and they waited in the vestibule for Mr. Latham, who had stayed behind to lock the car doors. On the second landing they waited again. Lymie glanced surreptitiously at the violets on Sally's coat. They were beginning to curl. He had never bought flowers for a girl before. Looking at them, and then at Spud, who was leaning against the wall, Lymie thought: *If anything should happen to him, if he should be killed in an accident or something, Sally would probably marry me, because I'm Spud's best friend and I would cherish his memory.* . . . That this thought might involve a wish, he didn't perceive. It was merely one of those mixed-up ideas that occurred to him sometimes when he was very sleepy. He put it out of his mind immediately, and didn't remember afterward that he had ever thought it.

When Mr. Latham put his key in the door and pushed it open, Lymie saw that nothing was changed since he had been here last at Christmas time. It was one of the reasons he liked to come here. Nothing ever changed. He slipped his coat off, and his scarf, and dropped them on the chair in the hall, and then he walked into the living room. There his eyes opened wide and he stopped right where he was. The others had to move around him in order to get into the room.

Mrs. Latham was still sitting on the sofa, and in her violently altered condition Lymie recognized one of those changes which happened, so far as he could make out, only to women. His own mother, usually so loving and tender with him, at certain times used to withdraw, leaving him stranded, the center of his life a void. When she had one of her headaches, which came fairly often during the last years of her life, after his father started drinking, she retired into a darkened room and there lay motionless on her bed, with a damp cloth over her eyes, without knowing or caring what happened to Lymie. When he got home from school he used to walk round and round the house before he went in. If the shades were drawn in her bedroom, he knew.

Helen was bending over her mother anxiously, and as the others filed in she turned and faced them with a hatred which made no distinctions; they were all included in it. Spud went up to his mother and said, "It's all over now," which was as near as he could come to telling her that he was sorry. When she didn't answer, he turned away and went out into the hall. Helen bent over her mother again, as if the others (including the girl they had brought home with them, whoever *she* was) were not in the room, or were there with no right and would soon perceive this and go away.

Sally glanced over her shoulder at Spud, for help, but he seemed wholly concerned with hanging his coat in the hall closet. And Lymie, whom she was able to count on under ordinary circumstances, looked frightened and uncertain of what to do. Something was wrong, obviously. It was a scene that belonged to a house with a crepe hanging on the front door and a coffin somewhere and the odors of too many flowers. At that moment, when the only thing she could think of was flight, she felt a strong hand close over her arm. The hand propelled her, unwilling, toward the sofa. She heard a voice that she recognized as Mr. Latham's saying firmly, insistently, "Mother, we've brought one of Spud's friends home with us. This is Sally Forbes."

Mrs. Latham's eyes, so lost in the recesses of her own grief, focused slowly upon Sally. She raised her head with an effort and extended a frail hand. Sally took it and smiled. The eyes that looked into hers were red from weeping, and there was no reassurance in them. But something—politeness, a sense of obligation, of responsibility toward a guest—gave Mrs. Latham the strength to take hold and manage her family again.

"You'd better take your coat off, my dear," she said, and then, turning to Helen, "She can sleep in your room tonight, and you sleep in here."

The atmosphere in the living room changed immediately. Mr. Latham's face cleared. He felt in the breast pocket of his coat and brought out a cigar. Lymie went up to Mrs. Latham and kissed her on the cheek. There was no answering pat, but tonight he didn't expect it, and wasn't alarmed when she merely said, "Good evening, Lymie."

Spud came back from the hall and tugged at his sleeve. "You can sleep with me," he said.

They had already turned toward the hall when the ax fell.

"I think Lymie had better go to his own home tonight," Mrs. Latham said.

"The bed's big enough," Spud said. "We've slept together in it lots of times."

"You need your rest," Mrs. Latham said.

Lymie wasted no time picking up his scarf and overcoat. He saw that Spud was looking at him apologetically, and so he said, "I'll call you in the morning. . . . Good night, everybody!" and closed the door behind him.

On the way down the stairs he remembered the feeling he had had the first afternoon that he came home with Spud. It was a kind of premonition, he realized. Everything that he had thought would happen then was happening now. He had been wrong only about the time.

45

During the early part of April there was a week of undeniable spring. It was in the air first, before the ground or the bare trees gave any sign of it; and its effect generally was to make people miss appointments and forget what it was that they had been about to say. Along with the marriage of the earth and the sun, other strange influences were at work—the renewal of grass, the northward migration of birds, the swelling of buds on the trees.

Classroom windows were flung open, and instructors

in economics and bacteriology and political science raised
their voices above the sound of power lawn mowers.
They spoke to empty seats, to a collection of figures that
looked alive but were actually made of pieces of colored
paper pasted over a framework of sticks, to ears that had
no hearing, to minds that, masquerading in leaves and
flowers, were even now on their way to the forest, up the
mountainside, down to the seashore, where, according to
ancient custom, certain rites were about to be performed
which would make the earth fertile and green.

The university tennis courts were weeded and rolled
and marked with new tape. All morning and all afternoon
tennis balls bounced and were struck back. The scoring
(*thirty-forty . . . love-five . . . deuce it is*) was added
to the other spring sounds.

With all the windows open and the sunlight streaming in, the men's gymnasium was like a pavilion. The trapeze performers set up their apparatus outside on the
grass, and there was a constant clatter of spiked shoes as
baseball players came in and went out of the building.
The empty football stadium (capacity seventy thousand)
was taken over by thin, tense-faced runners, hurdlers, and
high jumpers. Botany classes filed out of science buildings two by two. They were on their way out to the edge
of town where, in the cold running water of the drainage
ditch, spirogyra and chlodophora were to be found. The
girls had charge of the green laboratory jars. The boys
took off their shoes and their bright-colored socks, rolled
their trousers above the knee, and waded in slowly, their
bare feet searching for soft places in the gravel bottom.
They came out of the water bearing slimy specimens in
their hands and in their eyes the sorrowful realization of
all that they had lost by starting to school at the age of
six.

On the south campus two gardeners swept the cement bottom of the lily pond and then stood and watched

it fill with clean water. The apple trees in the university orchards were sprayed, according to the latest methods. Lambs that had been born in March in the big university barns were now let out to pasture. Dogs were seen in pairs on the Broad Walk, and one of them made an obstinate attempt to attend Professor Forbes's lecture on St. Anselm and his logical proof of the existence of God.

The nights were languid and soft with a tropical odor that had its origin in the thawing corn fields outside of town. Nobody could study. The brick terraces of Tudor and southern colonial fraternity houses were crowded long after supper with boys looking at the moon. Under lunary influence many of them went off and drank spiked beer. Although the university authorities had forbidden serenading, between ten-thirty and eleven o'clock shadows collected in the shrubbery outside sorority houses. There was a campus policeman but he couldn't be everywhere at once. Young male voices, not always on pitch, rose to darkened second-story windows. The serenaders sang the university anthem, "When Day Is Done" and various plagiarisms on "The Sweetheart of Sigma Chi." Then with applause following them, they moved off down the street, unmolested. Around midnight, mattresses and blankets and pillows were hauled out onto flat roofs. Boys who were so fortunate as to belong to a fraternity fell asleep with the moon shining on their faces. And boys who had had to be content with living in rooming houses awoke, morning after morning, with the sun in their eyes.

There were only five people in the English seminar the night of the annual spring celebration. The air that came in through the open windows was too soft to blow papers about, but minds were not, of course, immune to it. Of the five people, four were graduate students with a Ph.D. oral examination to face, and no time to admire the moon or make love on the damp ground. The fifth was

Lymie Peters. The scowling bitter face of Dr. Johnson looked down at them from the wall and approved of their industry, but the bust of Shakespeare was noncommittal.

A faint faraway sound was heard a little after nine o'clock. It might or might not have been cheering. One of the graduate students looked up from his barricade of books, took his glasses off, and announced the true cause of the disturbance. The others listened a moment and then all five went on reading. From time to time they also made crabbed, half-legible notes concerning the date of *Tottel's Miscellany* or the lavish use of similes in *Euphues and His England*. The cheering grew louder and more distinct.

Lymie, having finished the section of Dorothy Wordsworth's *Journals* recommended by Professor Severance, closed the book and restored it to the shelf where he had found it. He was ready to go home now and review separable and inseparable German prefixes. When he got outside the building, he saw that the sky to the south was pink from the glare of an enormous bonfire. The rooming house lay in one direction, excitement was in the other. Lymie started home, but he turned suddenly, hesitated, and then began to retrace his steps. Within half a block he was running.

The bonfire was in a muddy open field north of the stadium, and the field itself was swarming with dark figures. The boys nearest the fire stood out clearly. The firelight kept passing over their faces and hands. Others came out of the surrounding darkness, bringing fuel, and then went back again. Behind their movements there seemed to be some as yet unannounced purpose, some act of violence which would flare up all of a sudden and make the flames turn pale by comparison with it.

Lymie stood on the outer edge of the crowd, where he was not likely to get involved. The year before, in this same field, he'd lost a good coat and had the shirt torn

off his back, in a mud fight between freshmen and soph-
omores.

After climbing forty or fifty feet into the sky, the
flames, for lack of fuel, begun to subside, and darkness
gradually closed in on the field. A voice near the bonfire
yelled, "To the campus!" and there was an answering
roar which produced a stampede. Lymie was caught up in
it before he could retire across the street. He was swept
along willingly enough, his feet mingling with all the
other feet set so abruptly in motion. The running stopped
after two blocks and those who had no desire to be part
of the mob escaped from it. The rest proceeded through
the fraternity district in a shambling, almost orderly fash-
ion, filling the street and the sidewalks, and trampling
on new grass.

When they got to the Union Building, the editor of
the student daily newspaper, a tall, thin, hollow-cheeked
blond boy, appeared on the steps above them and made a
speech. "This is kid stuff!" he shouted. "What's the use
of it? What's the use of destroying a lot of valuable property and getting into trouble and maybe thrown out of
school?"

The mob, which had so far not destroyed anything,
answered, "Drown him!" "Throw the son of a bitch in
the Styx!"

"For what?" the thin-faced boy asked rhetorically.
"For a little fun, maybe, that will reflect on the university
and do serious harm. If you want to do something, then
do something constructive."

There was a surging forward and the boy ducked
hastily into the printing office and locked the door.

"Don't let him get away with that!" a voice cried,
and another voice screamed, "Smash the door down!" but
nobody wanted to be the one to do it. The mob had no
leader. Voices were heard frequently but they didn't seem
to be attached to a particular person, or at least not to

anybody who was willing to appear boldly in front of the others and take charge. The mob waited, milling around outside the Union Building until some of them grew bored and went home. The rest eventually started toward the center of town, which was two miles from the campus. Their destination was the Orpheum Theater, where they would undoubtedly have interfered with the performance of some Japanese acrobats if they hadn't been stopped.

On the way, as they were passing through a little park, they met a student with his date, coming home from the movies. They surrounded this couple and separated them. When the boy struck out frantically, dozens of hands grabbed hold of him, tore his shirt off, gave him a black eye and a bloody mouth. They took the girl's skirts and pulled them over her head and tied them there. Somebody tripped the boy, who was still fighting, and as he fell, they pushed the girl, unharmed, on top of him. This little unpleasantness, this token rape, seemed to give the mob confidence.

When a streetcar appeared around a corner, twenty boys ran to meet it, and one of them managed to pull the trolley off the overhead wire. The streetcar was plunged into abrupt darkness. Before it even came to a stop, it was being rocked from side to side by a hundred hands. The motorman got out, swearing, and put the trolley back on. The boys stood off, and watched him with apparently no thought of interfering. The wooden streetcar lighted up, the motorman climbed on and clanging his bell furiously, moved forward about twenty feet before the lights went out again.

This happened three more times and the last time they pushed a small bonfire under the car, which made a good deal of smoke and frightened the passengers. But the mob had already had enough when that happened, so they let the motorman continue and would have continued themselves except that the Dean of Men appeared miraculously in their midst. He was a slight, almost boyish man of sixty-two. His hair and his mustache were snow white. He looked kind, humorous, and fatherly, but the effect on the boys was as if a rattlesnake had materialized right in front of them on the streetcar tracks. As they backed away from him he began picking certain figures out of the crowd and addressing them by name. "Hello, Johnston . . . Feldcamp, are you here too? . . . Morrison, if I had as much trouble with physics as you seem to have, I'd be studying tonight. . . . Peters, I think you had better beat it for home. . . ."

Lymie thought so too.

On the way he had to pass Spud's fraternity. He went up on the porch, opened the door, and walked in. By that time it was nearly eleven o'clock, and Spud had finished studying and was straightening his desk before he went to bed. After the Golden Gloves tournament he had set to work with two cans of paint, one turkey red, the other black. Everything in the room that could possibly be painted—the door, the window frames, the woodwork, the two study chairs, the tables, the two goosenecked student lamps, the closet curtain rod, the ceiling light fixture, and even the glass ashtray—was either one color or the other. Spud glanced at Lymie's flushed and excited face and then at his muddy shoes. "Where the hell have you been?"

"Spring celebration," Lymie said. He pushed his hat on the back of his head and sank down in a chair.

"I should think you'd have had enough of that, after what happened to you at cap-burning," Spud said.

"This was different," Lymie said.

"What happened? Where'd you go?"

While Lymie was telling him about the riot, Spud got undressed and put his bathrobe on.

"I don't understand it," he said, when Lymie had finished. "If they'd started breaking into sorority houses and throwing furniture out of the windows, the way they did once before, you'd have got yourself into a lot of trouble."

"I thought of that," Lymie said.

"Well," Spud asked irritably, "what did you get mixed up in it for?"

"I don't know," Lymie said. "I honestly don't. Why are you staring at me like that?"

"Because you need to have your head examined."

"I saw the bonfire," Lymie said, "and I guess I just wanted to see what they were going to do."

"You're crazy, that's all that's the matter with you," Spud said. "Or else you've got spring fever."

"I've got something," Lymie said, and stood up and sneezed violently three times while he was buttoning his coat.

46

What Lymie had was a bad cold which lasted ten days, and by the end of that period the ground was once more covered with dirty snow. He took to his bed and started dosing himself. This, instead of forestalling the cold, seemed to make it worse. The boys brought food in to him but he was alone all day in the dormitory. With no one to talk to, he slept a good deal, and one day woke up with a feeling that he was in some unnamable danger. Something, a person, a presence (he couldn't quite imagine it but it nevertheless knew *him*) was waiting outside the door. In a growing uneasiness he got up and went downstairs and dressed. It took longer than usual because he was weak from staying in bed, but his cold, from that moment, began to get better.

In April nothing stays. No purpose in the heavens and certainly no need on earth can keep the wind in any one direction. It blew from the east, from the west, and finally from the south. There were rain clouds and when it rained, thunder and lightning as well. With so much uncertainty in the atmosphere it was not really surprising that again Spud was not himself. Lymie first noticed it when Spud walked past him and asked Armstrong to tie his gloves for him.

Lymie didn't know what the trouble was, but he was not dismayed. He had worn Spud down once before and he was sure that he could do it again. Every day between four-fifteen and four-thirty he appeared at the gymnasium and stood a few feet away from the punching bag where Spud, if he wanted his gloves tied on or any small service like that, wouldn't have to go far to find him. When Spud came up from the showers, Lymie was there waiting by the locker, like a faithful hound. He made no move to open the lock, or to touch anything inside the locker that belonged to Spud. Occasionally while Spud was dressing and afterward on the way home, Lymie would say something to him, but Lymie was always careful not to put the remark in the form of a question, so there was no actual need for Spud to reply.

One day it occurred to Lymie that if he also kept quiet, if he just gave Spud a chance, the situation might change. It did, but not in the way he had expected. Once having joined Spud in that harsh silence, he couldn't escape from it; he had to keep still himself. He walked along, hearing the unfriendly sound of Spud's heelplates as they struck the sidewalk, and watching the swing of Spud's knees. Once or twice his glance went as high as Spud's mouth, drawn in a tight line. It was all that Lymie needed to see. When they came to the corner where Spud turned off to go to the fraternity house, Lymie's hand would rise in a half salute which did not break the silence and yet spoke eloquently. And Spud would nod and walk away.

In German class he and Lymie sat side by side, four days a week, without speaking. When Spud had no paper, Lymie took a sheet out of his notebook and handed it to him, ready to take it back if Spud decided to refuse the offer and write on the bare desk top instead. At such times, Spud longed to lean over and whisper, "How'd we ever get started this way, when you're the best friend I've got. The only one, when you get right down to it. Sally is something different . . ." But he had never been able to say things like that, and besides, Miss Blaiser was at the blackboard writing: (*1*) *When do strong verbs change their stem vowel?* (*2*) *Give the meanings and principal parts of beginnen, beissen, binden, bleiben, finden, gefallen, laufen, lesen, nehmen, rufen, schlafen, schliessen, schreiben, sehen. . . .*

There were also times when Spud would have been willing to leave the fraternity house and move back with Lymie, if the brothers had given him the slightest excuse. Instead of treating him as they did the freshmen, they acted as if he were already initiated. He had no pledge duties, he was never called down in front of the fireplace and paddled on Monday nights, nothing was ever said to him about his attitude or about the right fraternity spirit. Without a grievance he couldn't act, and the brothers wouldn't give him one. He looked everywhere and the nearest to an enemy that he could find was Lymie, who was also his only friend.

One afternoon Spud cut his chemistry class and walked across the campus to the rooming house. He wanted to talk to somebody and he decided to spill everything to Reinhart. When he arrived at "302," Reinhart's room was empty. Spud looked at the schedule of classes tacked to the wall above the desk and saw that Reinhart had no classes the rest of the afternoon. He sat down in the sagging, overstuffed chair to wait.

He had only been there a few minutes when Mr. Dehner's spaniel caught his scent in the front hall and raced to the stairs. He threw himself on Spud, who picked him up, tossed him almost to the ceiling, and caught him on the way down. The dog squirmed in Spud's hands, rolled his bloodshot eyes ecstatically, and wagged his stump of a tail. When Spud put him down, he backed off and with his head turned slightly made a queer sound that was half whimper and half bark.

"Well," a familiar penetrating voice said, "if it isn't Mr. Latham! How that poor dog has missed you."

Spud turned and saw Mr. Dehner standing in the doorway with a dust mop in his hand.

"Have you come back to us? I was saying just the other day to Colter I think it was, or maybe it was Geraghty. I said, 'Some day Mr. Latham will be back. You wait and see. He's not the fraternity type. And if he saw the way Mr. Peters keeps that room—' My dear boy, you ought to go and look at it. Just like the town dump. I'm terribly fond of Mr. Peters. He's so sensitive and all, but I declare I don't know how he finds his books when he wants to study. He must have some sixth sense. . . . Be quiet, Pooh-Bah! . . . I had a cousin—she was my mother's cousin, actually, who always used to pray to St. Anthony when she lost anything. She lived right around the corner from a church so it was very convenient. She found ever so many things that way. A garnet brooch, and the key to her safety deposit box, and my mother's seed pearls. We used to go running to her the minute anything turned up missing, and I must say she got results, even though it was pure superstition. Mr. Peters is not religious, is he? Nobody is religious any

more. It doesn't seem to be fashionable. But it probably
will come back, just like Victorian walnut. And then the
churches won't hold them all. The intellectual types will
drop Spengler and Einstein and take up St. Thomas
Aquinas. For all I know they may be at him already. I
must ask Mr. Peters. He's the student of the house. He
looks like a student, doesn't he? So flat-chested. I
wouldn't be at all surprised if he were tubercular. You
don't think there is anything seriously the matter with
him do you, Mr. Latham? I'd hate to have somebody in
the house who was—you know. But probably he has
lungs like a jack rabbit and will outlive all of us. I used
to watch the two of you coming up the walk together.
So comic, the combination. One all brains and no brawn,
the other all brawn and—but grades aren't everything,
are they, Mr. Latham? And people with brains so often
seem to end up teaching school. That's undoubtedly what
will happen to Mr. Peters—he's been very absent-minded
lately—unless some kind fate intervenes. You never had
any courses under old Professor Larkin, did you? No, of
course you didn't. He died when you were in rompers,
poor man. He was an authority on Chaucer or Milton, I
don't remember which it was, and terribly absent-
minded. He was famous for it. He once took a letter that
he wanted to mail and left it on the hall table and went
with the lamp, plug and all, out to the mailbox. They say
that really happened. I don't know why absent-mindedness should go with teaching, but apparently there's some
connection. Probably teachers don't want to be teaching
any more than I want to keep roomers. They just wake
up some morning and find themselves on a platform
holding forth about Amenhotep III or heredity and en-
vironment. I do hope you're not planning to devote yourself to that sort of thing. You're not cut out for it, you
know. You've taught Pooh-Bah to sit up and speak nicely
for his biscuit, and he rolls over when you tell him to,

which is certainly more than he does for me. But I don't feel that you belong on the faculty somehow, and I don't know that I would want you to if you could. It's a very questionable life. Safe, up to a point. But there's too much emphasis on expediency. And except for a few professors who have relatives that die and leave them a little something, everybody is so poor. Mr. Peters I don't worry about. He looks like the kind of person who would some day inherit a small legacy. But you, my boy, you belong in the wicked world. Don't worry if there are people who are brighter than you are. They'll never get to the top. There'll always be some well-connected person above them. Over the last five thousand years the human mind has had every possible chance to make something of itself and so far—" Mr. Dehner crossed the room and threw open the window and shook the mop violently several times. "So far," he repeated, turning his head to avoid the lint that blew back in the open window, "it has failed." He closed the window with a bang. "Now my dear boy, don't look at me like that. I can see by your eyes just what you're thinking: 'What does that old fool know about it anyway?' And you're quite right. The answer is nothing. Nothing but what I see going on around me every day."

He went off mopping carelessly under desks and around chairs and humming:

> *Old Heidelberg, dear Heidelberg*
> *Thy sons will ne'er forget . . .*

47

When Professor Severance did not appear, his class in Romantic poetry waited the customary five minutes for a full professor and then walked out. Lymie, Sally, and

Hope did not separate until they were outside, and then only after considerable discussion. Lymie had a freakish black felt hat on—they were a sudden campus fad—and he pulled the hat, which was too small for him, down over one eyebrow, cocked the brim up in front, and said, "Now where are we going?"

"I've got a three o'clock gym class," Hope said. "I'm going back to the house and put my bloomers on. If you'd care to see me in a pair of bloomers, Lymie, you can hang around downstairs. It won't take me a minute to change."

"I think I'd rather go to the English seminar," Lymie said.

"Suit yourself."

"Well," he said, hesitating. "I don't have to see you in your bloomers to know what you would look like. I can imagine them."

"You may think you can," Hope said. "But I was never so surprised in my life as I was the first time I put them on. Forbes, are you coming?"

"I've got to go home," Sally said. "Mother's making me a new dress and I promised her I'd—"

"Do you have to do that today?" Hope asked. "I was thinking, if you and Lymie went to the Ship's Lantern I could meet you there before gym and we could do our French lesson together."

"Well," Sally said, "I'd rather, actually, but the thing is, Mother is expecting me. Also I want to wear the dress."

"Such selfish, disagreeable people," Hope said cheerfully, as she walked away. She had not had to drop out of school after the appendicitis operation because the sorority made her house manager, at a modest salary. As soon as she had something that set her apart from the others, she became pleasant to live with. Now her disparaging remarks were nearly always addressed to herself, and her opinions were no longer arrogant. When she stared at someone, it was obvious that she was worrying about unpaid house bills and didn't know that the person she was staring at was even there.

At the Broad Walk, Sally turned to Lymie and said, "Why don't you—oh, I forgot. You're going to the seminar."

"I don't *have* to," Lymie said.

"Well come on and walk me home then."

"All right."

They walked on in silence for almost a block before she lifted her head suddenly and said, "Spud's having one of his spells again."

Lymie nodded.

"I don't know when it began or what started him off," Sally said, "but every once in a while I catch him looking at me as if I were a perfect stranger to him. As if he were trying to size me up. We had a terrible fight last night, and then suddenly, when he was saying good night to me out on the front porch, he said, 'Hold me, Sally, just hold me!' It was terrible the way he said it. We sat on the front steps and leaned against each other and I held him as hard as I could for about half an hour, and when he went home he seemed a little better. He was all right, as a matter of fact, but I still don't know what was bothering him."

Lymie let her talk on and on until they reached the Forbeses' front walk. She put her hand on his sleeve then and said, "Somehow I can talk to you about Spud because I know that you feel about him almost the way I do."

She waved to him from the porch and then disappeared into the house. Lymie went on to "302." He had to go through Reinhart's room to get to his own.

When Lymie appeared in the door, Spud was there, and so was Reinhart. Spud stopped talking abruptly. The sight of Lymie's face, of his eyes blazing with happiness, was a too-exact, too-humiliating refutation of all that he had just been saying. There could be no question now

of whose fault it was. Reinhart, sitting deep in his chair
and twisting a lock of hair with his finger, would know
everything.

The silence expanded like a soap bubble; expanded
and expanded until it pressed against the four walls, the
floor, and the ceiling. It seemed to Spud that it took a
year for the light to go out of Lymie's eyes, for the expression on his face to change, for him to smile stiffly
and walk on to the next room.

48

Spud took longer than usual with the wrapping of his
wrists that afternoon, as if he were seeking for some kind
of perfection which would automatically dispose of all
his problems. The three o'clock gym classes had just been
dismissed, and the aisle around him was clogged with boys
opening lockers, pulling sweatshirts over their heads, stepping out of jock straps, arguing, singing, and snapping
towels at each other's buttocks. He was so accustomed to
this that he hardly saw them. He closed his own locker,
picked up the skipping rope and the boxing gloves, and
threaded his way through the crowded aisle without
touching or pushing anyone.

As he started up the stairs he was conscious of a
heavy feeling in his legs, though he had had plenty of
sleep the night before. When he reached the floor above,
he fought back an impulse to turn and go back down the
stairs. Up till now Spud had done all his fighting with his
fists and he didn't know how to cope with a stubborn, un-
yielding resistance that wasn't physical. He tried to pretend that this afternoon was like any other afternoon, to
keep his eyes under control, and above all not to look for
Lymie.

In spite of his lean, quick, well-trained body, in spite of the muscles in his arms and legs, there was a limit to Spud's strength and he had almost found it the night he got the cut over his eye. The cut had healed long since, but it had left a scar running through his left eyebrow. Spud drew a ringer that night—a Lithuanian who had no right to compete in that amateur tournament, since he was twenty-five years old and had been boxing professionally for years. He was tall and skinny with long arms. Spud took one look at him and was scared silly. He had reason to be. The Lithuanian hit him with everything but the ring post and Spud couldn't do anything about it. He couldn't get past those arms. The first three minutes seemed like three hours. It was the worst fighting Spud had ever come up against. In the second round he was knocked down and had sense enough to wait until the count of nine. Then he got up and the bell saved him. At the beginning of the third round he got the cut over his left eye. The blood ran down the side of his face and some of it went into his eye, so everything he saw was filmed with red. The floor kept slipping out from under him, and it took all his strength to lift his arms. During that fight Spud discovered that you can hit a man and hit a man and hit a man and finally if he is still there and you hit him with everything you've got, he has to fall down or you're licked. Fortunately the Lithuanian fell down. Spud hit him with his Sunday punch and knocked him out. If he hadn't, Spud would have sat down right where he was. He was too tired to go on.

Lymie was there. He was standing against the wall near (but not too near) the punching bag.

I don't want to hurt him any more, Spud said to himself. I just don't want to go on hurting him. . . . Apparently he had no choice. He couldn't blow up at the referee for not stopping the fight because there was no referee. He could walk up to Lymie now and say, *For*

Christ's sake, go away, will you? and Lymie would go away. But the next afternoon he'd be back again. And if he told Lymie to go away and not come back any more, Lymie would do that too. But he would stand outside the building waiting to walk home. Or if he wasn't allowed to do that, then he would follow at a distance. And even if he stayed away from the gymnasium entirely he would still be waiting, no matter where he was.

It must be something I did a long time ago, Spud thought suddenly—and don't remember. Maybe I didn't even know it at the time, but I must have done something to him or he wouldn't do this to me.

Ten minutes later while Spud was slapping half-heartedly at the punching bag, he felt a sharp, shooting pain all through his right wrist and up into his knuckles. He stopped and felt of his hand through the fingerless glove. It was okay as long as his hand was open and relaxed but it hurt when he moved his fingers. In disbelief that such a thing could happen to him, he drew his hand back, closed his fist, and hit the punching bag as hard as he could. Then he doubled up, holding his arms across his stomach.

Of the dozen boys working out in the gymnasium that afternoon only one realized that something was wrong and came up to him. Spud recognized Lymie's face, through a blur of pain. Lymie was staring at him, with his mouth open and his eyes filled with concern; and it was that, Spud decided suddenly, that he wanted. Somebody to be concerned about him. Somebody to understand what it would mean if he could never box again.

His eyes met Lymie's for the first time in weeks and he said quietly, "I hurt my hand."

49

The shiny new Chrysler sedan that was parked in front of Professor Severance's house belonged to Dr. Rogers, who had taken Hope Davison's appendix out (unnecessarily perhaps) and who was always pinching young girls. He was inside, in the upstairs front bedroom. He had been called to attend Mrs. Severance, who had had a stroke and was lying in her huge walnut bed. He could have pinched Mrs. Severance until she was black and blue and she would not have felt it. Her face was ashen gray and her breathing was terrible to listen to. It had a kind of rising-falling rhythm, like someone putting his foot on the second rung of a ladder, then stepping down one rung, then two rungs higher, then one rung down. When she got to the top of the ladder she started down. At the bottom there was an interval of perhaps twenty seconds before she started up again.

Dr. Rogers bent over the bed and forced one of the sick woman's eyelids open with his thumb. The eyeball was rigid. He let his hand move down to her wrist, which was lying outside the cover. His serene, pale blue eyes went round the room, resting by turns on various objects: sewing basket, sachet bag, brush and comb and oval hand mirror, small silver-framed picture of William Severance at the age of eight in a white sailor suit by the seashore. Next to this picture was a larger one of a middle-aged man, handsome and distinguished-looking, but severe. The face bore a family resemblance to Professor Severance—the shape and length of the nose especially. It was his father. From the two pictures Dr. Rogers' eyes moved on to the large green checkbook which Mrs. Severance had been trying to balance, sitting at her desk, when the

seizure occurred. Through daily use, all of Mrs. Severance's personal things seemed to have taken on her
warmth of heart, her indomitability, foolishness, and
charm.

The nurse that Dr. Rogers had brought with him
waited in her starched uniform and cap on the other side
of the bed. Professor Severance stood timidly in the doorway. When he was five years old his mother had taken
him to New York for a visit. They saw the Central Park
zoo and the aquarium. They observed the Statue of
Liberty from a little boat that went all around the harbor.
They rode on the elevated railway. He learned to take
his hat off in the elevators of the tall buildings, and his
mother, for the crowning treat of all, took him to the toy
department of a big department store where he saw all
the toys that he had ever dreamed of. She had an errand
to do on the floor above and she thought he saw her go,
but his mind was on a little piano with real keys, and
suddenly he discovered that he was alone, that his mother
had abandoned him. She was only gone five minutes, and
the saleswomen gathered around and tried to comfort
him, but a child lost goes on crying, right down to the
end of time.

The late afternoon sun came streaming in through
the open window and lay in squares on the white woodwork, on the polished floor, and on a section of wallpaper.
The small yellow roses climbing up the wall seemed almost real.

"Well," Dr. Rogers said finally, "there's nothing to
do but wait."

When he picked up his black bag and left the room,
the nurse remained behind. Professor Severance followed
him down the stairs and the two men stood talking on
the front porch for perhaps five minutes. They kept their
voices down, not because there was any danger that the

patient upstairs might hear them, but out of respect for the seriousness of her condition.

The doctor got into his car and drove away, and Professor Severance went back into the house. He picked up one of the little clay figures that were on the piano in the living room—the figure of the bridegroom in a red robe, with a gold sash and green lining to his sleeves. After a moment or two Professor Severance restored the figure to the wedding procession and went out into the hall to telephone. The colored maid, coming into the dining room to set the table for dinner, heard him say, "Apparently there's nothing . . . Yes . . . Yes . . . Yes, I will . . . Of course I will, but there's nothing anybody can do now. We just have to wait . . . Yes, I will, Alice . . . Yes, of course . . ." and knew that he was talking to Mrs. Forbes.

When he came back into the living room he sat down at the card table, in his accustomed place, and his eyes went searching, out of habit, until they found a jack of spades to go on a queen of diamonds, a nine of hearts that he could place on the ten of spades.

In the middle of the night, some time between two o'clock and three, the lights went on at Professor Severance's, first in one room and then in another, upstairs and then down. The houses on either side of it, all up and down the block, were dark, and so were the houses across the street, but Professor Severance's house looked as if it were all lit up for a party, one of the parties for which his mother was famous, with fiddlers for the Virginia reel and a staggering buffet supper afterward and none of the guests as gay as or having a better time than the old lady herself.

50

Those who are brave enough go straight into the center of any dangerous situation and often come out alive on the other side. Most people aren't very brave, of course, and to try and skirt around a danger looks safer than to go right into the center of it. Unfortunately it isn't safer, because if you don't go through the center you meet with an ambush later on, and there the chances are totally against you. But the odd thing is that if you keep walking around a danger, if you choose the indirect, cautious method, avoiding an open conflict, it will seem for a time to work.

Spud broke a bone in his hand, that afternoon at the gymnasium, and afterward a strange happiness set in for him, and also for Lymie and Sally; the kind of happiness that people sometimes describe as "like old times come back again." Included in this description is the knowledge that the happiness seemed, the first time, as if it would last forever, and that they now know better than to think that.

Spud was still jealous. All that was necessary to unbalance his feelings was for him to meet Sally and Lymie coming toward him on the Broad Walk and see with his own eyes how interested they were in what they were saying to each other, before they looked up and saw him. But since he now made no effort to fight it, Spud's jealousy didn't last as long. Sometimes it only lasted a few minutes. If Spud was silent, Lymie stopped talking. When Spud's face cleared, all that Lymie had been thinking burst out of him in a flood of conversation.

With his right hand and wrist held immobile between two splints, there was no point in Spud's going to the gymnasium. He and Lymie and Sally sat in the Ship's Lantern until suppertime, or if Sally was busy, Spud went home with Lymie to the rooming house. He even stayed all night there once. In the morning a hand shaking Lymie's shoulder wakened him, and for a moment he didn't know whose hand it was. But then he opened his eyes and saw Spud sitting up in bed, and happiness flowed back into him like sunlight entering a room.

Spud wanted to be at the fraternity house for breakfast. They got up quietly without waking anybody and went downstairs. Lymie sat in his bathrobe and slippers, with his legs drawn up under him, and watched Spud dress. Every move that he made delighted Lymie. The way Spud rubbed the sleep out of his eyes with his uninjured hand, the majestic way that he put one foot on a chair and then the other, for Lymie to tie his shoelaces were pleasures so familiar and so long denied. When Spud went off to the bathroom, Lymie followed and pulled the lid of the toilet down and sat on it. He was amused at the violence with which Spud soused his face with soap and water, and he enjoyed knowing that in a moment Spud, with his head bent over the washbowl, would reach out blindly for the towel that he knew Lymie would have ready for him.

Washing and dressing required only a few minutes, and no amount of observation and delight could in any way prolong them. Back in Lymie's room, Spud turned to the closet and shook his head.

"It's a mess, isn't it?" Lymie agreed.

"I don't see how you stand it," Spud said.

"I don't know either," Lymie said. "I guess I just didn't see it. I haven't any eight o'clock class today. I'll come back right after breakfast and clean it up."

Spud looked at the closet regretfully—he would have enjoyed straightening it himself—and then at his watch. "I have to be going," he said.

Lymie went to the head of the stairs with him, leaned over the railing, and watched Spud make his way like a hero between two drop-leaf tables. Lymie waited until he heard the front door close, and then he went back to his room. He was too happy and grateful to go back to bed, and it was too early to get dressed. He walked up and down with his hands clasped together, thinking. He was not grateful to Spud so much as he was grateful to life itself. Because you are born, he thought, and you learn to eat and walk and talk, and you go to school, thinking that that's all there is, and then suddenly everything is full of meaning and you know that you were not born merely to grow up and earn a living. You were born to . . .

On the back of a chair he saw a sweater. He picked it up, held it out in front of him, and smiled. The shape and size identified it beyond question, among all the navy blue sweaters in the world. In a sudden access of feeling he buried his face in it. He didn't do anything about the closet.

That night, after supper, the three of them met in front of the Forbeses' house and played football by the light of a street lamp.

Neither Sally nor Lymie could hold Spud alone but they tackled him together. Sally grabbed the upper part of his body and Lymie dived for his legs. Even so, and handicapped as he was by an injured hand, Spud often got away from them.

When they had worn themselves out, they went up on the porch and sat in the swing and talked about places they'd like to go to, if they had plenty of money and nothing to worry about, like school or earning a living. Sally thought it would be nice to take a long ocean voyage to India or China. The nearest she had ever come to it, she said, was the trip from Boston to New York, on the night boat, which left Boston at five o'clock on a summer afternoon. Her mother and father were with her, but she had a stateroom all to herself. Around one o'clock she woke up, after being asleep for hours, and decided that the boat was pitching and tossing. When people were seasick (and at that moment she felt very queer) they got up and walked on deck. When she got outside, she found that they weren't out in the ocean at all; they were going through the Cape Cod Canal, and the boat was moving along steadily and quietly as if it were on a millpond. That was when she was twelve years old, and she could still remember the sound the bottom of the boat made, scraping, and the little shacks along the sides of the canal. The shacks were so close that you could almost reach down and pick the geraniums that were blooming in window boxes. Men with lanterns called up to her from the towpath, the captain shouted from the bridge, and there was a little dog that barked and also a girl with a baby in her arms—a wonderful baby that was wide awake at one oclock in the morning.

The trip through the Cape Cod Canal was the first genuinely romantic thing that had ever happened to Sally. Until that time, her soul had been slowly perishing of a world where everybody was too well-bred and everything made too much sense. She wanted Spud and Lymie, her two closest friends, to understand about that inland voyage now, and share it with her, but unfortunately such an experience, the essence of it, cannot be communicated. And although Spud would have been glad of a chance to give blood transfusions or walk miles through deep snowdrifts for her sake, and Lymie would have sat for days at her bedside reading to her—on this occasion neither of them was willing to remain quiet and listen. Spud yawned openly, and Lymie kept fingering the chains which held the porch swing or pushing at a wicker chair to make the swing go sidewise. His eyes had a feverish luster that was not apparent in the dark, but when he spoke his voice

The evening of the first spring concert Lymie walked over from the boarding club with Reinhart. Here and there in the crowd he saw someone he knew—a boy who had sat next to him in botany the year before, two girls who were in his German class, his physical education instructor. Ford and Frenchie deFresne were there, each with a girl. No one looking at Frenchie now, with his hair parted in the middle instead of on the side, and wearing fawn-colored flannel trousers, a brown tweed coat, a snow-white shirt, and a yellow tie, would ever have guessed that he had once been through hell because he couldn't think of a nine letter word beginning with S and ending with N. And though the girl who stood with her arm drawn through Ford's called him "Diver," it was something she had picked up from the boys in his fraternity, and even they had no idea where the name originally came from.

Bob Edwards was at the concert with his public speaking instructor, a woman who was clearly too old for him; and Geraghty was there, but alone. His new girl had stood him up for an Alpha Delt with a Packard roadster.

Mrs. Forbes was standing under the low branch of an elm tree, near the Broad Walk. Professor Forbes was with her, and so was Professor Severance. She waved to Lymie, but the two men were deep in conversation and didn't see him. Professor Severance had not worn a band of black cloth on his left sleeve or made any public show of mourning, and many of his students didn't even know that his mother had died suddenly during the night. But Mrs. Lieberman saw it in his face the first day that he taught his classes again. Professor Severance looked not only older but smaller, and it was all she could do to keep from speaking to him after the hour. *Now you can lecture,* was what she wanted to tell him. *You've passed over. And I'd like very much to hear what you have to*

*say about Matthew Arnold or Swinburne or your-
self* . . .

She was at the concert with her two sons. She smiled
at Lymie and he smiled back, recognizing her vaguely.
The red-headed boy with her was the boy Spud got to
give him a boxing lesson, that day last fall. Hope was at
the concert also, with Bernice Crawford. Lymie stopped
to talk to them a moment, and then he and Reinhart
walked on.

Sally wasn't with her mother and father, and Lymie
assumed that she must be with Spud. He kept searching
for them in the crowd and finding people who looked
almost but not quite like them. The back of a girl's head
or the slope of a boy's shoulders would be almost right
but the carriage would be wrong or the girl would turn
and he would see what he had known all along—that the
girl was not Sally, not even like Sally.

He caught a glimpse of his logic instructor, a Welsh-
man with wavy hair, and, later on, of his last year's rhetoric instructor with a woman who looked as if she might
be his wife. Though dogs were not allowed on the
campus, there were several of varying sizes and breeds,
who pursued each other earnestly through the legs of the
crowd.

The music out of doors was like a part of the
weather. At one moment it sounded strong and clear and
touched the hearts of those who were listening to it. The
next moment it was scattered, lost on the largeness of the
evening. Lymie had almost forgotten that Reinhart
was with him when a remark, heard above the brasses and
the clarinets, made him turn and ask, "*What* can't you
stand any longer?"

"I don't know whether I ought to tell you," Reinhart
said.

"Why not?" Lymie asked, with his eyes on a chain
of migratory birds that were flying very high.

Reinhart shook his head. "It might make trouble."

"If it's something I ought to know—" Lymie said.

"Sometimes it's all I can do to keep from taking a poke at him. I'd probably get the shit beat out of me but it would be worth it. I'd feel better afterward. But anyway, I can't stand to see you following him around and getting kicked in the teeth whenever he feels like it."

Lymie looked at Reinhart oddly but said nothing.

"What the hell do you see in a guy like that?"

"A lot," Lymie said.

"I suppose you must," Reinhart said. "But if you feel that way about him, somebody ought to tell you something."

"What?" Lymie asked.

"You want to know?"

Lymie nodded.

"He's jealous of you. He's so jealous of you he can't stand the sight of you. He comes over to the house sometimes when you're at the library and he sits in my room and talks for an hour at a time about how much he hates you."

As a rule, Lymie's face gave him away. When he was embarrassed, he blushed to the roots of his hair. When he was frightened, he showed it. Now nothing showed.

"I guess I should have realized it," he said, and changed the subject.

The concert ended at eight o'clock with the playing of the university anthem. As the crowd began to drift toward the streets that led away from the campus, Reinhart tried to persuade Lymie to go to a movie with him, but Lymie said that he had to study, so they walked back to "302." Lymie went straight to his own room. He was loosening his necktie when Reinhart came in, sat down in the Morris chair, and lit a cigarette. He was in the habit of going from room to room during the evening, and Lymie was not compelled by politeness—since there was no pretense of it in the rooming house—to make conversation. He sat down at his littered desk and cleared a place in front of him. He knew that Reinhart was waiting for him to turn around, but instead he opened a book and pretended to read. Reinhart finished his cigarette and then got up and went on to Pownell's room. Five minutes later he was back.

"You're not sore at me, are you?" he asked hesitantly.

"Why should I be?" Lymie said.

"For telling you about Spud."

"No," Lymie said. "You did me a favor. Besides, I would have found it out sooner or later."

"That's what I thought," Reinhart said, and wandered back to Pownell's room.

A few minutes later he was back again. This time he didn't come in but lingered in the doorway. "Look, bud," he said, "I feel sorry about what I did. I shouldn't have told you. I know damn well I shouldn't. Now that I've made trouble between you two guys, I'm going out in a few minutes and get drunk." He turned away from the doorway and then came back one last time. "Why don't you come with me?" he asked. "You don't have to drink if you don't want to. Stay sober and keep an eye on me, because I'm going to need it." He saw by the expression on Lymie's face that he was getting ready to frame an excuse, and before Lymie could open his mouth, Reinhart said, "Never mind," and disappeared.

Between nine and nine-thirty, Colter and then Howard passed through Lymie's room without stopping. At twenty minutes of ten, Freeman came in and ransacked Lymie's closet for a sport coat which he had wanted to wear to the concert. He had gone through every other closet on the second floor without any luck, and so he thought he might as well try Lymie's. Lymie turned around and watched him. The sport coat wasn't there.

At ten o'clock Lymie undressed and went upstairs to bed. He was going to see Spud later. Beyond that he had no plan and yet he acted as if he had one, and as if it were essential to this plan that the other boys who lived at the rooming house should be in bed and asleep before he carried it out. The door swung open and closed, time after time. He thought he kept track of the boys who came in and got into their beds, but he miscounted. Reinhart and Pownell went out together, shortly after ten, and neither of them had come in when Lymie got up at midnight and slipped downstairs again.

Instead of getting dressed he put on a clean pair of pajamas and took his winter overcoat out of the closet. When he had combed his hair in front of the mirror he put the coat on, buttoned it, and left the house. It was a soft spring night and the moon, no longer full, was on its way down the sky. The houses Lymie passed were nearly all dark. Now and then a single harsh light burned in an upstairs room. In any other town a light in an upstairs window at that hour would have meant that someone was sleepless or sick. Here it was because a head was still bent over a book, a hand writing slowly. The campus was deserted. The massive familiar buildings were enjoying the peace and the silence in the corridors never allowed them in the daytime. The front door of Spud's fraternity house was unlocked, the brothers had no fear of being robbed by outsiders. There was a light in the front hall. Both the living room and the dining room were dark. The brothers had either gone out or up to bed, leaving the odor of stale cigarette smoke behind them.

Lymie went up four flights of stairs, with his right hand moving against the plaster wall, guiding him. The door which led to the dormitory had a pane of frosted glass in it, and groaned when Lymie pushed it open. He stood still, with his heart pounding, but no voice challenged him from the dark, no springs creaked suspiciously. Spud had shown him months before where he slept, and as soon as his eyes grew accustomed to the darkness Lymie made his way through the forest of double-deckers and found Spud asleep in his single lower, near the open window.

Lymie, who was always watching the others, who slipped into the water when it was his turn but never took part in the shouting and splashing, now for the first time watched himself. He was in the center of the stage at last, with an important part to play: he was the devoted friend, to whom a grave injury has been done.

52

Spud raised himself on one elbow and looked at Lymie without speaking. There was a second when Lymie was sure that he was about to fall back on the bed without ever knowing that anybody had awakened him. Instead he got up noiselessly and followed Lymie downstairs. At the door of Spud's room Lymie stepped aside. The door was padlocked and he didn't know the combination.

When they got inside Spud closed the door and went to his closet for a bathrobe; he had been sleeping naked. As Lymie took his coat off it occurred to him for the first time that Reinhart might have been mistaken. The whole thing could have been something that Reinhart had imagined, and the expression in Spud's eyes, the clouded look, might be due to the fact that his sleep had been broken. Lymie stared at the gray iris, the dark pupil, and then at the curve of the eyelids. There was no doubt about it, the expression was hate.

"There is something I have to tell you," he said.

Spud nodded.

"I went to the band concert with Dick Reinhart. He said you were jealous of me on account of Sally."

Spud's expression did not change.

"What I came over to tell you, you have to believe," Lymie said. "I'm not in love with Sally and she isn't in love with me. She doesn't love anyone but you and never has."

Spud nodded again, but it was not the kind of nod that means agreement.

"You believe me, don't you?" Lymie asked. "You have to believe me because what I'm saying is the truth."

To his horror he saw that Spud was smiling.

In the scene that Lymie had imagined, lying awake in bed on the other side of town, Spud had said to him, *I don't hate you, Lymie old socks. I couldn't hate you.* But there is so often a discrepancy between real life and the life of the imagination, and people tend not to allow for it, or at least not sufficiently. It hadn't occurred to Lymie that Spud would turn away, instead of speaking, and find a chair, and sit down with one leg crossed over the other and one fleece-lined slipper dangling in space. Spud was thoroughly awake now and his eyes were thoughtful, but the thought, whatever it was, remained locked inside of him.

Lymie saw that words were not enough. It would take some action, as yet unplanned but rising like a shadow behind him. On a sudden impulse he went toward Spud and knelt down and clasped Spud's knees. The movement came naturally to Lymie but it was also one of the oldest human gestures.

"Please listen to me," Lymie said. "Because if you don't, you'll be very sorry."

Spud had never read the *Iliad* and he was not moved by the pressure of Lymie's hands or the bright tears in his eyes. He had seen tears before and he himself never shed them.

When Spud lowered his eyes to his hands, Lymie looked at them too—at the tight bandage and the two splints on Spud's right hand, and the five fingers coming out of the gauze. When he is able to box again, Lymie thought, someone else will tie his gloves on for him. I no longer have access to any part of him.

There was a strange but not very long silence between them, and then Lymie got up from the floor, put his coat on, and turned the collar up around his throat. As he started for the door, Spud stood up too and followed him out into the hall. They went down the hall side by side, as if they were still on good terms with each other.

A door opened and Armstrong came out in his pajamas and bathrobe. His hair was rumpled. He had been studying late and he looked tired and sleepy. He glanced at Spud and then at Lymie, with interest. There had been a time when, if Armstrong had shown any knowledge of his existence, Lymie would have been pleased. Now when Armstrong said, "What are you doing up at this hour of the night?" Lymie didn't even bother to answer.

Spud followed him down the stairs and out onto the porch. The moon was going down behind the brick fraternity house across the street. Spud's face had relaxed and he looked almost kind. With this almost kindness Lymie would have no part. It seemed so unnatural, and so sad, to be separating for the last time. At the foot of the steps he turned and said, "I forgive you everything!" and then felt foolish, and wished he hadn't said it. It wasn't right. It wasn't even true. The sound of his voice had made it quite clear that he didn't forgive Spud anything.

53

Mr. Peters sat waiting in the outer office of the Dean of Men. His topcoat, neatly folded, lay on the chair beside him, and his gray fedora was on top of the coat. His eyes were bloodshot and he looked as if he hadn't slept well. Though he made no effort to attract attention to himself, the secretary to whom he had given his name managed to whisper it to the girl who was standing by the filing cabinet, and she in turn told the assistant dean, when he came out of his office to use the files. All three of them looked at Mr. Peters out of the corners of their eyes. They might as well have stared at him openly. He knew what they were whispering about.

He glanced at the clock on the wall, which said quarter after three, and compared it with his own gold watch. The clock was a minute fast. At twenty minutes of ten that morning he walked into his cubbyhole of an office, sat down with his hat on, reached into the top drawer of his desk, where he kept some aspirin, and took two, without any water. He lit a cigarette to take the taste out of his mouth, and as he put it down on the edge of the desk, the phone rang. He picked it up without having the slightest premonition of what was in store for him. "Mr. Lymon Peters?" the operator asked, and he said, "Yes, this is Lymon Peters speaking." "One moment please," the operator said, and then he heard a different voice. "Mr. Peters? Calkins speaking. George S. Calkins, Dean of Men at the University of . . . Can you hear me?"

"Yes," Mr. Peters said into the mouthpiece, and felt a cold sweat breaking out on his forehead. Lymie must have got into some kind of a scrape. . . . Mr. Peters hoped fervently that it wasn't a girl. If Lymie had got some nice girl in a family way. . . .

"Hardly hear you," the voice said. "Must be a bad connection . . . Operator?" The phone went dead for about thirty seconds and when Mr. Peters heard the voice again it was much louder. "Mr. Peters, I have something pretty upsetting to tell you. It's about your son."

"Lymon?" Mr. Peters asked, as if he had several. "What's he done?"

"Tried to commit suicide," the voice said. "Can you hear me now?"

Mr. Peters tried to answer but his throat seemed frozen and no sound came out of it.

"He's in the hospital," the voice said. "They took him there shortly after daylight this morning. And I've taken the liberty of hiring both a day and a night nurse. I hope that meets with your approval. Not that the floor nurse wouldn't do everything that's necessary, probably. But with cases of this kind, there is always a chance that they'll try again. So it's not safe to—"

"No," Mr. Peters said thickly. "I'm sure that's right, what you've done."

"I've looked up the train schedules for you," the voice said, "and I find there's one that leaves at . . ."

From the train Mr. Peters went to the hotel, registered, fortified himself with a shot of whisky, and then took a cab out to the university hospital. The dean had neglected to prepare him for the bandages around Lymie's throat and wrists, and at the sight of them the young man in Mr. Peters took his derby hat and departed.

Lymie was asleep. The doctor had given him a hypo and he had not even moved for nearly eight hours. Mr. Peters went over and stood beside the bed and looked down at Lymie's face. It was a dreadful waxy white, the thin skin drawn tight over the bones by exhaustion and revealing the secret shape of the skull. All the strength went out of Mr. Peters' legs, and he put his hand against the foot of the bed. There's only one thing to be thankful for, he thought, swaying slightly. And that is that the boy's mother isn't alive. It would have been too much for her. She couldn't have stood it. . . . He took out a handkerchief and blew his nose quietly. Then he turned to the nurse and said, "I don't suppose there is any use of my staying here. I have a room at the hotel, in case you need to get in touch with me. And I'll be back in the morning."

He had never been on the university campus before and what he saw, going from the hospital to the dean's office, wasn't very real to him. The sunshine and the big trees hanging far out over the street, and the sidewalks crowded with boys and girls Lymie's age, walking along with books under their arms, and all of them unconcerned, acting as if nothing were wrong anywhere in the world. But then the whole day was unreal to him.

The dean kept Mr. Peters waiting a full ten minutes before he was shown into the inner office, where the dean sat, at a heavy walnut desk, under a portrait of himself by a distinguished American painter. The money for this portrait had been raised partly by undergraduate subscription, partly by well-to-do alumni. The dean rose, walked around the desk, and offered his hand. His handshake, like that of most public men, was limp and impersonal, but the expression on his face seemed to Mr. Peters to be genuine sympathy.

"I'm very happy to meet you," the dean said, "though I regret the—er—circumstances under which we— Won't you sit down?" He regretted even more the alcohol which he detected on Mr. Peters' breath. . . . The dean was a teetotaler.

Mr. Peters settled himself in a chair beside the desk and waited for the dean to produce a letter addressed to him in Lymie's handwriting.

"It's not the first case of this kind we've had to contend with," the dean said. "At nineteen, you know, life often seems unbearable. I could show you statistics that prove—but you're not interested in statistics, I feel sure. Your son is in excellent hands, Mr. Peters. We have reason to be proud of our medical men. Dr. Hart is not my own doctor but I know him well and wouldn't hesitate to use him, if I were taken sick. He's both conscientious and thorough. I'm sure when you talk to him—"

"What did he do it with?" Mr. Peters interrupted.

"With a straight-edged razor," the dean said. There was a slight pause and then he added, "This must be very hard on you. I know how I'd feel in your place."

Mr. Peters looked at him and saw that the dean hadn't the faintest idea how he felt; that if anything, the dean was enjoying it, like the people in the outer office.

"I've talked to several of the boys in the rooming house where your son has been living, and to several of his teachers, and his two best friends—a boy named Charles Latham and a boy named Geraghty. You know both of them, probably?"

Mr. Peters nodded. He knew that Lymie had spent a good deal of time with a boy named Latham, when he was in high school, and that they had roomed together for a while when Lymie first came down here. "I've met Latham but not the other boy," he said.

"There is also a girl in the case," the dean said. "Her father is one of the prominent men here in the university. I couldn't get much out of the Latham boy. I found him sullen and distrustful. But Geraghty told me a good deal and so did the girl, without knowing it. She's a very open honest youngster. I've known her all her life. She says she didn't realize the situation, but it's obvious that your son was in love with her and tried to kill himself when he found out that she was in love with this Latham boy. I've been dealing with young people for thirty-five years now, and I've gradually come around to the belief that although they seem like children to us—to their parents especially—their problems, their emotional disturbances are not essentially different from the emotional disturbances of older people. The girl was rather distressed by our conversation this morning. She was crying when she left here, and she went to the hospital and tried to force her way in. We have a rule against mixed visiting at the university hospital, for reasons that I'm sure I don't have to explain to you. And in any case, the doctor doesn't want Lymie to have visitors for a day or so—that doesn't mean you, naturally. There are a couple of people that I have to talk to still—the president of Charles Latham's fraternity, a boy named Armstrong; and also the man who keeps the rooming house where your son has been living. I don't expect to find out anything from them that we don't know already."

Mr. Peters glanced uneasily at the pile of papers on the desk. "Did Lymie leave any word for me?" he asked.

The dean shook his head. "No word for anybody."

54

The statistics that the dean refrained from quoting show that there are more suicides in spring than in any other season of the year, that more single persons take their lives than married ones, that suicide is more frequent in peacetime than during a war, more common among Protestants than among Catholics.

Considering the whole of human misery, it is not unreasonable that now and then some unhappy person should want to take his own life. But certain customs and practices now fallen into disuse—the confiscation of the suicide's property, the brutal punishment inflicted on his corpse, the refusal of a Christian burial, and that strange practice of burying a suicide at a crossroads with a stake driven through his heart—testify to the horror aroused by this act. The horror may be due to the fact that all people share, in some degree, the impulse toward self-destruction; and when some one person actually gives way to it, all are exposed to the common danger. Or perhaps the horror stems from something else, something much less complicated: The suicide doesn't go alone, he takes everybody with him.

During the middle of the last century a French soldier hanged himself from the lintel of a doorway in the Hôtel des Invalides in Paris. For two years there had been no suicides there, and during the next fourteen days, five men were found hanging from the same beam. The passageway was closed off and there were no more suicides for a time at that institution, though men and women continued to jump from the Waterloo Bridge (also Highgate Archway and the Clifton Suspension Bridge), to swallow arsenic, to hold revolvers to their foreheads, and to throw themselves in front of trains.

The morning that Lymie was taken to the hospital, quiet descended on the second floor of the rooming house, and for nearly a week there were no fights, no wrestling matches at the head of the stairs. In one way or another each of the boys was affected. No one crossed the threshold of Lymie's room. The terrible expression that Freeman and Fred Howard remembered seeing in Lymie's face that night when they passed through this room was, of course, the work of their own excited imaginations. Colter remembered how Lymie had turned around sadly and watched him ransack the closet—and was ashamed. Pownell had come home about one-thirty that same night and heard someone being sick in the bathroom. He decided that it must be Reinhart, who had left him an hour before, good and drunk. He started to go in and hold Reinhart's head for him. But then he remembered that Reinhart owed him three dollars and had been asked for it repeatedly, so he went up the stairs to bed. For two days he kept from telling anyone about this, but finally he broke down and confessed that he was entirely responsible for Lymie's doing what he did, and there was no arguing Pownell out of it.

Amsler, who hadn't been home or allowed his mother to come and see him for over a month, sat down and wrote her a post card; she could expect him, he said, sometime late Friday. Mr. Dehner's reactions were perhaps the most peculiar, and made the least sense. When the telephone rang and he found himself talking to the dean at last, he was so confused he couldn't decide which boys, out of the dozen who lived in his house, were Lymie's friends. He saw Geraghty coming down the stairs at that moment and gave the dean his name. Mr. Dehner had been through a good deal. He had stood by while the plumber and his assistant had made the bathtub and the washbowl usable again, an experience that could easily have shattered a less nervous man. When he turned away from the telephone he went into his bedroom, locked the door, and lay face down on his four-poster bed, and wept; not for Lymie but for himself, because everything went wrong for him. No matter what he did or tried to do, the result was always the same.

After Geraghty left the dean's office he shut himself in a phone booth and called his old girl and they met in the Ship's Lantern and patched things up. Geraghty discovered that he was much fonder of her than he had realized. And he had not lied to the dean about his friendship with Lymie. He had always liked Lymie very much and had meant to be friends with Lymie, only he hadn't got around to it. What he told the dean was merely a statement of his intentions for the future—if Lymie survived. On the way home from the Ship's Lantern he stopped in to see his new girl, intending to tell her that it was all off between them. But for the first time in nearly a month she seemed really glad to see him and when she was like that, he didn't have the heart to tell her that he wasn't going to see her any more.

The only person in the rooming house who remained himself, calm and unexcited, was Reinhart, although it was he who had found Lymie at five o'clock in the morning, when he came home from a visit to the house on South Maple Street. He made Lymie lie down on the floor of his room, covered him with an overcoat, and then ran downstairs and called a doctor who lived in the next block. The ambulance came, twenty minutes later. Two interns brought a stretcher up the stairs. It was just getting light when they carried Lymie out of the house. The interns rode in the front of the ambulance and Reinhart rode in back with Lymie, who was conscious of everything that was going on but made no effort to talk. He didn't seem worried about himself or embarrassed about what he had done. Ordinary anxieties, the fear of what people might think, seemed to have dropped away from him. Reinhart took Lymie's hand and held it all the way to the hospital. At the door of the operating room the interns motioned Reinhart away but Lymie asked them to let him stay and so they put a sterile gown on him and a mask, and he stood near the door while the doctors questioned Lymie about the iodine he had swallowed and tried to find out whether he had cut his windpipe. Apparently he hadn't. The doctor took a long time cleaning and sewing up and dressing the wounds, and then he gave Lymie an injection for tetanus. The needles were inserted into his abdomen and they were an inch and a half long. Reinhart had to turn his eyes away when the needles went in. His body felt alternately hot and cold, and he thought he was going to faint.

When Lymie was wheeled off, Reinhart left the hospital and went to find Spud. It was six-thirty by that time and Spud was in his room getting dressed.

"Lymie?" Spud said. "Are you sure?"

"Yes, I'm sure," Reinhart said.

"But why?" Spud said. "What made him do a thing like that?"

"I didn't ask him," Reinhart said, "and he didn't tell me."

They both avoided each other's eyes.

Spud said, "I didn't think people—I mean, I thought he—"

Shorty Stevenson came into the room, in his pajamas, rubbing his eyes and yawning. They waited in silence while he put on his glasses, looked at them cheerfully, and stood scratching himself. "Did I interrupt something?" he asked, and when they still did not answer, he pulled his pajama coat off over his head, picked up a towel, and went off down the hall to the bathroom.

"Where's he now?" Spud asked.

"In the hospital. I just came from there."

"I guess I don't understand anything," Spud said, "but I thought— Tell me what happened."

He listened carefully with his eyes on the floor the whole time that Reinhart was talking. It was almost as if he suspected some trick, an April Fool's joke of some kind, and was on guard against it. But when Reinhart was finished, Spud said, "Wait a minute." While Reinhart stood there watching him, he finished dressing, picked up a couple of books and put them down again, looked around the room as if he were seeing it for the last time, then said, "Let's go."

On the way over to "302" they stopped at a dog-wagon and had breakfast. Reinhart lit a cigarette with his coffee and Spud asked him for one. Reinhart had never

seen Spud smoke before, and as he lit a match and held it
toward the end of Spud's cigarette, he thought: *this is the
strangest part of all.*

Reinhart had an eight o'clock class, but his head
seemed twice its natural size, from all the spiked beer that
he had drunk the night before, and he knew there was
no use trying to concentrate on anything. It would be
better to get some sleep, if he could. He gave up that idea
also when they started up the stairs at the rooming house
and Spud looked at him suddenly with the face of a
drowning man.

Reinhart stayed with Spud all morning, went to the
dean's office with him, and was waiting when Spud came
out from his interview with the dean. It was after twelve
o'clock then, so they started for the boarding club. Reinhart turned off suddenly, not wanting to expose Spud to
the curiosity of the boys from "302," and they ate in a
drugstore. Spud seemed all right by that time. When they
got to the rooming house, Reinhart went up to the dormitory and stretched out on his bed and fell asleep with
all his clothes on.

It was late afternoon when he woke and came downstairs. His room was empty and he thought for a moment
that Spud had gone back to the fraternity house. But then
he heard someone moving about in the next room. He
went to the door and looked in. Lymie's desk and the one
that had been Spud's and the closet were in absolute
order for the first time since Spud had moved out of
"302." It must have taken hours, Reinhart thought. He
looked at Spud, who didn't know that he was there. Spud
was standing in front of Lymie's dresser. Reinhart turned
away without making a sound.

A few minutes later Spud appeared in the door of
Reinhart's room. Reinhart was at his desk studying, with
his head supported by his hands. He didn't look up immediately. When he turned around, Spud was sitting in

the big overstuffed chair. His eyes were closed and he was shivering and shaking as if he had caught a chill, as if he were chilled to the bone.

55

At two-thirty the next morning, Lymie opened his eyes in a bare hospital room. The light was on, shaded by a piece of yellow paper. Miss Vogel, the night nurse, saw that he was awake, came over to the bed, and took his temperature. She was a plump, middle-aged woman with dyed black hair and a black fuzz on her upper lip. She took the thermometer out from under Lymie's tongue and read it. Then she wiped his forehead with a damp washcloth, and straightened the covers. These first threads of dependency having been established between them, she bent over the bed, so that her face was close to his, and said, "Why did you do it?"

Lymie's eyelids closed of their own accord.

I didn't want to go on living in a world where the truth has no power to make itself be believed, he said, without moving his lips, without making a sound. *There was a small bottle of iodine in the medicine cabinet in the bathroom on the second floor of Mr. Dehner's rooming house. I took the cap off and drank all of it. The iodine burned the lining of my throat on the way down and formed a solid knot of burning in my stomach. The burning got worse and worse until suddenly I flung myself on my knees in front of the toilet and vomited the horrible yellow stuff into the bowl.*

Someone came upstairs about this time and I was afraid they would come into the bathroom and find me but they didn't. Whoever it was went on up to the dorm. The burning lasted for a while and then it went away. I got up then and opened the medicine cabinet again and took out Mr. Dehner's straight-edged razor. With the warm water running slowly into the washbasin I began to cut my left wrist. The flesh parted with a stinging sensation and began to bleed. The blood turned pink in the lukewarm water and went down the drainpipe. I remember raising my eyes then, calmly, but with a wonderful kind of giddiness inside my head, and I looked at my face in the mirror. After a time the blood stopped flowing. The flow became single drops and the drops came slower and slower. I cut my wrist again, deeper. I made three separate incisions in my left wrist and each time the blood congealed, after a few minutes. So I transferred the razor to my other hand and cut wherever the veins showed through the skin.

There were moments when my strength failed and the light bulb dangling from the ceiling on a long cord seemed to grow much too bright. But these moments passed and I went on cutting. Finally (all this took a long time and I was very tired) I left the washbasin, knelt down beside the tub, and applied the edge of the razor to my throat. The blood flowed in a stream. The bottom of the tub was red with it almost immediately. The light dimmed and went out, and I remembered thinking then with surprise that this familiar thing, this comforting complete darkness that I had known every night of my life, was death.

When the blackness lifted, I was still there on my knees beside the tub. The razor was still in my right hand. I raised it and more blood flowed into the tub.

There is, for every person to discover, a limit, an end to his will, a wall before which he stands and has to say "This wall I can't climb over." At five o'clock, with the light showing gray in the bathroom window, I got up and acknowledged the fact that I was through. It had seemed so easy before I started, and it had proved to be so hard. I was too tired to cut any more. Some acts, particularly acts of violence, are not possible to certain people. Even when you try with all your strength, they just don't come off.

My white pajamas were soaked with blood. I picked up a bathtowel and wound it around my neck and then I started for my own room. Before I got there the front door opened and I heard singing. It was somebody coming home drunk, singing "Mary Ann McCarthy she went out to gather clams . . ." I went to the head of the stairs and waited there until Reinhart, lurching and stumbling and grabbing at the banister for support, looked up and saw me. "Want to pee, Lymie?" he said. "Do you have to pee?" Then his mouth fell open and he said, "Oh, my Christ, what have you done to yourself?"

56

"I expect Lymie has told you about me," Mr. Dehner said pleasantly. "My name is Alfred Dehner. I have the antique shop downstairs, and I'm his landlord, so to speak."

Lymie had never mentioned Mr. Dehner to his father, and Mr. Peters didn't like effeminate men. Instead of shaking hands he merely nodded.

"I just wanted to say how sorry I am. So shocking, wasn't it? Such an awful way to choose. Gas would have been much simpler, but probably he didn't think about it. And if he'd come downstairs and put his head in the oven I certainly would have heard him. I'm a very light sleeper. Have been for years. I fall asleep all right but then I wake up along about two o'clock and stay awake until daylight. And just before it's time to get up I fall asleep again. I said to Dick Reinhart this morning, 'Just when you think you're safe,' I said, 'and that everything has happened to you that can happen, that's the time to look out.' Lymie's always seemed like such a nice quiet boy. Not at all the sort that you'd expect to—although I must say, the first time I saw him, when I opened the front door and he was standing there, I had a feeling. Something told me that he—but that's the way life is. Always the unexpected. I've been horribly upset by all this. My nerves aren't strong, you know. I'm full of luminal right this minute. It isn't habit-forming, the doctor says, but probably if you took a lot of it, over a long period of time, it might be. I'm expecting some ladies who are interested in a piecrust table that I found in the top of an old barn. It had to be refinished, of course, and when I first got it, it smelled of sheep manure, but it's a very fine piece. I don't expect you're interested in antique furniture. So few men are. If you want anything, you'll let me know, won't you. I'll be downstairs. . . . Come, Pooh-Bah."

The spaniel sniffed suspiciously at Mr. Peters' pants leg, growled once, and then padded off after his master. Left to himself, Mr. Peters stood in the center of the room. He observed with satisfaction how neat it was. All the nagging he had done was evidently not in vain; Lymie had learned to pick up his things.

In a straight row at the back of the closet were a pair of rubbers and several pairs of scuffed shoes which couldn't belong to anybody but Lymie. I could have been a better father to him, Mr. Peters thought, looking at the shoes. *I could have stayed home oftener, and I could have been more patient. I could have spent more time with him, taken him to the movies occasionally, and gone to concerts and museums with him.*

While Mr. Peters was accusing himself, he heard a slight noise and turned around.

"There's something I want to tell you," Spud said. "I didn't know the money Lymie loaned me was from him."

Though Mr. Peters had only met Spud once, he recognized him immediately.

"I should have known it was from Lymie, but I didn't," Spud said.

"How much was it?" Mr. Peters asked.

"A hundred dollars."

Mr. Peters was shocked. A hundred dollars was a lot of money. Lymie couldn't have managed that on his allowance. He must have dipped into his savings. . . . The boy seemed to be waiting for reassurance, and so Mr. Peters said, "That's something Lymie hasn't told me about. But I'm sure that if he gave you the money, he wanted you to have it. You pay him back when you can."

"I will," Spud said, nodding. There was something about Mr. Peters—not his appearance so much as his choice of words—which reminded Spud of his own father. The silence between them was a comfortable one.

"Will you have a cigar?" Mr. Peters asked, reaching for his vest pocket.

Spud shook his head, but he was pleased. No grown man had ever offered him a cigar before. He watched Mr. Peters bite the end off of his and spit it in the wastebasket, and felt that he was on solid ground at last. Mr. Peters would never do some strange awful thing without letting you know beforehand.

"Have you seen him?" Spud asked suddenly.

"I saw him yesterday and again this morning," Mr. Peters said, searching for matches. Spud whipped out a package that he was obliged to carry as a pledge in a fraternity house. "Much obliged," Mr. Peters said. "He was sleeping both times. The doctor gave him morphine. He's in pretty bad shape, and of course he isn't a very strong boy to begin with, but they seem to think he'll pull through all right. I'm more worried about his mental condition than anything else. When he was younger, if I could have afforded it, I would have sent him to a military school. I wish I had anyway. It would have been good for him in lots of ways. The drilling, I mean, and the discipline. When Lymie was a child he used to have a terrible temper. You wouldn't think that now, would you? But if anybody teased him he'd fly into a rage. It was funny to see him sometimes—how anything so small could get so angry. Sometimes he looked almost as if he were ready to commit murder. After his mother died, I never had any more trouble with him, except that I can't teach him the value of— You wouldn't know by any chance whether he joined the Hospital Association this year? I'm sure he did because I told him to, and sent him the money, but at the dean's office they say they haven't any record of it."

"No," Spud said, "I'm very sorry but I don't know," and with no warning, he turned on his heel and left the room.

Mr. Peters stared after him and shook his head. First that business about the money, which the dean didn't know about. And the look of suffering in the boy's face. And what happened to his hand, that it was all bandaged up? Something was wrong somewhere. Nice boy, too. And probably not used to being mixed up in a thing like this. Probably very upset by it, like everyone else. . . .

Mr. Peters had always felt that he knew all there was to know about his son, and now suddenly it seemed as if he didn't know anything. Not even as much as the dean or this Latham boy, although there were probably things that they didn't know either. . . . He took a last look around, through layers of cigar smoke. What the room knew, it was not saying.

Mr. Dehner was waiting at the foot of the stairs with a folded sheet of paper in his hand. "I hate to bother you," he said, "when you have so much on your mind. But there's a small matter I'd like to discuss with you. I've been put to considerable trouble and expense by what happened the night before last. And I know that you'll want to do the right thing."

Mr. Peters glanced at the paper and saw that it was an itemized bill. "I'll attend to it," he said, and put the bill in his inside coat pocket. He started for the door, and Mr. Dehner followed him.

"There's one thing more. When Lymie is out of the hospital perhaps it would be better for everyone concerned if he found somewhere else to live. I can't have things like that going on in my house. I'm sorry but I just can't. The other boys would move out and it would give the place a bad name."

Mr. Peters waited until the front door had closed behind him, and then he drew the bill out of his pocket and looked at it.

To plumber on acc't stopped-up tub and
washbowl *$25.00*
New razor *$10.00*
Bathroom rug .... *$ 4.00*
Bathtowel .... *$ 2.00*
Total *$41.00*

There was no charge for the iodine.

57

When Lymie awoke it was late afternoon and he saw his father sitting in the chair by the window.

"Well, sport—" Mr. Peters said quietly and Lymie smiled at him. Neither of them said anything more for a moment. Mr. Peters drew the chair over by the bed. His hands trembled more noticeably than usual.

"The next time you do a thing like that—" he began.

"There isn't going to be any next time," Lymie said,

his voice low and rather indistinct. Mr. Peters leaned forward so that he wouldn't miss anything, but Lymie had finished. He lay perfectly still with his arms outside the covers.

"Well, anyway," Mr. Peters said. Sitting by the open window he had prepared this speech, and he felt obliged to deliver it, even though there seemed now to be no need. "I want you to remember that there are other people in the world, people who are very fond of you, and you have no right to hurt them, do you hear? You can't go on acting as if you had nobody to live for but yourself."

Lymie, who had not so far as he knew been living for himself, said nothing. His eyes moved toward the window. Just outside it there was a pear tree which was coming into bloom.

"There's something I wish you'd do for me," he said slowly.

"What is it?"

"There's a night nurse . . . I don't need her and I wish you'd tell them not to let her in here."

"Anything else?" Mr. Peters asked.

"No," Lymie said.

The day nurse came in with a box of flowers. She took the cover off and Lymie saw that they were long-stemmed red roses. There was a card tucked in among the waxed green leaves. The roses were from Mrs. Forbes.

When the nurse carried them off to put them in water, Mr. Peters stood by the bed, ready to go and yet not able to. He had decided not to say anything to Lymie about the Hospital Association. They could straighten that out later. Or about the itemized bill, which was outrageous. At least four times what any of those things could have cost. When he got home he'd cut the total in half and send the man a check.

"It wouldn't have hurt you to leave some word for

me, son," Mr. Peters said suddenly. "You could have written me a line or two and I wouldn't have felt nearly as bad."

Lymie looked up at his father. To lie, to make up a kind excuse, required effort and he wasn't up to it yet.

"Why didn't you?" Mr. Peters asked.

"I didn't think about it," Lymie said.

He simply spoke the truth, but for a long time afterward, for nearly a year, Mr. Peters held it against him. With that one remark the distance which had always been between them stretched out and became a vast tract, a desert country.

58

In desert country the air is never still. You raise your eyes and see a windmill a hundred yards away, revolving in the sunlight, without any apparent beginning and for years to come without any end. It may seem to slow up and stop but that is only because it is getting ready to go round and round again, faster and faster, night and day, week in, week out. The end that is followed immediately by a beginning is neither end nor beginning. Whatever is alive must be continuous. There is no life that doesn't go on and on, even the life that is in water and in stones. Listen and you hear children's voices, a dog's soft padded steps, a man hammering, a man sharpening a scythe. Each of them is repeated, the same sound, starting and stopping like a windmill.

From where you are, the windmill makes no sound, and if you were blind would not be there. A man mowing grass must be accompanied by the sound of a lawn mower to be believed. If you have discovered him with the aid of a pair of binoculars then you have also discovered that reality is almost never perceived through one of the senses alone. Withdraw the binoculars and where is the man mowing grass? You have to look to the mind for confirmation of his actuality, which may account for the inward look on the faces of the blind, the strained faces of the deaf who are forever recovering from impressions which have come upon them too suddenly with no warning sound.

But who is not, in one way or another, for large sections of time, blind or deaf or both? Mr. Peters passed the Forbeses' house on his way to the hospital and Mrs. Forbes saw him, without knowing who he was, when she glanced out of her living room windows. She saw him returning an hour later and, even so, failed to perceive that for the first time in many years he had tried to speak from his heart and had failed. A person really blind might have heard it in his step, a deaf person could have seen it in the way he turned his face to the sun. All that Mrs. Forbes saw was a man getting old and heavy before his time.

The desert is the natural dwelling place not only of Arabs and Indians but also of people who can't speak when they want to and of those others who, like Lymie Peters, have nothing more to say, people who have stopped justifying and explaining, stopped trying to account for themselves or their actions, stopped hoping that someone will come along and love them and so make sense out of their lives.

There are things in the desert which aren't to be found anywhere else. You can see a hundred miles in every direction, when you step out of your front door, and at night the stars are even brighter than they are at sea. If you cannot find indoors what you should find, then go to the window and look at the mountains, revealed after two days of uncertainty, of no future beyond the foothills which lie in a circle around the town. If it is not actually cold, if you aren't obliged to hug the fire, then go outside, by all means, even though the air is nervous, and you hear wind in the poplars, a train, a school bell, a fly—all sounds building toward something which may not be good. For reassurance there is also a car horn, a spade striking hard ground, a dog barking, and an unidentifiable bird in the Chinese elm. For further comfort there is the gardener, an old Spaniard, squatting on his haunches near the house next door. He is cleaning out the winter's rubbish and rotting leaves from the fishpond. While you sit on your haunches watching him, he will catch, in a white enamel pan, the big goldfish and the five little ones that have as yet no color. Day after day he tends this garden for a woman who is always coming back but who never arrives. Patience is to be learned from him. His iris blooms, his roses fade, his potted pink geraniums stare out of the windows of the shut-up house. It is possible that he no longer believes in the woman's coming, but nevertheless, from time to time, he empties the goldfish pool and puts fresh water in it.

If the sound of somebody chopping wood draws you out of the front gate and into the empty lot across the road, you will find blue lupines growing and see blankets airing on a clothesline, and you can talk to the man who is adding a room onto his adobe house. A great deal is to be learned from him. Also from the man chopping wood, who knows even now that there is a thunderstorm coming over the mountains, brought on by the uneasy wind in the poplars.

If you go and live for a while in desert country it is possible that you may encounter some Spanish boys, barefoot, wearing blue denim overalls. It is important that you who have moral standards but no word for addressing a stranger and conveying instantaneous approval and liking, no word to indicate a general warmth of heart; who sleep alone if you can and have lost all memory of a

common table and go to tremendous lengths to keep your
bones from mingling with the bones of other people—it is
vitally important that you meet the little Spanish boys.

If you speak to them too abruptly they may run
away, or they may even turn into statues; and how to give
them back their freedom and release them from their
fright is something that you alone can solve. One of them
will have patches on the seat of his overalls, which have
come down to him from many older brothers with some
of their animal magic still left. When he is sent for water,
his brothers are there to protect him. All through the day
he wears their magic, until night, when his brothers are
with him actually, crosswise in the bed, or curled against
him on a hard pallet on the floor.

One of the little Spanish boys will use expressions
which were current in the time of Cervantes. Another
will have a gray cotton sweat shirt with Pop-Eye the
Sailor on the back—the mark of the world and its cheap-
ness upon him, innocent though he is of any world beyond
this desert valley. And there will be another who is not
innocent but born knowing the worst, though perhaps
not where to find it. And two others will have Indians for
ancestors and, for reasons that are hidden from them
but urgent, will do things in a way that is different from
the way that the others, the pure Spanish, the Mexicans,
chose. Even the sleep of the little boys with Indian blood
is different, being (in all probability) full of dancing
and dreams which turn out to be prophecies.

The little Spanish boys have a word—*primo*, meaning cousin—which they use to convey their liking for
strangers, their willingness to share the clothes on their
back, the food on their table, their fire if they have one.
This same uncritical love is offered frequently to goats,
burros, dogs, and chickens, and it will be extended to
you.

59

There was a screen between Lymie's bed and the door, and for a second he didn't know who it was that had come. He saw Reinhart first, and then coming behind him into the room someone else. Lymie was too weak to sit up but he made a slight movement with his hands which Reinhart saw. He moved to one side so that Spud could get past him and backed out of the room. Spud came and sat on the edge of the bed. His eyes were filled with tears. The tears ran down his cheeks and he made no effort to wipe them away. Neither he nor Lymie spoke. They looked at each other with complete knowledge at last, with full awareness of what they meant to each other and of all that had ever passed between them. After a moment Spud leaned forward slowly and kissed Lymie on the mouth. He had never done this before and he was never moved to do it again.

60

In the middle of the night, Reinhart cried out in his sleep, and the sound was so sudden and so terrible that it woke every boy in the dormitory at "302." They lay in their beds shivering and waiting for it to happen again.

On the other side of town, Lymie was also awake. It was the eighth night that he had spent in the hospital, and something (the anti-tetanus serum?) had made him break out in a rash. His whole body itched. He couldn't sleep. He couldn't even lie still but kept moving his arms and

legs against the sheets for relief. After a while he turned
on the light and read, and while he was reading he noticed
a slight rigidness in his lower jaw. He put his book down
and waited for it to go away and it didn't. Instead it grew
worse. He tried not to get excited; like the rash, it could
be a reaction from the serum. But the doctor hadn't
said that his jaw would stiffen, and it was possible that
the serum hadn't worked. They might not have given him
enough of it, or they might have given it to him after it
was too late. . . . He didn't want to die of lockjaw; he
didn't want to die at all. He lay absolutely still, with the
light on, wanting to cry out for help and not knowing
where help would come from.

The truth is that Lymie had never wanted to die,
never at any time. The truth is nothing like as simple or
as straight-forward a thing as Lymie believed it to be. It
masquerades in inversions and paradoxes, is easier to get
at in a lie than in an honest statement. If pursued, the
truth withdraws, puts on one false face after another, and
finally goes underground, where it can only be got at in
the complex, agonizing absurdity of dreams.

When Lymie awoke at daybreak the rigidness in his
jaw had begun to go away. He realized that, just before
he woke, he had been dreaming. He was in a place by the
sea, and there were houses, and he made his way along
the street, searching for a particular house, which he
couldn't find. He was looking for No. 28. He stopped
people and they gave him directions which turned out to
be incorrect, and the street numbers changed in front of
his eyes, but finally he found the house he was looking
for—No. 28—and then those numbers changed too, while
he was looking at them.

61

The stiffness was entirely gone when the nurse came in at six-thirty to wash Lymie's face and hands. Though he had hardly slept all night long, he felt like singing. He was alive and he knew that he was going to live for a long time. He knew there were things he had not cared enough about, that he had taken for granted, that he would have missed if he had died. He wanted to get well and go back to school and study and walk under the big trees on the campus. He wanted to look into the faces of people that he didn't know and might never see again, hear rain in the night, and sleep, and turn in his sleep and have dreams. Good or bad, it didn't matter. The worst dream imaginable was better than nothing at all, no active mind, no waking up ever.

In the middle of the morning the nurse came in with a bowl of wildflowers—purple wood violets, Dutchman's breeches, jack-in-the-pulpit, trilium, and hepaticas. They had been dug up, dirt, roots, and all, and planted in a shallow blue bowl. They looked as if they had never been disturbed, as if they had grown that way, all in a cluster on the forest's floor.

"Who brought them to me?" Lymie asked.

The nurse didn't know. They had been left at the desk downstairs and there wasn't any card.

Lymie asked her to put the bowl of wildflowers on the night table beside his bed. While he was looking at them, his eyelids closed and he fell asleep. When he woke he went on looking at the wildflowers with all the strength of his eyes, and the narrow world he had lived in so long began to grow larger and wider. The world began to take on its own true size.

He slept on and off all day. That evening as it was beginning to get dark, he heard running footsteps in the corridor outside his room and then Sally put her head around the screen. She was out of breath.

"Well," she said, panting, "I finally made it. They wouldn't let me past the desk, so I sneaked in the ambulance entrance. How are you feeling?"

"I'm fine," Lymie said.

"You look a little peaked," Sally said. "And you've certainly got no business to be lying in bed on a day like today."

She came and sat on the edge of the bed and took his hand in hers. Then she turned her head and listened. There was no sound in the corridor. "Oh, Lymie!" she said, smiling down at him. Neither of them spoke for a minute or two. He was thinking how much she looked like a South Sea Islander, and she was trying not to look at the gauze dressings on his wrists and throat, and thinking that there are people for whom life just isn't going to be too easy, and that probably he was one of them and maybe she herself was another.

Putting her hand in the pocket of her red coat, she said, "Here's a letter for you."

Lymie took the envelope that she tossed to him. On it was written *For Lymon Peters Jr. Courtesy of bearer.* He pulled the letter out and read it.

Dear Lymie: I feel so important—I have just hired a janitor and fired a waiter. I suppose you would say the waiter was being abused, but really, Lymie, he was impossible— came when he pleased and was late then, sassed the cook and snooted me. So it is "check" for Mr. D. Evarts. I also have just completed 31 lines of blank verse for Professor Severance. It is very putrid blank verse but it is blank verse and I love it with a mother's love. I started out to

*ask you, Lymon, if you would care to come to our spring
house dance? May twenty-eight. Reply by courier.*
> *Faithfully,*
> *Hope*

When he had finished reading, he turned, frowning
slightly, and looked out of the window. He'd have to wear
a turtleneck sweater instead of a white shirt, and everybody there would know why he was wearing it . . . If
Hope had the courage to ask him, if she wanted him,
knowing that he. . . .

The pear tree was in full bloom.

"I have another message for you," Sally said. "Mother
wants to know if you'd like to come and stay at our house
for a week or so after you leave this dump."

"I'd like to very much," Lymie said.

"Then that's settled."

"What's settled?" a stern voice asked, and Sally
glanced at the screen in alarm, but it was only Spud. He
came in and sat down on the other side of the bed. He had
moved back to the fraternity house, but every morning
before he went to his first class, he came to the hospital.
Today was the first day that he had come twice. The
bandage and the splints had been removed from his right
hand, and he held it out for Lymie to see, flexing the fingers slowly and then doubling up his fist.

"Do you want to know why my mother is so fond
of you, Lymie?" Sally asked. "It's because she's sure that
you are going to be a professor. She says she knew it the
very first time you came to our house. You walked in,
she says, and all you saw was the books."

"Doesn't your mother think I'm going to be a professor?" Spud asked.

"No," Sally said. "And you'd better not be, if you
know what's good for you."

There were footsteps in the hall but they went on past.

Sally also knew who had sent the bowl of wild-flowers. Mrs. Lieberman had stopped her after class and asked about Lymie.

"They're beautiful, aren't they?" Sally said. "Do you know her? Do you know who she is?"

He shook his head.

"She asked me to bring you to see her, and I said I would."

"That was very nice of her," Lymie said, turning to look at the flowers. The violets had closed for the night.

"She seemed like a nice woman," Sally said.

Spud walked over and examined the flowers closely. "They're just like the kind that grow in Wisconsin," he said.

When he came back he sat on the bed again, beside Sally this time. She took his hand in hers and Lymie's hand in her other hand, and with her eyes shining with mischief she said, "Well, here we all are!"

"You guys," Spud said disparagingly, and made Lymie raise his knees, so that he and Sally could go on a camping trip up and down the cover.

It was some time before the nurse came in and put an end to this childish game.

Nonpareil Books

FICTION

Reuben Bercovitch
Hasen
160 pages, $8.95

José Donoso
The Obscene Bird of Night
448 pages, $12.95

Stanley Elkin
The Franchiser
360 pages, $10.95

Searches & Seizures
320 pages, $10.95

Marian Engel
Bear
144 pages, $9.95

Paula Fox
Desperate Characters
176 pages, $9.95

William H. Gass
In the Heart of the Heart of the Country
340 pages, $10.95

Paul Horgan
A Distant Trumpet
628 pages, $16.95

Joy Kogawa
Obasan
250 pages, $11.95

William Maxwell
The Chateau
416 pages, $12.95

The Folded Leaf
288 pages, $11.95

The Old Man at the Railroad Crossing
192 pages, $10.95

Over by the River
256 pages, $10.95

Time Will Darken It
320 pages, $10.95

They Came Like Swallows
192 pages, $9.95

So Long, See You Tomorrow
174 pages, $9.95

Wright Morris
Collected Stories 1948-1986
274 pages, $10.95

Plains Song: For Female Voices
232 pages, $10.95

Howard Frank Mosher
Disappearances
272 pages, $10.95

Robert Musil
Five Women
224 pages, $10.95

Liam O'Flaherty
Famine
480 pages, $12.95

Mary Robison
An Amateur's Guide to the Night
144 pages, $9.95

Days
192 pages, $9.95

Oh!
224 pages, $9.95

Peter Rushforth
Kindergarten
208 pages, $10.95

Maurice Shadbolt
Season of the Jew
384 pages, $12.95

Among the Cinders
218 pages, $10.95

Nonpareil Books returns to print books acknowledged as classics. All *Nonpareils* are printed on acid-free paper and are produced to the highest standards. They are permanent softcover books designed for use and made to last. For a complete list, please write to David R. Godine, Publisher.

David R. Godine, Publisher
300 Massachusetts Avenue
Boston, Massachusetts 02115